# Driving
# Whiskey
# Wild

## The Whiskeys

## MELISSA FOSTER

ISBN-10: 1-948004-81-X
ISBN-13: 978-1-948004-81-7

Cover Design: Elizabeth Mackey Designs
Cover Photography: Wander Aguiar Photography

WORLD LITERARY PRESS
PRINTED IN THE UNITED STATES OF AMERICA

# A Note to Readers

When I first met Bullet Whiskey, I knew it would take a special, strong, and patient woman to break through his barriers. The instant I met Finlay Wilson, I knew she was his one and only. I hope you love them as much as I do and that you enjoy their sexy, emotional story. Each of their witty and wonderful family members and friends will also be getting their own happily ever after. Several books are already published and available for your enjoyment (TRU BLUE, TRULY, MADLY, WHISKEY, and RIVER OF LOVE). If this is your first introduction to the Whiskey family, each book is written to stand alone, so dive right in and fall in love with the Whiskeys.

Remember to sign up for my newsletter to make sure you don't miss out on future Whiskey releases:
www.MelissaFoster.com/News

For more information about my fun, sexy romance books, all of which can be read as stand-alone novels, or as part of the larger series, visit my website:
www.MelissaFoster.com

If you prefer sweet romance, with no explicit scenes or graphic language, please try the Sweet with Heat series written under my pen name, Addison Cole. You'll find the same great love stories with toned down heat levels.

Happy reading!
~ Melissa

# Chapter One

THE DOORS TO Whiskey Bro's blew open and Dixie Whiskey, Bullet's youngest sibling, barreled toward him with *that* look on her face. Her long red hair hung loose and wild, and in her cutoff T-shirt, skinny jeans, and black boots, she looked like a force to be reckoned with. There were very few things the ex–Special Forces biker couldn't handle, but today of all days he didn't have the patience to deal with whatever had crawled up her ass and died. Not after the fucked-up, restless night he'd had.

Dixie crossed her arms, her fingers drumming annoyingly on her tatted-up forearm. The smirk she was wearing told Bullet this could go one of two ways. She needed him to do something he would not want to do, or she was about to give him shit.

He stopped wiping down the bar and tossed the rag on the counter behind him. "What's up, Dix?"

"You look like hell."

He poured himself a shot of bourbon.

"You're drinking on the job?"

"You see any customers?" At six five and two hundred and forty pounds, it would take a hell of a lot more than one drink to affect him. He downed the shot, set the empty glass in front of him, and placed his hands flat on the bar, letting the burn soothe the demons of his past.

Locking eyes with Dixie, he said, "Did you come here to give me shit?"

Dixie held his gaze. "Nightmares, up all night fucking some girl you can't remember, or was someone in trouble?"

He'd taught her never to back down when she was just a lanky redheaded pistol with a big mouth and not enough sense to know when to shut up. He'd had to teach her to be tough so she wouldn't get herself in trouble. She hadn't changed much, except now she wasn't scared of anything. Including *him*.

He picked up the shot glass and turned to wash it out. "Whaddaya need?"

"I need you to behave when Finlay Wilson gets here."

Bullet stifled a curse. "Finlay? The catering chick from Tru and Gemma's wedding?" How many Finlay Wilsons were there in Peaceful Harbor, Maryland? It wouldn't matter if there were a dozen. This Finlay had already gotten Bullet's attention—and blown him off, which was probably a good thing. She was sweeter than sugar and had no business agreeing to help them expand their family-run bar to include lunches and dinners. She belonged in an ice cream shop like her sister, Penny, where she could flash that sparkling smile for friendly families. She'd be eaten alive in a place like Whiskey Bro's.

"One and the same," Dixie said.

"That tiny flick of a woman does not belong in a bar. Especially *my* bar. Don't you have someone else to harass?"

"First of all, we're all equal partners in this place. You, me, Bones, Bear, Mom, and Dad. So cut the bullshit about it being *your* bar."

He gritted his teeth. Technically she was right. They were all equal partners on paper, but it didn't quite work out that way in real life. Bear had run the bar after their father's stroke and had also taken over their family auto shop across the street when they lost their uncle. Bullet had stepped in five years ago and had taken over the day-to-day responsibilities of the bar, so Bear could cut back to part-time. Dixie ran the books for both their family businesses, waitressed at the bar, and had recently taken charge of the expansion of Whiskey Bro's kitchen. But his younger brother, Bones, a doctor, hadn't ever gotten his hands dirty inside the bar. Not that Bullet cared about that. Bones would jump in if asked, but Bullet didn't ask for help. Had never asked for it a day in his life.

*With one fucking exception*, but he wasn't going there now.

He pushed the harsh memories aside and focused on Dixie's narrowing green eyes. The bar might be as much theirs as it was his, but he was the one who was there every goddamn day.

"Don't fuck this up, Bullet, or I swear I'll make your life a living hell. She's agreed to work with us for a month, and we need her if we're going to pull this off. She knows about menus, hiring kitchen staff, and health regulations."

"She doesn't belong in a place like this, Dix. She's not like us." Finlay looked like a frigging angel with her silky blond hair and innocent blue eyes. It was that innocence that had flipped some switch inside Bullet and made him want to *sin her up* and *protect* her at the same time. *Fucking Finlay Wilson*. The wedding was four weeks ago, and he hadn't been able to stop thinking about her since. If she wasn't starring in his X-rated fantasies, she was flitting about town in those frilly dresses she wore, spreading smiles like fairy dust.

"You didn't seem to mind that when you hit on her at the

wedding." She arched a brow. "Or did you think I didn't notice the way you were watching her every move when Bear and Crystal also decided to tie the knot? Sidling up to her every chance you got during the reception, like a puppy chasing a treat?"

Bullet scoffed. He'd been looking at her long before Crystal and Bear's impromptu proposal and subsequent wedding the day Tru and Gemma got married. "She's a hot chick. So what? I didn't want to marry her—just have a little fun."

"Then you shouldn't mind seeing her in here for a few hours a day while we pull things together."

"It's a mistake, Dixie." He moved around the bar and stood beside her. "A pretty little thing like her is just asking for trouble in a place like this. Why are you so hung up on hiring Finlay anyway? Did you even check with our club members to see if anyone needed a job?"

"You know, sometimes I forget that you have so much *Dad* in you, it's like beating my head against a brick wall."

"What the fuck does that mean?"

"That you're as hesitant to hire outside the family as he is. That you think if someone's not in the club or one of us, they can't do shit."

"Jed's working here, isn't he?"

Bear had recently given up bartending and was now designing motorcycles for the elite Silver-Stone Cycles. For the first time in the history of the bar, they'd been forced to hire outside the family *and* outside their motorcycle club, the Dark Knights, which was as solid as family. Although Jed Moon, who was not only their new part-time bartender but also worked as an auto mechanic for the shop, was Bear's new brother-in-law. So technically, he *was* family. Finlay Wilson was *not*. Finlay Wilson was trouble waiting to happen.

"Give me a break." He shook his head. "We always hire family first."

"Yeah? Well, which of our club members do you think knows how to run a restaurant? *Gutter*, the home repair expert? Or maybe one of the Bando brothers, who pour concrete for a living? Do you realize Finlay went to one of the best culinary schools in Boston? She's worked in a restaurant, and she's run her own catering company for years, and soon she'll be opening a catering company right here in town."

He didn't give a rat's ass about her credentials. If anything, she was overqualified. But the thought of her flouncing around the bar with a bunch of horny, drunk guys going after her made Bullet's blood boil. The fact that she was not his to worry about did not escape him. "We're offering sandwiches and fries, not gourmet meals."

"Which makes her the perfect person for this job. She knows how to keep costs down, and she's from Peaceful Harbor. She's putting down roots here, which means she'll want to see the business do well—so it doesn't reflect poorly on her. What do you have against Finlay, anyway?"

"*Against* her? Nothing." Though he'd like to be buried deep inside her. "But she'll get eaten alive in a place like this and she'll go cowering out the door. Then we'll be left trying to figure shit out anyway. Besides—"

The creak of the front door opening drew their attention. Bullet looked over his shoulder, meeting the innocent blue eyes of the angel peeking in at them.

FINLAY SMILED AND waved as she slipped into the dingy bar. "Hi. Am I interrupting?" From the scowl on Bullet's face, she was not only interrupting, but she'd somehow pissed him off. Well, good for him. Let him be angry, the big, tattooed bully. What kind of man comes up to a woman at a wedding and says, *Hey, sweetheart, whaddaya say I take you for a ride on the Bullet train?*

She smoothed her sundress over her hips, trying to gather her wits about her. *Bullet train.* She had no doubt he had a train in his pants. The man was larger than life in too many ways to count, and when he set those cold, dark eyes on her, she swore they ignited right in front of her. *Lordy, now my pulse is racing.* She'd been thinking of that flash of heat ever since the wedding, and she couldn't deny that it scared her and turned her on in equally frustrating measures. If she were honest with herself, she'd thought she was too damaged after losing Aaron to ever feel this type of spine-tingling excitement over a man again— and the fact that she felt it around a guy like Bullet scared the heck out of her. But this was not the time for honesty. She needed to pull herself together so she didn't make a bad impression.

Dixie pushed past her massive brother to greet her. "Not at all! I'm glad you made it in." She gave Finlay a quick hug and then glared at Bullet. "*Right*, Bull? Aren't we *glad* she made it in?"

He lifted his chin in a half-cocked greeting before stalking around the bar and busying himself pulling bottles from shelves. Was he upset that she'd refused his magical penis ride? If so, he was going to have to get over it, and fast.

"Don't pay attention to him. He had a rough night." Dixie waved a hand as if Bullet didn't matter.

Finlay forced a smile, knowing the big oaf mattered a heck of a lot. She'd grown up in Peaceful Harbor, although she was several years younger than the Whiskeys and she hadn't known them then. She'd moved back into town two months ago, hoping to put down roots near her sister, Penny, after leaving to attend college in Boston nearly a decade ago. Penny had filled her in on the Whiskeys when she'd accepted the catering job for their friends' wedding. Apparently, the Whiskeys and their motorcycle gang owned her small hometown. Only, according to Penny, it wasn't like the stories she'd heard about bikers causing a ruckus or scaring people. No, the Whiskeys were known to be good folks, and apparently their *gang* was more of a *club*. She didn't know the difference, but understood that they protected the community, keeping crime down and helping with bullies—except, apparently, for their own big, pushy son. From what Penny had said, they might look intimidating, but beneath all those tattoos and dark leather, they were kind, caring, generous people. She'd noticed that at the wedding, and in the weeks since, as she'd seen Dixie, her other brothers, and their parents around town. They were all as nice as could be. The jury was still out on big, bad Bullet.

But if she was going to spend any amount of time in his presence, he needed to respect her. This was why Penny had pushed her to take this job, wasn't it? Because she'd been hiding behind her past, living a safe, comfortable, *lonely* life for so long she'd all but forgotten how it felt to be hit on? *And how to handle it.* Well, that ended *now.* She straightened her spine, the way she'd learned to do in culinary school, when top chefs came in to teach and they'd ream the students for the smallest errors. There was no room for thin skin in catering—and she'd be darned if she'd let Bullet Whiskey intimidate her one bit.

"It'll be fine," she assured Dixie, and walked directly behind the bar to the mountain of a man who was trying his best to ignore her. Every step made her heart beat faster. Holy moly, she hadn't remembered him being *that* tall. She was only five three, but even though she had heels on, he was well over a foot taller than her.

She reached up and tapped Bullet's shoulder. It was like tapping stone covered with a black leather vest. He turned slowly, his broad chest and massive arms suddenly taking up all the extra space. She stared up at him. His dark beard and eyes gave him a menacing look. She swallowed hard, steeling herself to say her piece. In the next second those angry eyes turned even hotter and hungrier than they'd been at the wedding.

Her traitorous insides flamed.

*Oh boy.* She was in way over her head. This man probably got everything he wanted from women with that look. He cast some sort of spell with his leather wrist cuffs, scary-looking silver and black rings, and *go-ahead-just-try-to-mess-with-me* attitude.

Forcing her sternest expression, she said, "Bullet, if we're going to work together, I expect you'll let what happened at the wedding go and get behind me on this project."

He cocked his head, his lips curving up in a wicked smile that brought goose bumps to her entire body as he said, "I'm happy to get *behind* you anytime, sweetheart."

"Bullet." Dixie glared at him.

Finlay felt her jaw drop open and snapped it closed. She needed the money from this consulting job to help get her catering business off the ground, and she really liked Dixie and the rest of the Whiskeys. She felt good about helping them and couldn't let this Whiskey scare her off.

"First of all, I am *not* your sweetheart, and if you think for a second that your dirty talk will scare me off, you're wrong."

He leaned in so close she could smell alcohol on his breath. "You haven't begun to hear dirty talk, darlin'. And scaring you is the *last* thing I want to do. But you working here is a mistake."

The front door swung open and two loud-talking, burly men walked in. They wore grungy T-shirts and jeans, with black leather boots, much like Bullet's. One had scraggly gray hair pulled back in a ponytail. The other was bald and broad, with tattoos on both arms. Finlay was so far out of her element, she could no longer *see* it. But she wasn't about to admit that. She felt Bullet watching her intently and tried to school her expression. Once again, she gathered her courage, realizing that if she had any hope of earning Bullet's respect, she had to prove she wasn't the mouse he seemed to think she was. She'd done enough bartending when she was in college to make ends meet, and she could make drinks in her sleep.

She spun on her heels as the men sat down at the bar and flashed them her warmest smile. "Hi, y'all. What can I get for you today?"

They glanced at Bullet, who chuckled.

"What will it be? Beer, bourbon, or Biker's Poison? Knuckleheads?" When they stared at her, dumbfounded, she set her hand on her hip and smiled at Dixie, who was clearly getting a kick out of her little show of authority. "Shy boys, huh? How about I surprise you?"

She turned, and Bullet grabbed her arm, glowering at her again. Whatever amusement had caused his chuckle was flat-out *gone*. She looked at his hand on her arm and smiled. "I'm sorry, Bullet, but you seem to think manhandling me is an appropriate way to get my attention." She peeled his hand off and placed it by his side. "Now, if you'd like to say something, feel free while I mix these good men their drinks."

With her heart in her throat, she grabbed two lowball glasses and a bottle of tequila while Bullet breathed fire beside her.

"This is *my* territory," he seethed.

"Hm. Seems you're a bit possessive about your space." She pointed to a bottle of Kahlúa. "Can you please hand me that, and the ouzo?"

Teeth clenched, he handed her the bottles, and she began mixing the drinks. This time the chuckles came from the other men. She couldn't see Dixie, but she heard the heels of her boots clicking along the hardwood toward the kitchen. She reached in front of Bullet to grab two napkins and grazed his stomach, which earned something between a grunt and a dangerously sexy sound she didn't want to think about.

She set the drinks on the bar and wiped her hands on a towel that was hanging beneath the counter. "Two Boot Knockers just for you two beautiful men."

Stepping closer to Bullet, she crooked her finger for him to bend down so she could speak quietly. To her surprise, he did, and she said, "I'm really not comfortable with *territories*. It feels outdated. Like women being seen and not heard."

Bullet rose to his full height, face pinched tight.

She patted his chest and, in her sweetest voice, said, "You do your job and I'll do mine. But there will probably be occasions when I need to get behind the bar, or you need to get into the kitchen. Think you can handle that?"

One of the men at the bar lifted his glass and said, "This is the best drink I've had in a long time. I can handle this pretty lady making my drinks."

Finlay batted her eyelashes just for dramatics, enjoying the irritated look on Bullet's face. "Thank you. I'm pretty good behind the bar. Oh, and in the kitchen," she added with a smile.

She felt something thundering against her palm and realized her hand was still over Bullet's heart. She lowered her hand, and he growled something indiscernible.

"Now, if you'll excuse me, I have a meeting with Dixie."

# Chapter Two

WEDNESDAY EVENING FINLAY was talking to her best friend, Isabel Ryder, on speakerphone when she pulled up in front of Whiskey Bro's. Isabel bartended and waitressed at the restaurant in Boston where Finlay had worked before opening her small catering company, Finlay's. They'd become fast friends, and a year after Finlay had opened her company, Isabel had begun working for her part-time, helping at the events. Finlay had been back in town for two months, and even though she'd made lots of new friends and had rekindled some of her old childhood friendships, she missed her bestie.

"You won't believe what the new chef, Paolo, is doing with the kitchen," Isabel said. "The guy might be a great chef, but he's a total a-hole. I wish I could quit right now and come down to Peaceful Harbor and just work for you."

"Sorry, Iz. Hopefully one day, but I don't have things ironed out yet. I am catering a baby shower in two weeks for one of Penny's friends. You know how much I love themed parties, and the mom is having twins, so I get to do boy and girl goodies."

"They have no idea what they're in for. Do they realize that when it comes to food, you're the queen of all things baby-themed, which is second only to your affinity for heart-mending comfort food?"

"That's why they hired me."

When Finlay had first started her business, she'd catered a baby shower for a mom who was having quadruplets, and she'd come up with different baby-themed foods for four very distinct babies. She'd quickly become known as the go-to baby shower caterer in her area, and referrals to her website had taken off.

"How's it going working from home?"

"Limiting. I can only take on small parties, but I think I was really lucky to find a rental with two wall ovens. I did see two more retail spaces today, and they were okay, but something was missing."

"Yeah, *me*."

Finlay smiled, picturing Isabel's short dark hair and big, almond-shaped eyes looking at her like she was a fool for not realizing she'd left her behind. "Oh, please. It's not like you can just pick up and leave. And now that I'm helping the Whiskeys, it's going to be another month before I can dig my feet in, anyway, so I'm not in a rush to find space right now."

"And?" Isabel asked curiously.

"And what?" She cut the engine and took Isabel off speaker-phone.

"The *train guy*? Did you see him today?"

Finlay shoved her keys in her purse and stepped from the car. "He goes by *Bullet*, and no. Not yet. I don't have to work at the bar very much yet. Just when I'm trying new menu items, or setting up the kitchen, or interviewing. It's a process. But I'm on my way there now. I want to measure the counter space and check out the appliances. I was so busy talking with his family yesterday that I forgot to see if it was all up to snuff."

"Bullet," Isabel said softly. Then louder, "*Bullet train.* What do you think he believes about himself? That he's really powerful, or that he fucks fast *and* hard?"

"Izzy!" Finlay felt her cheeks flush. She wasn't a prude by any means, but she wasn't as crass as Isabel. She looked around the parking lot, which was full of motorcycles and trucks, and wondered which one was Bullet's. She spotted a shiny black Harley, and just as she decided it was his, she shifted her gaze to the scuffed-up one parked beside it. *Yeah, that's yours, I bet.* "All I know is that he isn't the type of guy to do anything *slowly.* I told you he's part of a motorcycle gang or something, right? His whole family is, and the bar..." She glanced at the run-down building and sighed. "It could be cute if the windows weren't blacked out and they spiffed it up a bit. But as it stands, it looks like it's on its last legs, which is probably part of the allure for these guys. They're really rough, totally different from—" She stopped herself before *Aaron* could fall out and said, "The guys who frequented that hole-in-the-wall bar on the corner by the restaurant."

She'd met Aaron Rush almost nine years ago, during her first year of college, and it had been almost seven years since he was killed. Long enough to get past the physical pain of missing him and still recent enough to remember what his carefree laugh sounded like. His smile was beginning to fade from her memory, but the way that smile had made her feel? That would never leave her. She'd been just a girl of nineteen when they'd met, with no real-world experience and away from home for the first time ever. But she'd fallen hard for the confident, blond man of twenty-three who had already completed one military tour and had just reenlisted for another.

"They didn't hire you to redecorate," Isabel reminded her.

"I know, but…" She slung her purse over her shoulder and headed up the front steps.

"'But every place should bring a smile to the patrons' lips, whether they get a glimpse of the restaurant, the kitchen, or the bathroom.'"

"Okay, Miss Parrot," Finlay said with a smile. "Maybe I have a thing for liking my surroundings." She pulled open the heavy door and was assaulted by the smell of leather, metal, and *Whiskey*. She whispered into the phone as she stepped inside, "Remind me to bring some air freshener tomorrow."

The din of the bar quieted, and all eyes turned to her. The combination of leers and confusion on the customers' faces made her wonder if she'd spilled something on herself, and she looked down at her outfit. But her sea-foam-green dress was clean, the frills at the bottom neat and orderly. Her nude heels weren't broken or even scuffed. Her stomach pitched south.

"Everyone's staring at me. I gotta go," she whispered into the phone, and ended the call. Aware of every set of eyes watching her—especially those of the monstrous man behind the bar, who seemed to be chewing nails—she tossed her long blond hair over her shoulder, lifted her chin, and tried to ignore the buzzing of her nerves as she made a beeline for the kitchen.

Someone whistled, and she made the mistake of looking over. The whistler was sitting on a stool by the bar. He winked, and she quickly shifted her gaze to Jed, the friendly guy with dirty-blond hair whom she'd met at the wedding last month. He was now busy bartending beside Bullet. Jed was kind and funny and not nearly as intimidating as some of the people she was walking past.

Jed smiled and said, "How's it going, Finlay?"

She managed a quick wave as she weaved between tables, stepping over so many leather boots she could have been in a shoe store. She heard Bullet growl something at Jed, but she couldn't make out the words.

A guy wearing a bandanna around his head said, "Hey, baby," as she passed.

*Not on your life.*

She quickened her pace, passing a good-looking guy with short-cropped hair and tattoos snaking down his arm and a couple of guys wearing matching leather vests who lifted their drinks as if they were toasting her. What the heck? She felt like she was back in high school, running out onto the field to cheer for a football game, minus the cheerleading outfit *and* the desire to be appreciated for her looks. *Nope. Not happening.*

She finally pushed through the kitchen doors and, after scanning the room and making sure she was alone this time, exhaled loudly, silently chiding herself for being so nervous. They were just people.

The doors flew open behind her, and Bullet filled the door-frame. His dark eyes locked on hers, and her heart rate kicked up even faster. He was looking at her like he either wanted to devour her or kick her out of the bar. Right that second, she might not have minded the latter.

His gaze slid down her body, slowing at her breasts before taking a lustful stroll down her legs, all the way to the tips of her closed-toe heels.

*Devour. Definitely devour.*

She cleared her throat, and his eyes jerked up to hers, dark and desirous. In the blink of an eye, anger, or something similar, pushed all that desire away. He moved as slowly and silently as a humid afternoon, closing the distance between them—and sucking the oxygen from the room. Then he was upon her, standing so close she had to lift her chin to see his face. His brows were drawn into a concerned slant, worry lines so deeply etched across his forehead she wondered if they ever went away. Even with his beard, the tightness of his jaw was evident. His hulking body dwarfed hers in breadth and height, but it wasn't the don't-fuck-with-me aura surrounding him that had her trembling in her heels. It was the conflicting messages in his eyes.

"Everything all right?" he asked gruffly.

She nodded, unable to breathe.

"What are you doing here so late?"

His arms arced out from his body from the sheer size of his muscles, and she realized he could literally crush her if he wanted to. His fingers curled up, as if he was stopping himself from touching her. It reminded her of having seen him at the wedding with his friend's children, Kennedy, a three-year-old little girl, and Lincoln, a toddler who had walked down the aisle holding Bullet's hand. He'd been putty in their sweet little hands, as gentle and protective as could be, without a hint of aggression. She looked for that man now, and the longer she stared, which was about all she could do at the moment, the clearer it became that he was looking at her like she was an alien he didn't understand. That's just what she felt like, because she'd never met a man like him before. Tough as a truck tire and unafraid to speak his mind. The depth of those dark eyes that flashed hot and cold like railroad crossing lights gave her the sense there was a lot more he wanted to say than the gruff and sexy comments he tossed at her. While that made her nervous, the realization that he was probably just as confused by her as she was by him somehow eased the knot in her chest. She had only glimpsed at the women in the bar, but they seemed hard, street savvy in a way she wasn't. They were obviously used to dealing with guys like Bullet. Facing him down was one thing, but a room full of Bullets? She needed to toughen up if she was going to hold her own and help the Whiskeys with this place.

He stared at her expectantly, and she realized she hadn't answered his question. "I...um...I came to measure a few things."

His eyes moved around the ample, though antiquated, kitchen. "Measure?"

She nodded again, focusing on the tattoo of a snake peeking out of his collar. What other tattoos were hidden beneath that shirt? She had a feeling they held the answers to his closed-off personality. Then again, his whole family was covered in tattoos, even Dixie, except she hadn't seen any on his brother Bones. She imagined that was because he was an oncologist and it wouldn't suit his professional image. But she found that curious, too. Bones seemed to be the only one of the Whiskeys who had chosen to follow a more professional path. Was that a reflection on their upbringing, or who each of them were at their core?

"You should work in the daytime." His deep voice pulled her from her thoughts, and she must have been quiet too long for his liking, because he said, "You shouldn't be here at night."

The comment tweaked her nerves, and she found her voice. "I'm fully capable of deciding where and when I should go places."

He chuckled, which infuriated her, turning her jitters into irritation.

She slipped her purse from her shoulder and slammed it on

the counter, *hard*. "Are you pushing my buttons on purpose, or are you really a jerk?"

She felt him watching her as she rooted around in her purse for her measuring tape and notebook, trying not to let him see how nervous he made her.

"I definitely enjoy pushing your buttons, and I'm pretty much an asshole. So, I'd say both."

Her hands stilled, and she glared at him. He shrugged with a half-cocked smile, which she found strangely endearing.

"At least you're honest," she said, and began measuring the countertops. "Why do you care when I work?"

"Why do you care about the length of our countertops?" He crossed his thick arms, watching her with a stern expression.

"Because you need enough space to prepare food. We need a deep fryer, and if we replace the oven and the refrigerator with slightly larger appliances, we need to make sure you'll still have enough room to work."

He motioned toward the table in the back of the room. "We can make sandwiches there."

"Yes," she said as she wrote down the dimensions. "But that's not efficient."

"Why? Your legs broken?" He lifted his brows, and his eyes went hot again. "Because they're looking mighty fine and functional to me."

Her cheeks flamed. Instead of responding, she turned her back to him and began measuring another counter, telling herself to calm the heck down. She felt him move behind her, as stealthily as a ninja. His proximity made her acutely aware of the heat filling the miniscule space between her back and his front. Her pulse raced as she finished measuring and scribbled the dimensions down in the notepad while he watched over her shoulder.

"That's wrong." He reached around her and picked up the measuring tape.

He stretched the tape out between his big hands, measuring the countertop while still standing behind her. The farther his arms reached, the more his body pressed against hers. Her girly parts tingled and clenched like they'd been starved for a man's touch. Okay, maybe they were. She closed her eyes, trying to focus on anything but the hardness of his thick thighs against her ass, the feel of his belt buckle pressing into her back—

"See? You missed an inch." He showed her the measuring tape.

It was all she could do to blink up at him, over her shoulder.

"Every inch counts," he said as he set down the measuring tape. "I thought all sweethearts knew that."

Nervous laughter bubbled out before she could stop it. "Sweethearts? Really?"

"What? Women are sweet." He ran the back of his knuckles lightly up her arm, then wrapped his long, strong fingers gently around her upper arm and slid them down to her elbow, leaving flames in their wake.

Her entire body shuddered with his strong touch.

"And you're extra sweet, like a sugar rush."

She bit her lower lip, caught between being turned on by his touch and amused at his lines. Then he leaned in closer. His hot breath slid over her ear, and his beard scratched her cheek, tipping her toward the turned-on side. The man was a walking roller coaster.

"Don't fight it, Finlay. You know you want to take me for a ride," he whispered, deep and raspy.

"Take you for a *ride?*" She giggled and peeled his hand from her arm, turning in the sliver of space between them. He pressed his hips against her, and while she tried not to react to the size of his package, she knew by the look in his eyes she'd failed—epically.

"A long, hard ri—"

She reached up and put her hand over his mouth. "Don't even say it. I'm not sure what type of girls you're used to, but all this"—she waved toward his body—"is not working for me."

He glanced down at her pert nipples, which pressed against the thin material of her dress, and a cocky smile lifted his lips. "Your body says otherwise."

"Ugh. You are so arrogant!" She pushed out from between him and the counter, and cooler air swept over her, making her nipples pebble even tighter. "It's the air in here."

"Uh-huh." He stepped toward her, pinning her in place with his piercing gaze.

What was it about him that was drawing her in even as warning bells went off in her head? She needed a distraction, enough space to regain control. She snagged the measuring tape from the counter to give her hands something to do and began measuring the refrigerator. Her darn hands were trembling.

He moved behind her again. "Why do you want to replace the appliances? This refrigerator works just fine."

"There's not enough space in it, and it's old as dirt. You want your appliances to function properly so your ingredients don't go bad." She moved to the counter again and jotted down the dimensions.

"It's fine," he said sharply.

"Are you always like this? Hitting on women one minute and arguing with everything they say the next? Don't you have to mind the bar?" She measured the stove, then quickly shoved her notebook in her bag, needing an escape.

"Jed's got it covered." He put his hand on her bag. "In a hurry?"

"As a matter of fact, *yes*. I'm meeting friends and I don't want to be late."

His fingers fisted in her bag, and his brows furrowed again. He tucked her bag against his side like a football and headed for the door.

"Hey!" She hurried after him. "That's my bag."

He pushed open the door and held it for her. "I'm carrying it to your car."

Confused, she passed by him and walked into the bar. His arm swept possessively around her, and suddenly all eyes turned toward her again. Only this time, there were no heated glances or haughty whistles. Both were replaced with respectful nods directed at Bullet. Anger simmered inside her.

She hurried out the front door and twisted from his grip. "What the heck was *that* all about?" She ripped her purse from his hands, unable to stop her voice from rising. "I am *not* your property, and that was…Oh my gosh, Bullet. I don't even know how to classify what you just did. It was the equivalent of dragging me by my hair into your *cave*."

"You work there now," he said evenly.

"What the heck is that supposed to mean? Just because I work for your family doesn't mean you own me."

He stepped closer, and she held up her palm. "Stop. Why do you always do that?"

"What?"

"Encroach on my personal space. Stay there. Say what you have to say, and it darn well better include an apology, because I don't need this job enough to deal with this every time I'm here."

FINLAY GLARED AT Bullet as if she could visually cut him to shreds. "I am *not* some biker guy's *old lady*! I am a professional woman, and if you refuse to treat me like one, then I'm gone, Bullet. And you can explain to your family why I left."

"What the fuck are you so pissed off about?"

"You! You think you can just push your way between my legs? Maybe other girls like all that bad-boy mojo you have going on, and I'll admit, there's something hot about it, but all that heat tends to fizzle when you treat a girl like property."

*There's something hot about it* glowed in his mind like a beacon. "I was putting a stop to the bullshit leers you were getting. Would you prefer I let you throw yourself to the wolves and allow those guys to eye-fuck you like that's all you're worth?"

For the second time in twenty-four hours, her jaw hung open, and she snapped it shut. She stepped closer, a hair more than five feet of confident bravado, all wrapped up in a frilly dress with a sweet little ribbon tied around her waist. He'd never met anyone like this feminine, smart little waif, and even though he knew he should probably take the golden ticket she was offering and let her walk away, he couldn't do it.

"Isn't that exactly what *you* have been doing to me?" she said in a calmer, accusatory voice. "Leering and making lewd comments? Trying to get me to *ride the Bullet train*?"

Aw, fuck. She had a point. "Yeah, but that's just because I'm into you. It's different."

She wrinkled her nose, as if she couldn't believe he'd said

that, so he tried to explain.

"You may not be ready to ride yet—"

"Oh my gosh," she said under her breath.

"But one day you will be, and I'm not going to let those horny bastards look at you like you're a piece of meat."

"But it's okay for you to do it?" Her eyes bloomed wide.

He nodded, then quickly realized what she'd said. "No. Wait. That's not what I'm doing."

"Yes, it most definitely is." She reached into her purse as she spoke. "Look, Bullet. I don't know what your deal is, but I like your family, and I want to help make this place better. I'm sure I'm not the type of person you're used to, but I know my way around the kitchen, and I could do this job in my sleep." She pulled out her keys and said, "Obviously I have to pull up my bootstraps and be more confident around your customers, but now that I know that, I'll do it. What I won't put up with is having to fend off your advances every time I come in. So let's lay it all on the line, right here, right now."

"Great." He crossed his arms. "Go out with me."

She laughed.

"Not the response I was looking for," he grumbled.

"How can you even ask me that after everything that just happened?"

He splayed his hands and felt a smile creep across his lips. "You put up a few roadblocks, and I'm navigating around them."

"Roadblocks?" Her shoulders dropped. "Okay, listen, we're not going to go out. Like, *ever*."

"Yes, we are, Finlay. Maybe not today or tomorrow, but one day you're going to go out with me."

"*No*, I'm not."

Refusing to play this game, he looked around the parking lot, zeroing in on a pale-pink Suburban parked by the road, and stifled a laugh. "That yours?"

"Don't laugh. It's for my catering company. I have to stand out. I want people to take notice and wonder why there's a big pink truck on the road."

"You don't need a pink vehicle to stand out. All you need to do is flash that traffic-stopping smile of yours."

"Bullet," she said softly, and headed toward her truck.

"You do have trouble with honesty, don't you?"

She turned and glared at him. "No."

"Bullshit."

"Do you always curse?"

He shrugged. "Only when I feel like it."

She studied him for a long moment, her big blue eyes moving from his face to his chest and down his arms. He wondered what she was looking for. Just as he was about to ask, she said, "Are we clear about everything now?"

"I am, but you obviously have a few things clouding your vision." He reached for her keys, and when she lifted her hand up, as if she could hold them out of his reach, he smiled and covered her hand with his. "Keys, lollipop."

She huffed out a breath and let go. As he opened her door, she said, "Lollipop?"

He wasn't about to tell her that he'd like to lick her all over. "Best type of sugar rush there is."

"I'm not sure if I should slap you or thank you."

As she climbed into the van, he put a hand on her back, and she glared at him.

"Put that scowl away, lollipop. If you think I'm not going to help you into your truck, you're wrong. And as far as slapping

25

goes, if that's what you're into, you can try it. But don't be surprised if that gorgeous ass of yours sees its turn."

She turned bright red. "I can't believe you talk like that."

"Like what? Oh, *right*. You have that thing about honesty. A proper girl like you? I'd think you were all about honesty. Where are you headed?"

She settled into the driver's seat and started the engine. "Out."

"Drinking?" He couldn't imagine her drinking anything stronger than a Shirley Temple, but he felt the need to know she was safe.

"After tonight? Most definitely."

He imagined her in a bar and immediately envisioned sleazy guys trying to pick her up. "Give me your phone."

"What? No."

"Jesus." He pulled his phone from his pocket. "What's your phone number?"

"Why?"

"Because I'm your boss and I should have it."

She rattled off her number and he sent her a text. Her phone dinged from within her purse.

"Now you have my number in case you need me." He put his hands on the roof of her car and leaned in, purposefully encroaching on her personal freaking space. "Or if you *want* me."

She blinked up at him, cheeks flushing, eyes heating.

*Yeah, that's right, lollipop. I want to get so deep in your personal space you won't be able to tell where I begin and you end.* "I'm only a phone call away."

# Chapter Three

WITH A TINY straw between her lips, Finlay leaned closer to Gemma, simultaneously draining the last of her strawberry lemonade vodka and trying to hear her talking over the blaring music. She'd always thought it was funny that the club was called Whispers when it was never quiet. She had been there a few times since she'd moved back to Peaceful Harbor, and there had been a live band playing each and every time. Tonight she was with Penny and Dixie, who were dancing in their chairs, and Gemma and Crystal, who were talking about their weddings. She took in Dixie's long, flame-red hair and tattooed shoulders and arms and Crystal's black leather miniskirt and boots. Her jet-black hair hung thick and shiny over her shoulders. Penny had come from work at her ice cream shop, looking sweet and sexy in a pair of jeans and a striped top. And then there were Gemma and Finlay, both wearing dresses and heels. They all appeared to be so different, but they got along like sisters. Finlay counted herself lucky. Back in Boston, when she wasn't running her catering company, she would hang out with Isabel. She'd worried that when she moved back to the harbor she'd be too busy trying to get her business off the ground to make friends. But she'd quickly met Gemma and Crystal when Penny's friend Tegan had referred her to cater Gemma's wedding, and they'd all hit it off right away. When they'd introduced her to Dixie, it had been another godsend. Not just for her friendship, but because of Dixie, for the next month Finlay had a job she was excited about that allowed her enough time to get things in order for her own catering company.

If she could get her arms around the situation with Bullet. The trouble was, she didn't know if she wanted to get her arms around the situation—or *him*.

*Oh boy.*

She held her hand up as the waiter walked by, then pointed to her glass when she had his attention. She was on her second drink, which wasn't much compared to how many drinks Dixie and Gemma had consumed, but Finlay rarely drank. One drink made her silly. Two would make her not give a darn about what she said. Tonight she was on a mission. If she couldn't figure out Bullet, at least she could drown her dangerous desires, and with Crystal as their designated driver, she didn't have to worry about getting home safely.

"I still think the way you proposed to Bear at our wedding was the most romantic thing I'd ever seen, other than Tru's proposal to me, of course," Gemma said to Crystal.

The waiter brought Finlay's drink, and she sipped the deliciously fruity cocktail, letting it numb her curiosity. "It was definitely the most romantic thing I've ever seen," Finlay agreed. She'd never forget the way Bear and Crystal had whispered across the aisle while Tru and Gemma had said their vows. Or the look on Bear's face when Crystal proposed, and the look on Crystal's when he'd dropped to one knee and presented a ring. Even now, weeks later, she got a warm feeling all over just thinking about it.

"Thanks," Crystal said as she tucked her dark hair behind her ear. "But wait until you hear about our *legal* wedding. You might remember that we didn't have a marriage certificate when he proposed, but we had the guy perform the ceremony anyway, and to us, that will always be our real wedding day. But we went to the courthouse two weeks later with Jed, Dixie"—she smiled across the table at Dixie—"and the rest of Bear's family."

"And my family!" Gemma reminded her.

"I was getting there," Crystal said. "Anyway, almost everyone from the wedding was at the courthouse, and it was *finally* our turn to get 'officially' married. I was more nervous than I've ever been in my life, which is crazy, because in my heart we were already married. Anyway, just as the clerk tells Bear to recite his vows, this woman *screams*. And it wasn't just a scream; it was a bloodcurdling, terrifying scream, like in a horror movie."

"My brothers and Tru bolted out of the room like bats outta hell," Dixie said, and downed her drink. She flagged down the waiter, indicating she'd like another, and said, "I'm telling you, the room *shook*, and that poor clerk had no idea what was going on."

"Clerk?" Gemma interrupted. "How about poor Kennedy and Lincoln? Lincoln started crying, 'Daddy, Daddy, Daddy,' and Kennedy, the ever-protective big sister, tried to wrench him from my arms, while at the same time screaming, 'Uncle Boney! Uncle Bullet! Uncle Be-*ah*!'"

"I love how she says 'Be-*ah*.' Don't ever teach her to say her r's," Crystal said.

Gemma rolled her eyes. "That'll be real cute at sixteen."

Penny leaned into Finlay and slurred, "We need a baby in our family."

Finlay took Penny's drink from her hands and gulped it down. "Don't look at me." Her hormones were all messed up. They had to be for her to be getting so hot and bothered over Bullet Whiskey that even Crystal's story wasn't distracting her from him. She looked at Crystal and said, "What did you do?"

"We rushed out of the room and found Bones kneeling beside a woman with a broken nose. Bear and Tru were standing in front of them like bodyguards, and Bullet's holding the asshole who hit her six inches off the ground, with his back against the wall, like this." Crystal wrapped her hand around the front of her neck. "And Kennedy yells, 'Uncle Bullet, did he hurt that lady?' Bullet turns, and I swear he melted right there in front of us."

"Yup. He turned to a big puddle of goo for my baby girl," Gemma agreed.

Finlay had seen that sweet side of him with the kids, but it worried her that she could just as easily picture him with his hand around a man's neck. "What did he do?"

Dixie laughed. "He did what Bullet does best. He kept the guy against the wall, didn't flinch, smiled at Kennedy, and somehow, without a hint of anger, he said, 'Yes, baby girl, but I'm going to make sure he never does it again.'"

"Wow," Finlay said a little breathlessly. "That's scary and chivalrous at the same time." Her eyes skirted over the dance floor, and somewhere in the back of her mind she cataloged how different Bullet looked from anyone in the bar.

"It's only scary if the guy didn't deserve it, but he literally broke that woman's nose," Crystal said. "He deserved it."

"I was worried when the police pulled Bullet off the guy,"

Gemma admitted. "But Bullet didn't seem concerned, and the guy didn't press charges, so…"

Finlay couldn't imagine seeing anything like that firsthand. "Did you have to reschedule the wedding? I would have been a mess."

"Are you kidding?" Crystal asked. "Nothing would have stopped us from getting married. Once a Whiskey man makes up his mind about something, nothing will dissuade him."

Bullet's voice thundered in her head. *You may not be ready to ride yet…But one day you will be…*

"All of them?" Finlay asked.

Dixie nodded as she checked out a dark-haired guy walking by. "We were brought up that way." The waiter brought her drink, and she tucked a five-dollar bill into his pocket and winked. She patted his butt and said, "Thanks. Now get outta here. I've got to chat with my girls."

"Dixie!" Finlay laughed.

"What? He's cute, right?" Dixie took a drink.

Crystal pushed away from the table, holding her stomach. "I think those nachos want to come back up. I'm going to the ladies' room. Back in a few minutes."

"Want me to go with you?" Gemma offered.

"No, I'm good." Crystal hurried toward the ladies' room.

Dixie leaned across the table and said, "For once my brothers aren't around. I'm going to have some fun. See? We Whiskeys *all* go after what we want." She gathered her hair over her shoulder, and her expression turned serious. "Wait. Are you worried about Bullet? Because he acted like he didn't want you to work at the bar?"

Finlay finished Penny's drink. "Yeah, that's it."

"She's lying," Penny announced. She leaned in so close her

nose nearly touched Finlay's. "You're lying. Your eye is twitching."

Finlay turned away. "It is not."

Gemma squinted at her. "Your eye *is* twitching."

"It's like Pinocchio's nose," Penny said. "But why are you...? Oh my God. You *like* him."

There was a collective gasp.

"That's why you're suddenly drinking like a fish. You never drink, except when you feel overwhelmed, which is *never.*" Penny's long lashes fluttered over her mischievous blue eyes as she patted her hand over her heart. "*Buuuullllleeeeet—*"

"*Ew!* That's my *brother.*" Dixie downed her drink.

"It's not true! I drink sometimes," Finlay insisted. "I drank when I decided to move back home. Izzy and I went out to celebrate and I had a margarita."

"*One* drink?" Penny pointed to the empty glasses in front of Finlay. "You're *totally* hot for Bullet."

"I am *not!*" Finlay insisted, purposely looking out at the dance floor instead of meeting the girls' curious gazes. *Geez! Am I?* She needed another drink, no matter what it told Penny about her feelings. Trying to figure out how she felt toward Bullet should not be decided on the heels of hearing about Bullet's convictions toward taking care of others. That was like an aphrodisiac.

"Fin, why are you lying?" Penny pushed. "Bullet's a good guy, and Lord knows you could use a man who knows what he's doing to shake things up between the sheets."

"Penny! *Please!*" She made a mental note not to share her sex life with her sister *ever* again. She never should have told Penny she'd been intimate with only one man since Aaron, or how bad that experience had been. "I'm just...*curious*, or something.

He's nothing like any of the other guys I know."

"What's going on between the sheets?" Gemma asked.

"Or *not* going on?" Dixie added.

Finlay closed her eyes, but it made her a little dizzy, so she opened them and said, "*Not* going on, thank you very much, and nothing. We're *not* talking about this."

"What are we not talking about?" Crystal asked as she slid into the seat beside Gemma. Her face was sheet white. "Whatever it is, you'd better *not talk* about it too fast. My stomach is beyond sick. I just threw up, so I called Bear. I need to go home."

"Threw up?" Gemma put her hand on Crystal's forehead. "You don't have a fever, and you didn't drink anything."

"Nachos…" Crystal put her hand on her stomach and said, "I'll have Bear come back and drive you guys home after he takes me home, but I don't think I can be in the car for that long without puking."

"We can get an Uber," Penny assured her, and the girls all agreed.

"I'm sorry you don't feel well," Finlay said. "I'd offer to drive you home, but…" She pointed to all the empty glasses on the table.

"None of you are getting behind the wheel. Got it?" Crystal demanded.

They all nodded.

Crystal leaned back, holding her stomach. "Now, please talk so I think about something other than my stomach."

They all talked at once about clothes, movies, and other nonsense to distract her. Fifteen minutes later, Bear appeared by the table, concern written all over his handsome face.

He helped Crystal to her feet and slipped an arm around her

waist. "I've got you, sugar. Can you make it to the car, or should I carry you?"

*Carry her?* Finlay's heart swelled at the love billowing off him.

"I can walk, but we may need a bucket." Crystal smiled at the girls and said, "Sorry, you guys. Gem, I'll call you if I'm still sick in the morning, but hopefully it's just the nachos."

They said their goodbyes, and after a few minutes of gushing over Bear's love for Crystal and hoping she was okay, Dixie said, "I think we need to dance."

She grabbed Finlay's hand and dragged her toward the crowded dance floor. Gemma and Penny followed them out. It had been a long time since Finlay had gone dancing, and even longer since she'd been this tipsy. She felt *amazing!* She gazed up at the colored lights misting over the dance floor, where couples swayed seductively, bumping and grinding, their skin glistening with sweat. Finlay was right there in the middle of it all, lost in a topsy-turvy world. Guys cut in to dance with her, and she sang along with the lyrics, without a care about anything other than having fun. But as men cycled through, dancing with her for a few songs, bumping and grinding, her inebriated mind turned them all into the scowling, bearded giant she was trying *not* to think about. The one who stood up for a total stranger at the risk of being arrested.

The one who wanted her to ride his *Bullet train.*

She gazed up at the blond guy she was dancing with. He was hot, with sexy dark eyes and serious dance moves. Maybe *he* could take her mind off Bullet. She swayed her hips and tried to give him a seductive look, bracing herself for the tingling sensation in her belly and the fluttering inside her that had hit full force every time she was near Bullet.

But nothing came.

Her body was numb. *Or dumb.*

*Come on,* she pleaded with herself. She needed a night of freedom and flirting, and kissing. Gosh, she missed kissing so much! She wasn't even sure she remembered how to do it. Maybe she'd really get wild and touch all this guy's muscles, too. That's what she needed. A good fu—

She couldn't even *think* the word, it went so strongly against her grain.

*Just like Bullet.*

BULLET KICKED HIS feet up on the porch railing and cracked open a beer. Tinkerbell, his rottweiler puppy, named by Kennedy, rested her chin on his leg. "How's my girl?"

He set the beer down and patted his stomach. Tinkerbell hopped up on his lap and licked his face. He grabbed her furry head between his hands and planted a kiss on her snout. "I missed you too, sweetheart."

She rested her head on his chest and curled up like a giant lap dog. His brothers were always giving him shit about allowing Tinkerbell to sit on his lap, but he didn't give a fuck if she grew to be a hundred and twenty pounds. He'd happily love her up. There weren't many things that made Bullet truly happy, but Kennedy, Lincoln, and that eighty-pound pup always put a smile on his face. Finding Tinkerbell had changed his life for the better, and he only hoped he made her life just as good. He'd been up late one night when insomnia had dug its nasty nails in deep and refused to let go. He got in his truck and got stuck behind a beat-up black Cadillac on his way out of town, when the car slowed and tossed a load of garbage into the road. Pissed off, and worried someone might get into an accident, he'd pulled over to clear the debris. He'd never forget the sick feeling that had consumed him when he'd lifted the garbage bag and felt something move. He'd found the rail-thin pup inside. He'd torn every fucking trash bag open to make sure there were no other animals, and then he'd taken the rottie straight to his buddy Marty "Paws" Miller, a veterinarian who was also a Dark Knight. The first few days were rough, with Tink puking up her food nearly every time she ate, out of nerves or because her stomach was just not used to food, he wasn't sure. But she'd soon acclimated, and she'd been Bullet's companion ever since. Neither of them could sleep without the other. Tinkerbell had become so attuned to Bullet, that on the rare occasions when the nightmares he'd experienced after first returning to civilian life claimed him, she'd wake him before they pulled him too far under.

To this day, he kept his eyes peeled for a black Cadillac with a big-ass dent in the right rear fender. God help the owner if he ever caught him, because while there were many things Bullet wouldn't put up with, hurting children, women, or animals topped the list.

He stroked Tinkerbell's back and reached for his beer. There had been a time when Bullet was a big drinker, but that, along with everything else in his life, had changed when he was in the military. Now he had an occasional beer, but for the most part he liked to remain sober just in case someone fucked up and needed his help. But it had been a long night, made longer by a stroke of unexpected jealousy that gnawed at his gut. Tonight he wanted to try to drown out thoughts of Finlay Wilson.

As he lifted the bottle to his lips, his phone rang. *Goddamn it*. He remembered that Finlay had his number, and a spear of ridiculously embarrassing hope rang through him.

Tinkerbell lifted her head as he dug his phone out of his pocket and glanced at the screen. *Bear*. He set the bottle back on the table and put the phone to his ear. "Hey, B, what's up?"

"You at home?"

"Yeah."

"Drinking?"

He glanced at the open and untouched beer. "Not yet."

"I need a favor. Crystal was out with the girls and she was the designated driver. She got sick, and I had to go pick her up."

"Where are they?" He gently nudged Tinkerbell off his lap and rose to his feet.

"Whispers."

"Aw, fuck. Seriously? Was Dixie with her?" He hated that place. Unfortunately, Dixie liked going there for exactly that reason.

"Yup."

"I'm on my way." He patted his leg and headed for his truck, with Tinkerbell trotting beside him. "How's your girl?"

"Not well, but I've got her. She thinks she ate bad nachos, but if she's not well in the morning I'll call Bones and have him check her out."

"You need anything while I'm out?"

"No. We're good. Thanks, Bullet. Take your extended cab. You'll need the space."

With Tinkerbell on the passenger seat, Bullet drove down the rural road and pulled onto the main strip. Picking up the girls was no big deal, even if he had to drag his ass out of the house after working a fourteen-hour shift. He'd spent his later teen years driving drunk customers home from the bar. That was when his father had still run the place, before his stroke. Before Bullet had enlisted and entered the Special Forces. Before he'd seen too many men take their last breaths. Before he'd found out that he wasn't invincible.

Before PTSD.

He rolled down the window as he cruised toward the night-club. The cool air helped clear his head. He reached across the seat and petted Tinkerbell, glad for the company. When he pulled into the Whispers parking lot, he spotted Crystal's car and made a mental note to pick it up with Bear if Crystal was still sick tomorrow. *Poor girl.* He added one more item to the list of things that made him smile. The way his family took care of each other. They always had each other's backs. Knowing his family was safe, that might just take the cake.

Thinking of cake, his mind turned to Finlay. She was a sugar rush if ever there was one. He felt himself smiling, and just as quickly, that smile faded. Where the fuck was *she* tonight? He threw the truck into park and patted Tinkerbell's head. "I'll be back in a few minutes. Don't go for a drive."

He cracked the windows, locked up, and headed inside to collect his sister and whoever else was wasting their night in this douche bag place.

Bullet strode into the dimly lit, testosterone-laden bar. The heat was almost as oppressive as the aura of yuppiness. He was a good head taller than the crowd, making it easy to scan his surroundings. A sea of sexed-up women danced with too-pretty men sporting manicured eyebrows and buttoned-up shirts. The guys were probably hoping for a fuck, the girls, dreaming of their frogs turning into princes, complete with a diamond ring and a white picket fence.

Bullet knew he was a menacing force, and he was used to crowds parting for him, as they were now, eyeing him up as if he might pound the hell out of someone for no damn reason. *Idiots.* Goddamn kids, living their safe little lives, afraid to step outside of the harbor and experience the harsh real world.

*Fucking Dixie.* Why did she get off on this shit? His gaze locked on her red hair, and he plowed through the crowd. She was dancing with Gemma and Jon Butterscotch, the doctor dude who came into the bar with Bones sometimes. Bullet lifted his chin in greeting. Jon was a good guy, but not for Dixie. She didn't need a stuffed shirt who drove fancy cars.

Bullet grabbed Dixie's arm. "Let's go."

Dixie spun around with fire in her eyes, grabbed his wrist the way he'd taught her, and twisted out of his grip. The anger in her bloodshot eyes morphed to irritation when she realized it was *him* who had grabbed her.

"What're *you* doing here?" She continued swaying to the music, or maybe she was swaying because of how much she'd had to drink. Bullet couldn't be sure.

The music blared so loud he had to raise his voice to be sure she heard him. "Driving your drunk ass home. Let's go."

"I can take her," Jon offered, his gaze sliding to Dixie.

*Over my dead body.* "That's okay. I've got her."

"I'll grab an Uber," Dixie insisted.

"My ass you will."

"Bullet!" Gemma clapped her hands. "Are you here to dance?"

*Jesus fuck.* They were both blasted. "No, sweetheart. I'm taking you home to Tru."

"Oh! Okay, thanks! I miss him. And my babies. I should be home with my babies." Gemma craned her neck, looking around the dance floor. "We need to find Finlay and Penny!" she hollered. "There's Fin! With that guy!"

Like a scope on a rifle, he zeroed in on Finlay's blond hair, her slinky little body dancing too damn close to some prick. Bullet glared at the guy as he closed the distance between them, drawing the weasel's attention. The guy stumbled back, putting space between him and Finlay as Bullet's arm swept around her waist. "Come on, lollipop. Time to go."

"Bullet? What are you doing here?" she yelled, pointing to her ear. "I can't hear you!"

He bent to speak into her ear and she threw her arms around his neck and said, "Dance with me!"

*Christ. You're plastered too? So much for Shirley Temples.* "We're leaving."

He took a step, and she squirmed from his grip.

"I'm not leaving! I'm *dancing*." She reached for the guy she'd been dancing with, and Bullet gave him a dark look.

The guy held his hands up and disappeared into the crowd.

"You scared him away! Now you *have to* dance with me." She plastered herself against him, and he caught Penny's sleeve as she stumbled past, yanking her against his side and holding on tight as he pried Finlay's delicate arms from around his waist. He hauled her against his other side and demanded, "Gemma, Dixie. Front door. *Now*."

Groaning, arms flailing, Dixie traipsed ahead of him, while Gemma hummed with a smile on her lips.

"I don't *want* to leave!" Finlay pleaded.

Bullet glanced at Penny, who said, "She doesn't get out much."

Ignoring Dixie's pouts and Finlay's struggles, he managed to get them to the front door. He pushed it open, and Finlay spun around, heading into the bar. He grabbed the back of her dress and pulled her against him.

"Not happening, lollipop. You're too drunk."

"I am *not* drunk!" she said, leaning against him. "Right, Pen? I can hold my liquor." Her eyes bloomed wide as he led the stumbling, swaying lot of them toward his truck. "I can hold my booze, my bar liquid. My…I don't want to go home."

Penny laughed and buried her face in Bullet's side. "I can't believe we have to be escorted home by a Whiskey."

"More like taken against our will," Dixie said as she tilted, grabbing Gemma's shoulder to steady herself.

Bullet grabbed ahold of the back of Finlay's dress again to keep her from running off, holding on tight as he unlocked and opened the truck door. She came face-to-face with Tinkerbell—and *screamed*. All at once, Penny squealed, Tinkerbell barked, Gemma turned and puked, and Finlay scrambled behind Bullet, clinging to his hips, her face pressing into his leather vest.

*Christ.*

Dixie stood by the truck, arms crossed, taking it all in with an amused smile.

"Get in, Dix. Tink, *back. Floor*," he commanded, and Tinkerbell jumped into the backseat and lay down on the floor. He turned to Gemma and helped her upright, searching her face. She had the relieved look of someone who had spewed poison from their body. A good sign. "You okay, sweetheart?"

Gemma nodded.

Bullet swept an arm behind him and pulled Finlay around to his front. Her face remained buried in his leather vest. She clung to him, eyes slammed shut. At least she wasn't running. "I've got you, lollipop."

She whimpered.

"She's afraid of dogs," Penny explained.

"You afraid of dogs, too?" he asked Penny.

She shook her head.

"Great. You and Dix, in the back with Tinkerbell."

Finlay laughed against his stomach. "Tinkerbell? Big, bad *Brutus* has a dog named Tinkerbell?"

He cursed under his breath. Dixie stomped around to the other side and climbed in as Bullet peeled Finlay from his body and helped her into the front seat. "Slide all the way over."

"You just want me next to you," Finlay snapped as she scooted across the bench seat.

He wasn't going to touch that one with a ten-foot pole. He reached for Gemma and helped her in, taking an extra second to be sure she was okay. Truman, Gemma, and their babies might not be blood relatives to Bullet, but he considered them family. And since the girls had obviously taken Finlay into the fold, she was, too, which meant Bullet would take care of her from here on out, regardless of whether or not she ever gave him a second look. Because that's how the Whiskeys rolled. *Love, loyalty, and respect for all* wasn't just the Dark Knights' creed. It was how they lived their lives. And when you entered the Whiskeys' circle, you became family.

"Buckle up, girls." They were all within reach. *Safe.* Bullet exhaled with relief. "Let's get you home."

"She's got a fancy pink collar, Fin!" Penny said as she loved up Tinkerbell. "Aw, look how cute."

Finlay covered her face, doubled over in laughter. "Tinkerbell."

Bullet pulled the seat belt across Finlay's lap. She spread her fingers, peeking out at him, and whispered, "Sorry. It's a good nam—" Laughter swallowed her voice.

Bullet spent the next hour driving Gemma, Penny, and Dixie home and walking them to their doors, all the while Finlay gave a play-by-play of their evening. He gritted his teeth through descriptions of enough guys to gag a man. After dropping off Dixie, who hugged and thanked him despite all her bitching, he climbed back into the truck.

Finlay rested her head on his shoulder with a long, drawn-out sigh. "You're, like, a *hero*."

"Far from it. Where's your place, lollipop?"

"Lolli." She snort-laughed and started singing a song about lollipops he hadn't heard since he was a kid.

Even drunk off her ass she was too fucking cute. He scrubbed a hand over his face, but couldn't suppress his smile. "Fins, where do you live?"

"His kiss is sweeter than a cherry pie, and he's shakin', rockin', dancin', ploppin'…"

"I don't know that song, but I'm pretty sure you've got the words wrong. Come on, let's get you home."

She continued singing a drunken rendition of the Lollipop song, only now she was shaking her shoulders and waving her hands. "Oh, lolli, lolli, body, body, candy *stick*."

"*Christ*," he muttered as he drove onto the main drag. "Where to, Fins?"

"Whispers!" she said far too cheerily. Then sang, "Lolli, lolli, *pop*!"

"Not a chance."

"No, I mean, head *over* there. That's near where I live." She sat up straighter, pressed her knees together, and folded her hands in her lap.

He realized she was trying to rein in the carefree woman she'd unleashed. Some people needed alcohol to get a stick out of their ass, and some needed it to escape life. He knew Finlay didn't need it for the first, and he had a feeling she loved her life as it was, which made him wonder what she was trying to escape.

"How often do you drink like this?"

"Never," she said happily, and began humming.

"Why'd you drink so much tonight?"

"I'm not drunk," she insisted, and began bobbing her head as she hummed.

"Don't stop singing on my account," he said, earning one of her effervescent smiles.

She sang and hummed, and sang some more, until she collapsed with another long sigh against him. She smelled like warm vanilla and sugar. Like freshly baked cookies, and *damn*, would he like to eat her up. Her body melted against his side, which he liked way more than he probably should considering she might not remember it in the morning.

Her hand fell to his thigh, and she sang, "Thick thighs, cherry pies," as Whispers came into view. "Turn right at the next light."

He tried not to make too much out of her hand on his thigh, but his body had other ideas. As he turned down the road and drove toward a residential area, he said, "You live across the street from the bar? Why didn't you tell me before I drove you all around town?"

She grinned up at him and squeezed his thigh, which sent heat straight to his groin. "And miss all the fun? Besides, we *needed* this time alone."

Yeah, they needed time alone all right, but not with her ten sheets to the wind.

She traced the tattoos on his forearm, whisper-singing, "Call me babypop, lollipop, lollipop." She hummed as she directed him down two more streets to a quiet residential cul-de-sac. "I'm renting the one at the end. Why are you so gruff all the time when everyone else thinks you're a hero?" she asked out of the blue.

He cut the engine and wondered who had been filling her head with bullshit. "I told you, I'm no one's hero." He unhooked her seat belt. She curled her fingers around his forearm, gazing hungrily into his eyes. Her hair was tousled, and her cheeks were flushed. He wished he'd been the cause of those things. It took all his restraint not to lean forward and kiss her.

Tinkerbell's head popped up behind the seat and she barked, startling Finlay into Bullet's arms. If this was how she reacted to dogs, maybe they'd take a stroll through the pound.

"Lie down, Tink."

"Thank you," she whispered, as if talking alone might call Tinkerbell into the front seat. "You didn't answer me," she said quietly, looking temptingly innocent. Her hand moved up and down his forearm, slow and painfully soft. "Why are you so gruff?"

He wasn't used to women like her, all pure and honest. She made him *want* to talk, and the feeling was so foreign, he forced himself to climb out of the truck rather than contemplate it. She scooted over to the door, her frilly dress bunched around her thighs. A tiny gold heart hung around her neck on a sparkling chain, and she had a sad look in her eyes that nearly dropped him to his knees.

"*Talk* to me," she pleaded. "You can't hide behind all that bigness forever."

*Wanna bet?* "How about we get you inside."

He helped her to her feet, steadying her as she swayed, and

then grabbed her purse from the seat. He peered into the back and said, "Hold down the fort, Tink. I'll be back."

As he cracked the window for Tinkerbell, he took in the incredibly small house. The covered porch was barely wider than the front door. A small picture window overlooked an even smaller garden, and a single window was centered in the gable. It looked more like a dollhouse than a residence.

"You remind me of that guy in that show," she said as they walked up a narrow walkway. "The big guy. The one everyone hated."

He put an arm around her to keep her from tipping backward as they ascended the porch steps. He had no idea what show she was talking about, but he had a feeling neither did she.

He held up her purse, and she dug out her keys. When she dangled them in front of her eyes like they'd magically appeared, he took them from her and unlocked the door.

She leaned against the wall fidgeting with the little bow at her waist. "Why do you open doors and help drunk girls? It doesn't really go with your bad-boy image."

She pushed from the wall, swaying forward. He caught her before she could fall, and lifted her into his arms, reveling in her softness and her heavenly scent. It had been too long since he'd gotten laid, and his dick instantly rose to the occasion.

"Whoa!" She wrapped her arms around his neck and rested her cheek against him. "Your chest is so *hard*."

He bit his tongue against a filthy retort and carried her inside, closing the door softly behind him. His gaze swept over the room, taking in the white shag rug, a beige sofa and love seat, fluffy pink, purple, and flowered pillows, and a host of neatly stacked notebooks and a giant calendar atop a glass coffee table. Across the room, a round kitchen table littered with ledgers, colorful sticky notes, a cup full of pens, and several cookbooks sat in front of a set of glass doors. The walls were decorated with photographs of Finlay, Penny, and he assumed, their parents, intermixed with happy and inspirational sayings, like, *Make today beautiful!* and *Believe you can and you will.*

He headed for the couch and she pointed down the hall. "Bedroom, *please.*"

Clenching his jaw, he hesitated. Finlay Wilson's bedroom. The place he'd been fantasizing about since he'd met her at Truman's wedding. He'd fantasized about the feminine beauty having a dark side that came out in the bedroom. He'd also fantasized about taking her in a soft, frilly bed that was all *Finlay.*

She leaned up and ran her finger over his beard as she whispered, "Bedroom, Brutus."

*Brutus.* Why did that make him even hotter? Against his better judgment, he carried her down the hall.

Her hand slid down his neck, playing over the skin just above the collar of his T-shirt. "Why did you get a snake tattoo? What else do you have tattooed on you?" She tugged at his neckline, peered beneath his shirt, and gasped. "Chest hair! I *love* chest hair."

Her hand dove down the front of his shirt, grazing his nipple. *Christ.* She wrecked him.

"Male models don't even have chest hair anymore." Her fingers moved along his pecs. "I bet they shave *everywhere.*" She leaned up again as he crossed the threshold to her bedroom and whispered, "I bet you don't shave *anywhere.*"

He tried to quell his mounting desire, but it came out in the form of a groan. Her bedroom looked just as soft and innocent as she did. Floral-patterned pillows rested against a tufted white headboard, and cutesy knickknacks in light colors filled the room.

She peeked down his shirt again. "I see ink. What is it? Show me?"

He set her on the edge of the bed, and she grabbed the hem of his shirt and pulled him so close he could taste her sweet breath.

"Finlay," he warned.

"*Brutus,*" she said with a giggle, and pushed his shirt up.

The feel of her warm hands on his stomach sent heat streaming through his veins. He grabbed her wrists and shook his head.

"The guy in that movie had tattoos, too. You could be him, you know. You're big and burly, and I bet you're good at being naked like he was." She covered her mouth and whispered, "Oops! Did I say naked?"

He cocked a brow.

"I meant...*naked.*"

*Fuck.* Hearing her alluring voice say that word made him hard as stone. "Finlay, stop. You're drunk, and I don't want you to regret anything tomorrow."

She glared at him. "For your information, I'm *not* drunk."

"Are you sober?" he asked.

She leaned forward, and the neckline of her dress shifted, giving him an eyeful of her gorgeous breasts straining against pink lace. She pressed her lips together. "No, but I'm not drunk. I'm *tipsy.*"

"Right, we'll see if you remember any of this tomorrow."

She pushed to her feet, using his hip to steady herself, and said, "You think I don't know what I'm saying? Well, guess what, Brutus?" She accentuated her words, which flew from her mouth at breakneck speed, by poking him in the sternum. "I know exactly what I'm saying. I *wanted* to drink too much tonight so I could stop thinking about you and your dirty talk. I *want* to see you without your shirt on. I want to see your tattoos because I want to know why you have them, and what they mean, and how you got them with chest hair? Did they shave it? I *do* think you look like that actor Jason Mammoth, or whatever his stinking name is. And I *know* I want to see you nake—"

A slow smile crept across his lips.

Finlay slapped her hand over her mouth, eyes wide. "I think you'd better go," she said from behind her hand as she lowered herself to the bed.

"Sure you're okay?"

She nodded.

"For the record—"

She closed her eyes and held up her hand, silencing him.

"I want to see you naked too," he said honestly.

Her eyes popped open, her cheeks flamed red, and her jaw gaped again. He used his index finger to lift her chin so her mouth closed.

Thrusting a thumb over his shoulder, he said, "I'm going. Lock up after I leave."

Chuckling, he headed out to his car. For the first time in years, he couldn't wait to go to work the next day.

# Chapter Four

"I'M GOING TO slaughter you," Finlay said to Penny over the phone the next afternoon as she stood by the kitchen counter, cracking eggs into a bowl.

"Why? You needed to cut loose, and it's not like you got into any trouble."

"Oh no?" She began beating the eggs. "What would you call telling Bullet Whiskey that I wanted to see him naked? You *know* I can't hold my liquor. You're my sister. You should stop me from doing bad things."

"Then you've got the wrong sister, because I was thrilled that you finally had some fun, Fin. You haven't gone out and had any fun since you lost Aaron."

Finlay added more ingredients to the bowl and beat them as hard and fast as she could. She did not want to think about Aaron, or how long it had been since she'd been interested in a man. She'd finally gotten some perspective on Aaron's death. And talking about the fact that she hadn't dated much since she'd lost him wouldn't change it. She only wanted to figure out how to walk into Whiskey Bro's today and look Bullet in the eye without feeling like she was standing there buck naked now that she'd revealed her innermost thoughts.

"You're baking," Penny said.

"Of *course* I'm baking! Didn't you hear me? I told *Bullet* I wanted to see him *naked*. And I knew I was saying it when it came out. It wasn't like I was too drunk to think straight. I was just drunk enough to think straight *and* tell the truth." She had always turned to cooking when she was emotional. When she'd lost Aaron she'd come up with five new recipes in one weekend, and when they'd lost their father she'd baked enough desserts for three homeless shelters in the first five days. It was a wonder she didn't weigh three hundred pounds.

Penny laughed. "Aren't you the one who preaches honesty?"

"Yes, but I'm working for his family, and he's the kind of guy who probably sleeps with women like other guys eat chips. And you know I am not that kind of girl."

"Maybe not, but how do you know he's like that? I'm so glad you moved home, by the way. You really have been out of the real world for too long. There's more to life than just work, Fin. And besides, be careful what you say. Maybe I'm one of *those* girls. I'm no saint."

"I'm sorry." Finlay set the bowl aside and sank down to a chair at the table. She knew Penny wasn't the kind of girl who slept with lots of guys, but her sister did have a more active sex life than she did. Then again, didn't most socially active twentysomething women?

"Fin, it's been years since you lost Aaron. Why can't you explore a little?"

"I did explore, remember? Last year?" The last time she'd had sex was at the end of last year, and it hadn't gone well. She hadn't felt any pleasure, and definitely not the type of connection she should have. That experience had been the catalyst to her decision to move back home. Even with Isabel's friendship, she'd been lonely. If she wasn't whole enough to love a man, then she could at least be near her sister, who loved her unconditionally.

"I know, but one bad experience does not mean that you won't find a connection with someone else. Listen, Fin, I've had more sex than you have, and I'm four years younger than you. Maybe you should admit to remembering everything. Tell Bullet the truth, that you think about sleeping with him. Go out with him. Heck, sleep with him if you want to. This is your life and your body, and no one is going to judge you, if that's what you're worried about."

"I'm not worried anyone will judge me. I just...I can't tell him that. I don't even know if I want to sleep with him. I just know that he makes me confused, and hot. Definitely hot. But that doesn't mean I need to jump his bones."

"Then you could lie and say it was a minor lapse in judgment due to alcohol consumption, or just act like you don't remember anything from last night. He'll probably believe that. And don't be embarrassed, which I know you will be. It's not like he knows you well enough to realize that the side he saw last night has been kept under lock and key for years."

"Ugh. Why does everything sound so easy when you say it?"

"Because it is. You have choices. Lie or be honest. I personally think you should take a ride on the *Bullet train* and *then* figure it out. What do you have to lose?"

"Only my mind. I can't believe my baby sister is telling me to sleep with a biker."

"Hey, you're the one who wants to get naked with him. I'm just being supportive. Besides, I *like* the Whiskeys. I'd date one of them in a second."

"How are we even sisters?" Finlay laughed. "You jump into things with your eyes closed, and I have no idea what I want. All I know for sure is that he's got this way of looking at me, and it makes me nervous, but the good kind of nervous, you know? With Aaron I felt sparks, but this is like *lightning*. And I don't understand it, or know what to make of it. He's everything I *never* wanted. You know me. Clean-cut guys all the way. But I haven't been able to stop thinking about him since I saw him at Tru and Gemma's wedding with their kids when he made that ridiculous pass at me. Remember?"

"I'll never forget that one. Heck, I want you to sleep with him just so I know if he really is a *Bullet train*."

They both laughed.

"Listen," Penny said in that I-have-all-the-answers-little-sister voice that Finlay knew so well. "You're curious because he's tough and confident and strong. He's everything *you* are—"

"What? Have you lost your mind? I'm none of those things. I'm like a flower and he's a lawn mower."

"You're so wrong. You're one of the strongest women I know. When we lost Dad, you were my rock. And now you're here. Do you know how much courage it takes to pick up your life and start over?"

"Do you know how much courage it takes to open your own ice cream store with your inheritance and have no idea if you'll sink or swim?"

"See?" Penny said. "We are definitely sisters, 'cause you're doing the same thing with your catering company. Will you bring me some of whatever you're making?"

"Sure. They're cookies. I'm going to spend the morning choosing new appliances for the bar, and this time when I go there, I'm not going to run like a scared kitten into the kitchen.

I'm going to pretend the customers are my catering clients, and put myself at ease."

"In other words, you're going to distract them from your blond hair, blue-eyed goody-two-shoes image with food."

"Pretty much. But really, it's about distracting *me*, not them."

"Throw some jeans on, and a pair of boots. That'll help you fit in."

"This is about *me* being comfortable, and I'm comfortable in skirts and dresses. I've got this. You'll see. I'll come by before I head over to the bar."

After she ended the call, she noticed her message light was on and scrolled to her text messages. She didn't recognize the number, but when she opened the text and read it—*Here when you need me. B*—she realized it was the message Bullet had sent her last night, and lightning ricocheted inside her.

She stared at the text, thinking about the way he'd plowed into the bar last night and had dragged them all out of there, no questions asked. Was that the way the Whiskeys did things? Or was that just Bullet's way? What if she hadn't been tipsy? Would he have let her stay to find her own way home?

*Would I have wanted him to?*

She added his name to her contacts, then set about making the cookies. She mixed and kneaded, rolled, and cut, creating dozens of motorcycles, leather jackets, and boots. She was excited to see the customers' faces when they tasted her special recipe. *Yes, it's the customers I'm hoping love them. Not Bullet. Nope. Not him.*

*Yeah, right. I can't even lie to myself!*

While the cookies baked, she shopped online for appliances, comparing prices, sizes, and warranties. She called the companies and negotiated discounts for her top three choices, printed out the spec sheets, and put them in a folder alongside the budget she and Dixie had come up with. She and Dixie were meeting again Friday morning to discuss the kitchen renovation.

After the cookies cooled, she took her time decorating them, copying pictures from the Internet to define the motorcycle parts from the seats and fuel tanks (which she'd had no idea was the big thing in front of the seat), to the spokes on the wheels and fenders. As she studied and copied, she learned the locations of shock absorbers and other mechanical parts, making mental notes to try larger motorcycle cookies so she could include those details. She used black frosting on the jacket- and boot-shaped cookies, added silver zippers to the jackets and soles to the leather boots. She wrote WHISKEY BRO'S or WB's on each one, and made a special cookie for Bullet. Then she set them carefully on her pink catering trays, wrapped them up, adding her standard pink ribbons with FINLAY'S printed on them. She changed into a pretty coral-colored dress, and because Penny might be right, she wore her brown leather knee-high boots.

She stuffed her folders and phone into her bag and hoisted it over her shoulder, taking one last look around her living room. Her gaze caught on a yellow sticky note on her calendar. She plucked the calendar from the coffee table, laughing and shaking her head as she read what could only be a note from Bullet, written in red ink and stuck to that coming Friday. *This is when you need me.*

She vacillated between smiling and stewing nervously all the way to Penny's ice cream shop. When she arrived, she was in a *smiling* stage. She breezed in the door, the bells chiming overhead, and it took her sister less than thirty seconds to say,

"Holy crap. You either got laid or you're about to." Penny looked at her watch. "It's five thirty. I'm going with about to get laid."

Finlay wrinkled her nose. "Do you kiss your mother with that mouth?" She handed her a bag of cookies.

"Mom's too far away to kiss, but I do lots of dirty things with my mouth." She stuck out her tongue and wiggled it. Their mother had moved to Montana two years ago and had since remarried.

"Ew! Pen!"

Penny peeked into the bag and inhaled. "Ah, sugary goodness. I am so glad you're back."

"You run an ice cream store. You can have sugar anytime you want."

Penny bumped her with her hip and said, "But not cookies made with love by my favorite sister. Now, about getting laid…"

"Not happening. I'm just happy, that's all."

"Because…?"

Finlay didn't know exactly what Bullet meant by her *needing him* on Friday, but she knew if she said anything to Penny she'd push her to *explore*, so instead she said, "Even though it freaks me out, it's easier knowing that *he* knows I have thought about him as more than just some pushy guy."

"You always did love open communication. You get that from Dad. Remember what he used to say when we'd go out and give him vague answers about where we were going?"

"'How can I keep you safe if I don't know where you're going?'" they both said in unison.

"I miss him," Penny said. "I think he'd like knowing we are both here in Peaceful Harbor, and doing well."

"He knows." Finlay hugged her. She'd always believed that her father was watching over them. They'd been close to their parents, and when their mother had moved away because the memories of their father made it too hard for her in Peaceful Harbor, she and Penny had understood. And when she fell in love with another man, they were happy for her. Though neither believed their mother would ever love anyone the way she had their father. He'd been funny, loving, and he worked hard to support their family. He was one of the hardest workers at the power plant.

"I've got to go. I have a lot to do today," Finlay said, and headed for the door. "I have to start menu planning!"

"Fun, fun. Just make sure there's room on your menu for dessert." Penny winked. As Finlay walked out the door, she called after her, "That means sex!"

Finlay spun around, mortified that the woman walking by had heard what her sister had said. "Penelope Anne!" She glared at Penny.

Penny thrust her hips forward while pulling her arms back and made a face like she was in the throes of an orgasm.

*Great.* Now she was thinking about Bullet *and* sex.

As she drove toward the bar, she couldn't help wondering what Bullet, who was all power and forward motion, would be like in bed. *He's a Bullet train.* Her stomach fluttered, and her pulse quickened. *No, no, no.* She tried to think about work, cookies, the cars on the road. Anything other than Bullet. But his seductive, demanding eyes plagued her. And now, thanks to Penny, so did the *rest* of his body.

*I want to see you without your shirt on...I know I want to see you nake—*

Shivers tickled up her spine.

*This cannot be happening.*

Bullet's raspy voice slithered through her mind. *Don't fight it, Finlay. You know you want to take me for a ride.*

She shoved her hand beneath the wrapping that covered the cookies, grabbed one of the motorcycle cookies, and shoved it into her mouth. *Three hundred pounds, here I come.*

BULLET SLID A glass of beer across the bar to Lance "Crow" Burke, one of the Dark Knights. His family owned Mid-Harbor Housing Supply and Renovation, and Bullet had known him since they were kids. He had pitch-black hair and angular features, almost too angular, like a model—hence his road name, Crow. Asking him to come in and talk had been a double-edged sword for Bullet, as Crow had a reputation for being a womanizer, and he'd always had a thing for Dixie. Both Dixie and their mother, Red, were waitressing tonight, which Crow was enjoying far too much.

"About that project I mentioned," Bullet said to get his attention off his sister. He'd hoped Finlay would show up at some point, but either he'd pissed her off or she was sleeping off a hangover, because he hadn't heard a peep from her. But that didn't stop him from thinking about her every damn minute of the day.

"The kitchen, right?" He took a swig of his beer. "Dixie mentioned it a few weeks ago." He glanced over his shoulder at Dixie again, then turned back to Bullet. "She said y'all are doing some renovations in the kitchen, but she wasn't sure what you'd need. She also said not to do anything unless I spoke to *her*."

"She's busy," Bullet said. He had agreed to let Dixie manage the renovations, hiring, the whole shebang, but after seeing Finlay measuring and moving so quickly, he wanted to make sure things got done without holding up her plans.

"Still, Bullet. You're a force to be reckoned with, but that one?" He glanced at Dixie again and whistled. "I'm not dumb enough to go against the fire in her belly."

Bullet flattened both hands on top of the bar and leaned across it, bringing them eye-to-eye. "Don't think about her body parts, got it?"

Crow laughed and took another drink.

Dixie stalked over to the bar. "B, I need two whiskey sours, one Heiny, and one Coors." She set her hand on her hip, and her features softened as she faced Crow. "Hey there. Have you given any thought to the renovations I mentioned?"

Crow's appreciative smile practically slapped Bullet in the face. "You know I always give thought to your propositions."

Dixie rolled her eyes.

"Cut it out, Crow," Bullet warned.

Crow pulled something out of his back pocket and handed it to Dixie. "It's all there, babe. Everything you asked for. Prices, timelines." As he lifted the beer to his lips, he eyed Bullet, as if to say, *Calm down. I'm riding a fine line and you have no reason to pound the shit out of me.*

Bullet leveled the smirk on his face with a dark stare before turning his attention to filling Dixie's drink order. He wanted to see that damn list, but the truth was, this was Dixie's area to manage. He didn't need to piss her off any more than he already had.

"Jesus, you two. Cut the shit," Dixie said, and stalked off to help another customer.

It was a constant job keeping his family safe, but it was one

Bullet was good at, even if it ruffled their feathers. He couldn't do anything about the way Dixie dressed in skinny jeans, Daisy Dukes, miniskirts, half or tight shirts, and boots, all the things guys got off on, but he could yank the men's leashes when they needed reining in.

He filled several drink orders, talked with his usual customers, and shot the shit with Crow, all the while keeping one eye on the front door in case Finlay showed up.

"I hear Penny's sister is helping y'all get the kitchen up and running," Crow said. "What's she like?"

As if beckoned by the stars, Finlay backed into the bar in one of her sexy short dresses, carrying some sort of tray in each arm and with a big bag over her shoulder.

"Who is *that*?" Crow's gaze flamed as he drank her in.

"Eyes back in your head. It's Finlay." Bullet came out from behind the bar as she practically twirled, her dress whisking around her thighs. She almost ran right into him. He grabbed the trays to keep them from falling out of her hands.

Every eye in the frigging place was watching her, including his.

"Whoa!" She smiled up at Bullet. "Sorry. I didn't see you there."

Her eyes sparkled with happiness, and he felt himself falling into them. He focused on the trays to keep from making a fool of himself. "What's all this?"

"Cookies," she said cheerfully as she walked around him and took a tray from his hands. She set it on the bar, then turned back for the other, setting it beside the first. She plopped her bag on a barstool beside Crow and began taking things out of it—pink napkins and plates that read FINLAY'S in swirly white letters, and at least a dozen tiny pink notepads with the same logo at the top.

"What's going on, lollipop?" Bullet asked as she untied a pink ribbon from around one of the trays.

She stepped in close, surprising him, and motioned for him to lean down. The scent of warm vanilla and sugar seeped beneath his skin, and it *wasn't* from the cookies.

"I know I need to feel comfortable here, and I also need to get to know your customer base so I can figure out the best menus for them. Cookies are a great ice breaker." She grabbed something wrapped in pink tissue paper from a tray and handed it to him. "This one is yours. I hope you love it! But if you don't, it's okay. I have thick skin."

She spun on her sexy-as-sin boot heels and walked around to each table, delivering her goodies.

There was nothing *thick* about Finlay Wilson. The muscles in Bullet's neck knotted up as she flitted from table to table, smiling and chatting, touching the arms and shoulders of each customer as she leaned in close to catch every word they said. The men ate up her attention. The quiet ones became motormouths, the dicks shamefully leered, and she made fast friends with the women. His fingers curled into fists, stopping short of crushing the gift she'd given him.

He didn't have time for gifts. He needed to draw some very dark lines in the sand. Fuck, he needed a goddamn backhoe.

He strode across the floor, eyes locked on Finlay. *His* Finlay. Yeah, he might not have the right to claim her, but he didn't care. In his mind she was already his, whether she knew it or not. He stepped around a table and Red came out of nowhere, blocking his path.

Standing before him in a black Whiskey Bro's shirt, black jeans, and a smile that said, *I love you, but...*, she wrapped her hand around his arm and said, "Come on, sweetheart." His mother never called them by their road names. While she'd chased after four wild kids, it had probably been easier to call them the endearments that still rolled off her tongue so easily—*sweetheart, babe, honey*. On the rare occasions when she used their given names, she meant business.

She took a step toward the bar, but Bullet's boots were rooted to the floor. His gaze darted to Finlay, who was now standing by the pool tables, talking with two guys while holding out a paper plate with cookies on it.

*Fucking cookies.*

His mother sighed, worry settling in her eyes as she patted his arm. "Brandon Whiskey, trust me on this. You do *not* want to do what you're dead set on doing."

"*Red*," he said, knowing when his mother set her mind on something, like the rest of them, there was no dissuading her. They'd called her Red since they were kids, when Bear had heard her friends calling her by her name, Wren, and thought they'd said Red. The name had stuck.

"Come with me, babe. Let's have a little chat."

He tried to clear his throat, but it came out as a growl, and she laughed.

"Well, this is *new*." She guided him away from the tables, but he kept his eyes trained on Finlay. "Eyes down here, baby boy."

He met her amused gaze.

"I thought your brothers were crazy when they said you had a thing for Finlay at Tru and Gemma's wedding. Clearly, I was slow on the uptake."

"Your point?"

"My point is"—she lifted his hand holding the tissue-paper-wrapped gift from Finlay—"that sweet little thing over there is not a biker girl. You can't bully your way into her heart, or scare away every man who looks at her with the hopes that she'll only see you."

"I can try." He was only half kidding.

"Yes, and you'll push her away faster than you can grovel to get her back."

He stroked his beard, mulling over what she was saying and hating every word of it. "I'm not walking away from her."

"Did I say you should?" She arched a slim red brow. "I'm not sure you could if you wanted to. I've waited forever to see that fire in your eyes."

"You always say I was born with fire in my eyes."

"And you were. The fire you were born with made you the man you are." She glanced at Finlay, and then his mother's green eyes found him again. "But this fire will make you the man you're supposed to be." She paused, as if she wanted her words to sink in, which they did.

All the way to his bones.

She smiled and said, "Don't go after your sweetheart with your brawn, baby. Go after her with your heart. That's the biggest and best thing that sets you apart from every other tough guy out there."

He watched her stroll away to help another customer, and he wondered why women had to talk in riddles. What the hell did it mean to go after her with his heart? He glanced at Finlay, who was reaching across a table, which gave him a perfect view of her ass. His cock twitched. *Calm the hell down. You're not my fucking heart.*

As he went behind the bar, Jed showed up for his shift and snagged a cookie.

"These are awesome." Jed wiped his forearm across his mouth. His thick blond hair flopped over his eyes. It was hard to put him and Crystal together as siblings, with her jet-black hair.

Jed had a history of theft, but Bullet had recently learned about Jed and Crystal's painful past, which had led Jed to do what he'd had to in order to help his family, and had led to Crystal's total transformation.

Bullet became aware of the gift in his right hand again. "You can take off tonight."

"No, man. I'm supposed to work, and it's busy."

"Schedule change. I need you to work Friday night. That cool?" *Please fucking say it's cool.*

"Seriously? I told you I'd work whenever you needed me. I can stay tonight, too, if you want me to."

"Nah. Go have some fun. Just stay out of trouble. And thanks for Friday."

Jed pulled on his leather jacket and patted Bullet's shoulder. "Thanks for tonight. Now I can meet up with Quincy and head down to a bonfire on the beach." He snagged another cookie from the near-empty tray on his way out.

Quincy was Truman's younger brother and Jed's roommate. He'd also had a shitty upbringing. Unfortunately, he'd followed in his mother's footsteps down a drug-infested path. But he was clean now, and on a safe and healthy track. And Bullet would do everything within his power to make sure he stayed that way.

There was an influx of drink orders after Jed left. Bullet set the tissue-paper-wrapped gift on the counter behind him and tended to customers. Finlay was still on her cookie-inspired mission, moving from patron to patron, but now she was passing out little notepads and tiny pink pencils, asking people to write down their favorite bar foods. She set a bowl in the middle of each table for the customers to put their suggestions in. She'd gone from a deer in the headlights to driving the truck in the blink of an eye. Her confidence and determination were as big a turn-on as her innocence and beauty.

As soon as there was a break in orders, Bullet turned his back to the bar and unwrapped the tissue paper, unveiling a cookie that looked a hell of a lot like him, from his beard and tattoos right down to his black leather boots. While all the other cookies had WHISKEY BRO'S or WB scrawled across them, his cookie read, BULLET TRAIN.

# Chapter Five

THE NEXT MORNING Finlay let herself into Whiskey Bro's. The bar didn't open for a few hours and she knew she'd have time alone to go through the customers' suggestions from last night before her meeting with Dixie to go over the appliances. She could hardly believe she'd pulled off getting to know so many customers without being a nervous wreck. But Bullet had taken care of that when she'd walked in the door and nearly slammed into him. After blurting out all the secret thoughts she'd been having about him, she'd been most nervous about facing *him*. And for whatever reason, after she'd nearly bowled him over when she'd arrived, he'd kept his distance for the rest of the evening. When she'd gathered her things to leave for the night, he'd been tied up with customers, and she'd slipped out the front door without a confrontation.

Now, as she sat at the bar, sifting through customer menu suggestions, her mind traveled back to the night Bullet had carried her into her bedroom. He'd never answered her questions about why he was so gruff or why he'd come to get them. Dixie had told her that after dropping all of them off Wednesday night, Bullet had picked up Bear and taken him to get Crystal's car. She found it curious that he was always willing to drop what he was doing for his family. Didn't he have a social life? She'd assumed he was out on his bike at all hours, picking up women and doing Lord only knew what. But he'd been stone-cold sober every time she'd seen him, including when she'd met him at the wedding, which was more than she could say for herself in the last forty-eight hours.

She unfolded a piece of notepaper and read another customer suggestion. *More cookies, and buffalo wings.* She smiled, pleased at the response. There were several more requests for cookies, along with sandwiches, burgers, salads—which surprised her—and a host of other easy-to-make dishes. She wondered what Bullet had thought of his cookie. Did he notice that it was different from the rest? Did he care? She thought of the note he'd left stuck to today's date on the calendar. *This is when you need me.* What did that mean?

*What do I want it to mean?*

She wasn't ready to answer that question, so she pushed it aside and made her way through more than a hundred suggestions. When Bullet walked through the kitchen door, she was so deep in concentration, she was startled, knocking a handful of the notepapers onto the floor. Her hand flew to her chest, as if that might calm her racing heart.

"Geez, Bullet. You scared me. How'd you get in the kitchen without me seeing you walk by?"

He wasn't wearing his leather vest, and he looked even more commanding without it. His faded black T-shirt stretched tight across his body, defining each and every muscle in his torso. There was a tear on his left shoulder, and the edges of the sleeves were frayed. On anyone else it might look ratty, but on Bullet it looked *right*. His dark jeans were faded and nearly worn through in the thighs, like a favorite old pair, and his scuffed black leather boots made him look edgy—and *hot*.

"Back door," he said, pulling her from her secret inspection.

In three long strides he was standing beside her, his heady stare making her heart beat even harder.

"What's that look for?" she asked.

His eyes twitched, but he didn't say a word, just scanned her notebook, where she had written down the menu suggestions, looked at her bag and her other items spread out along the bar, and then glanced down at the notes littering the floor. When his gaze landed on her again, he looked deeply into her eyes, as if he was searching for something. The intensity of his stare made it hard for her to breathe.

"Do you remember what happened two nights ago?" he asked.

It would be so easy to say she didn't remember, but no part of her wanted to lie to him. "Of course. I told you I wasn't drunk." She set down the pen she was holding and crossed her arms, needing the barrier between them, because the longer he stared at her, the more intrigued she became.

"Everything?" He set one hand on the bar, the other on the arm of the stool, caging her in. "Loose lips sink ships."

Holding his gaze, she said, "There is no ship to sink. I remember every word."

"Then we're both on the same page," he said in a low, gravelly voice.

An after-sex voice.

She swallowed hard, remembering the last thing he'd said to her Wednesday night. *For the record...I want to see you naked, too.*

"You know you want to go out with me, Finlay." He slid his

hand along her back, and heck if her body didn't heat right up like she'd been torched. "Don't fight it, lollipop. Tonight's our night."

Her head spun with thoughts, desires, *worries*. She pushed from the stool to her feet, needing the distraction of pacing, but he blocked her path, towering over her. His closeness made her knees weak.

His features softened, and just when she began to catch her breath, she remembered how his entire demeanor had changed in an instant when he'd held her after she'd come face-to-face with Tinkerbell. *I've got you, lollipop.* So much for catching her breath.

"Do you want to go out with me, Finlay? Or are you playing some sort of game?"

"I don't know," she said honestly, throwing her hands up, frustrated with her own confusion. "Yes...Wait, *no. Yes...*"

He cocked his head with a perplexed expression.

"I'm sorry! I'm really confused. You mess with my head. Or rather, you've been messing with my head since the wedding. But that's not your fault. And now I'm rambling, but I want to be honest with you. The truth is, I'm *curious* about you. Maybe more than curious," she said, moving around him so she could pace. "But I don't know what you expect from women, and I don't know anything about your biker lifestyle. I don't think I'm a biker girl. But I don't *really* know that. I do know I'm probably not like the women you're used to, and motorcycles scare me. And sometimes you scare me. Not *you*, you, but the idea of you, because I'm not sure who *you* really are. But you also turn me on, which makes it all even more confusing."

A slow grin spread across his face.

"See? That smile makes my stomach go all sorts of crazy."

"Call me nuts, but I think that's a good thing, Fins."

The endearment *also* made her insides flutter. But none of that came close to the worries welling up inside her right that second as the big, confident caretaker to all around him stood looking at her like he was hanging on her every word, and the truth came tumbling out. "I haven't been with a lot of guys, and like I said, I don't know what you expect. You're all power and"—she tried to use her hands to emphasize her thoughts, but she ended up looking like she was imitating a bear, with claws extended—"*sexuality*, like you're ready to swoop in and devour me. But I'm not sure I can handle being devoured, because it's been so long since I've even kissed a guy that I might have..."

He stepped closer as slow as could be and placed a hand on her hip. She was mesmerized by his gentle approach and the touch of his hand as he brushed her hair over her shoulder, holding her gaze so intensely, she couldn't speak. His hand slid softly to the nape of her neck, then into her hair, until his long fingers cradled the back of her head. His other arm circled her waist, holding her against him.

"Forgotten how..." she whispered.

He gave her plenty of time to pull away, to tell him *no*, but her voice was silenced by the throbbing of her heart, the wanting in her head. As he lowered his face toward hers, she went up on her toes, bracing for a fierce, possessive kiss. But his mouth came gently down over hers, drawing a breathy sigh. His lips were warm and soft, his hands hard and hot, and her body was a vibrating mess. His beard scratched her cheeks, sending swirls of desire spiraling through her core. He pressed her tighter against him, angled her head and kissed her harder. His tongue swept across the seam of her lips, and she surrendered to his masterful seduction. His whole body beat against her like a pulse, bringing a surge of lust from some forgotten place inside her. He took the kiss deeper, tasting every dip and swell of her mouth, and a heady sound rumbled in the back of his throat. And oh, how she loved that! She'd never been kissed so thoroughly, been wanted so desperately. She never imagined that the man who was forward motion personified could harness that power and deliver it with such all-consuming passion. She couldn't resist lifting higher on her toes, clawing at his shoulder, trying to taste more of his sweet and sinful desire. He was right there with her, gripping her waist as he lifted her off her feet, holding her against his hard frame, her legs dangling off the ground as he kissed her breathless.

She was so lost in the slide of their tongues, the purely male, utterly unique taste of him, time failed to exist. They could have been kissing for hours, maybe even days. By the time her feet touched the ground, her noodle legs refused to work. But they didn't need to. Bullet was still holding her tight, kissing her softer now, his scratchy beard trailing after his lips across her jaw, all the way to her ear.

His warm breath seeped into her skin as he whispered, "I think you remember how to kiss just fine. Go out with me, lollipop. You don't have to be a biker girl. Just be *my* girl."

"'Kay," came out embarrassingly breathy.

"*Fuck yeah*, lollipop," he said louder.

She was reeling from his exclamation when his mouth came down roughly over hers, with all the fierceness and fervor she'd braced herself for earlier. Gone were the slow sensual kisses he'd lavished on her, replaced with an aggressive, celebratory rush of excitement, which she felt from her head all the way down to her toes and every tingly inch in between.

Did they really have to finish working? Did they have to

move from this very spot...*ever*? Couldn't she stay in his arms, being kissed into the heavens, forevermore? She'd never known a kiss could be so intense and electric, and smooth and entrancing at the same time. Even her fantasies couldn't come close to measuring up to the graceless power of his kisses.

When they finally came up for air, she was a boneless, needy mess.

How was she supposed to speak after that kiss? She was still clutching his shirt. She couldn't recall grabbing it in the first place, and for some reason, she couldn't unfurl her fingers. Nervous laughter fell from her lips. Good Lord, he'd kissed her silly!

She touched her forehead to the juncture of his rib cage. His big hands pressed against her cheeks, and he tilted her face up toward his, which only made her laugh more.

"I'm sorry," she managed. "That was a pretty amazing kiss. How am I going to work, to function after that?" If he could make her lose her mind with kisses, what would happen when he touched her? When *she* touched *him*? Oh Lord, how she *wanted* to find out.

"Work can wait."

His eyes were coal black and his voice was thick with desire, snapping her out of her fantasy. She lowered her gaze, concentrating on the hole in his shirt instead of the look in his eyes, reminding herself that she wasn't one of those girls who lost her head over men. But she couldn't resist stealing another glance at him, and his lips curled up in a wicked smile, causing lust to coil tight and hot, low in her belly.

*Okay, maybe I am one of those girls who loses her head over...Bullet.* Was that so bad?

No, she decided. It wasn't bad. It was very, very good.

"We good? Play now, work later?" He said it with a tease in his voice, and she was glad for it, because her normal sure-of-herself-goody-two-shoes personality seemed to have fled the premises, leaving a lusty, horny, want-to-be-bad woman behind.

"Yes, we're good, but no, we're not going to 'play.' You're taking me on a proper date tonight, remember? Despite losing my head for a few minutes, I'm not the kind of girl to kiss and then jump into bed. Besides, Dixie's going to be here soon to go over the renovation plans. And I have some things I want to show you, too."

His gaze ignited, and she swatted his arm. "Not like that! Gosh, Bullet, a few hot kisses and you think that's a green light and you can take home the prize?"

"I happen to like green lights and prizes."

Why did she find everything he said exciting now, instead of inappropriate?

*Because now I know how fun inappropriate can be.*

"Calm down, *Brutus.* We've got work to do." She took a step toward the stool and turned back, seeing him through new eyes. Less judgmental, kinder eyes. She went up on her toes, hands pressed to his hard pecs, and kissed the tattooed snake on his neck, which was as high as she could reach. Without a word, she climbed up on the stool, strangely calm and focused for the first time in days.

FINLAY LEANED OVER a mass of documents as she explained to Dixie the technical differences between several appliances she'd deemed "the best for your money." She seemed to have a mental checklist she was ticking off with each point she made and went on to explain why it was worth an extra few thousand dollars to opt for a twelve-burner stove rather than the eight-burner options. Though he was busy doing inventory, Bullet got caught up in her enthusiasm and the passion in her voice over something as boring as kitchen appliances. The more she explained, the clearer it became that she really cared about the future of their family's bar.

"Based on the customer suggestions," she said to Dixie, "they really do want mostly finger foods like sandwiches, fries, wings, you know, standard pub fare. But there were enough requests for other, more complicated dishes that I think you should renovate for the future of what Whiskey's could easily become."

"That makes sense, but how far out of our budget is it?" Dixie asked.

Finlay pushed a spreadsheet in front of Dixie. "It's really not bad."

Dixie studied the numbers. "Less than seven thousand dollars? That hardly seems enough to worry about."

"Exactly," Finlay said. "And with the increased profit from the kitchen, you should make it up fairly quickly. I'm glad you agreed to hire two cooks and two dishwashers, even if part-time, in case someone gets sick. I have some other ideas, too. I think once we make a few decorative changes, you could pull in a whole new crowd."

Bullet's enthusiasm came to a screeching halt. "Decorative changes?"

"Just a few small things," Finlay explained. "Like clearing the black from the windows and maybe spiffing things up out front so it doesn't look like such a dive from the road. Curb appeal goes a long way, and with a little love—"

"Hold up, sweet thing. We aren't looking for a new crowd. Whiskey's is a biker bar. It's been a biker bar for several generations, and that's what it's going to stay. I thought Dixie covered all this with you."

"I did. Don't you have inventory to do? Finlay and I are capable of dealing with this on our own." Dixie glared at him.

"It's okay, Dixie," she said. "Yes, Dixie went over it with me, but don't you want it to be the type of establishment that people are drawn to? That *new* bikers in the area want to check out?"

"Um, not really," Dixie said. "That can be tricky around here."

"What do you mean?"

Bullet came around the bar and said, "The first problem with your idea is that Whiskey's isn't an *establishment*. It's a *bar*. A dive. A place guys can come to after a hard day's work and shoot the shit, have a few drinks, play a few rounds of pool, hook up with a hot chick. We're not looking to be some fancy place like Whispers. And as far as new bikers go, babe, you've got to learn about our world before you can make those suggestions."

"You know what? You're absolutely right," Finlay said enthusiastically. She picked up a pen and started jotting down notes. "I'm going to check out other biker bars here and in the neighboring towns. That will tell me what your competition is, and I'll take a look at their menus, too."

Bullet put his hand over hers, stopping her from writing any more nonsense. "Like hell you will."

Dixie glared at him.

Finlay wrenched her hand free. "What is *wrong* with you? First of all, I'll do whatever I think is right, and second of all, market research is important."

"Putting your pretty little ass in danger is stupid. We've got all the market research we need right here in the history of the bar. I don't give a flying fuck what other bars are doing. I only care about ours, and it's *not* changing."

Finlay gasped, shock rising in her wide eyes. "Just because I agreed to go out with you does not give you the right to demean me and call me stupid. In fact, it makes me wonder what the heck I was thinking." She pushed to her feet, the shock in her eyes morphing to hurt, slicing right through his heart.

"You agreed to go out with Bullet?" Dixie asked.

Finlay looked at him with disdain. "Yes, but now I think it might have been a mistake."

Bullet's gut clenched. "Like hell it was."

He pulled her closer and sank down to a stool, bringing her between his legs so they were eye-to-eye. He finally realized what his mother had meant when she'd said, *Don't go after your sweetheart with your brawn, baby. Go after her with your heart.* The last thing he wanted was to hurt Finlay, and he'd done just that. He didn't have much experience with apologies. In fact, he avoided them at all costs, living his life how he wanted to without anyone telling him what to do or how to feel. Now, faced with the pain he'd caused Finlay, he not only wanted to apologize, but he needed to. The nightmares from his military days wouldn't come close to the haunting her sad eyes would inflict on him.

"Oh my God," Dixie whispered. "Penny was right."

He had no idea what the hell Penny had to do with this, but he wasn't about to slow down enough to find out. He regretted hurting Finlay's feelings, even if he stood behind his statement.

"I'm sorry, Finlay. I wasn't calling *you* stupid. I meant the *idea* of a sweetheart like you going into biker bars wasn't smart because you have no idea of the danger you'd be putting yourself in."

"Well, you need to think before you speak." Her gaze softened slightly, but the hurt remained palpable.

"You can say that again," Dixie mumbled, and this time Bullet glared at her.

"I'm not very good at that," he admitted, "but I can try to be more careful about the way I say things."

That seemed to soothe a little of the hurt, but he'd damn well try to be more careful.

"Thank you," she said with more politeness than he deserved. "I think I proved that I can handle myself around bikers."

Grinding his teeth against a knee-jerk reaction of, *Bullshit. You have no fucking clue*, he said, "Babe, you proved that you could handle yourself around *my* type of bikers, in *my* bar, where they know I'll pound the life out of them if they wrong anyone in my circle. Bikers are not all the same."

"But aren't most of those guys in your gang?" she asked. "They weren't aggressive with me."

She tucked her hair behind her ear, looking so sweet he wanted to put her in protective armor and stand sentinel over her, keeping all the ugliness away. The fact that he had spouted off something so hurtful without even a hint that he was saying something wrong did not escape him. He was part of that ugliness, and he knew he'd have to figure shit out or let her go, because causing the pain he'd seen in her eyes again was *not* an option.

"The Dark Knights is not a gang, Finlay. We're a motorcycle *club*, which means we're a group of people who have an interest in biker culture. We have rides and events that are family friendly, and in our case, help the community. Gangs are completely different beasts. There is a lot of drugs and violence, parties that, trust me, you do *not* want to know about or be part of the shit that goes down there. The last thing we want is for some gang to ride through town and think they're welcome in our bar."

Her expression was taut, her eyes contemplative. "But how can anyone possibly tell the difference? You guys all look the same."

"But they're not," Dixie said.

He'd heard it his whole life. *You guys all look the same.* Growing up in the club environment, he'd had the same observation and questions when he was young. There were plenty of times when his family was out and his father, who went by the road name Biggs, because of his six-five stature, and whom Bullet took after, would see a rough rider and suddenly send Bullet and his siblings off to the car with their mother, or into a store. Or there would be a knock at the door in the middle of the night and one of the club members would show up, bloody and angry, and his father would take off for hours. He learned about loyalty, and as he got older and stupider, he'd made his own mistakes, causing trouble to come crashing down on his family. Getting into the military was his savior, and his demise. His stomach knotted up with the memories. Those weren't things Finlay needed to hear about, but she had to understand that bikers' turf wasn't something she should fuck with.

"You know the leather vest I wear?" Bullet asked. "The patch on the back represents the Dark Knights. Every club and gang has patches that represent their club and members' statuses in the club."

Finlay drew in a deep breath and blew it out slowly. "So…what? You have them all memorized or something?"

"Pretty much," Dixie said.

"Listen, Finlay," Bullet said carefully. "I admire you for wanting to do right by our family's bar, but there are reasons Whiskey's is the way it is."

Her lips thinned with displeasure, and he knew he wasn't going to get off without a clearer explanation.

"Do you know why the bar is on the edge of town? Why Peaceful Harbor isn't overrun with gangs and all the bullshit that goes on in other towns?"

"I can't even imagine Peaceful Harbor with gangs." Finlay's gaze moved between him and Dixie. "I get it. You don't want me to change the bar. But I still think it's a mistake. You're asking me to make the bar better, but no one will know it is except your current customers."

"Finlay look at me." He waited until he had her full attention. "I didn't want this expansion in the first place, but I understand why everyone else did and why we need to bring in more income and change things up a little. I'm on board with that. But there are things that cannot change. Once you understand the history, you'll realize I'm not just being a dick."

She winced. "I hate that word."

"Yeah, well, you probably hate half my vocabulary, and that's not going to change either. This is who I am, Finlay. I curse and I protect my family and this town at all costs. Period."

Her gaze darted to Dixie, who nodded. "It's the Dark Knights way, and cursing? That's Bullet's way. He's honest, Fin. I don't think he knows how to be any other way."

Bullet was warmed by his sister's words. "There's never a

reason to lie. We were brought up to be straight shooters, and I'm not about to try to pretend I'm something I'm not. I'm a Whiskey, and I'm proud to be a Whiskey. Our great-grandfather founded this bar and the Dark Knights, and he protected this town. Whiskey's was built on the edge of town because that's where you *stop* trouble from coming in. Once bad news comes over the bridge into Peaceful Harbor, it's got only one way to go—forward—and all sorts of hell can break loose until it finds its way back outta town. *If* it finds its way out."

"I know this probably sounds far-fetched to you, Fin," Dixie said, "but Peaceful Harbor is *peaceful* because the riffraff has been kept out."

"Our ancestors, and the Dark Knights brotherhood, spent years claiming this town, defining our territory," Bullet explained. "And every generation of the Dark Knights since has protected it. And we'll continue to. If a gang came in and tried to claim this territory, or even tried to operate within it to sell drugs, or whatever, our family—the Dark Knights—would take whatever action was necessary to defend it."

Finlay looked nervously at Dixie. "Okay, now you're just scaring me. You make it seem like my quaint hometown could turn into a nightmare at any time."

Bullet and Dixie exchanged a knowing glance. They knew how real that possibility was. They also knew it would take a hell of a battle for any other group to overtake the Dark Knights.

He took Finlay's hand in his and said, "You don't have to worry about that. We've got this town. Nobody's going to mess with us."

"But..." She looked pleadingly at Dixie. "You said whatever action is necessary. Does that mean you'd fight? You just got done telling me that you were different from a gang."

"We are," Dixie insisted. "Nobody goes looking for trouble."

"But if it comes here, we'll take whatever measures we need to."

Fear rose in Finlay's eyes. "Like fighting? *Killing?*"

"Do you think I'd ever let any harm come to my family?" Bullet asked.

"No."

"To Tru's kids? To Gemma? Crystal? To you, or Penny, or anyone else in this town? *Our* town? The town my ancestors fought to make great for us?"

Finlay shook her head.

"It scares you, and I get that. I'd rather you didn't think about it," he said honestly. "But it doesn't scare me. This is my reason for being here, to *protect.*"

"You say it like it's your calling," she said anxiously.

He shrugged. "It is." *Just because you get out of the military doesn't make you any less of a soldier.*

Dixie nodded in agreement. "Now do you see why he doesn't want you going into biker bars?"

"Yes," she said. "But how can this whole underworld exist without some sort of...? I don't know. Without anyone knowing?"

Bullet chuckled. "People know. More people than you think. The principal at the high school? He's family."

"Mr. Martin? He's not a Whiskey," Finlay said.

"Our motorcycle club is family," Bullet explained.

"That docile man is a member of your motorcycle club?"

Bullet nodded. "The owner of the flower shop, the CFO at Peaceful Harbor Bank, several doctors, the pharmacist at CVS. I could go on and on."

She lowered herself onto a stool. "Wow. I had no idea." Her brow furrowed. "So, I *could* go check out other club bars, right? I'm not a member of your club, and clubs aren't like gangs, so that would work for research."

Dixie smiled.

"No wonder you hired her," Bullet said to Dixie. "She's as determined as you, only sweeter."

"I'm sweet." Dixie smirked. "I just hide it well."

"I think you're very sweet," Finlay said. "Tough, too, but sweet and nice and funny."

"Thanks." Dixie made a dramatic show of fluttering her lashes at Bullet.

"*Christ*. If you're dead set on going to a biker bar, I'll take you to the Snake Pit," Bullet relented. "It's at the other end of town and owned by two members of the Dark Knights. It's classier than our joint, but it'll have to do."

"Thank you. I think that'll help."

Dixie pushed to her feet. "I'm going to the bathroom. I'll be right back, and then we can go over your other ideas. We kind of got sidetracked."

After Dixie was out of earshot, Bullet pushed his hands into the front pockets of his jeans and tried his best not to sound like an arrogant ass. "I didn't mean to put you down, and I won't make that mistake again. You have my word, lollipop. I'm a hard-ass, but I'm not intentionally a dick."

She lowered her gaze, her face a mask of contemplation.

He bent so his face was lower than hers and looked up at her, earning a sweet smile, which soothed the ache in his heart from accidentally hurting her. "Let me rephrase that to something more *lollipop appropriate*."

She smiled again, and this time it was warm and genuine and gave him hope that she'd forgive his comment.

"I'm tough and crass. Some might say I'm not easy to like," he said apologetically. "We're from totally different worlds, and I'll never be a collared-shirt yuppie, but I'd never in a million years try to hurt you."

"I believe you," she said softly.

"Think you can bear with me? Help me learn to keep my fucking mouth shut?"

"Bear with you? Yes. Help you keep your mouth shut?" She shook her head, laughing softly. "What time are you picking me up tonight?"

He leaned forward, his lips grazing hers. She inhaled a ragged breath, and he whispered, "Seven thirty."

"No motorcycle."

"No motorcycle," he agreed.

"No Tinkerbell."

"No Tink. *Yet.*" He pressed his lips to hers, vowing to never accidentally hurt her again and hoping he could figure out how to lead with his fucking heart, because he knew better than anyone that being given a second chance was the gift of a lifetime.

# Chapter Six

"WHAT DO YOU wear on a date with a *Bullet train*?" Isabel's teasing voice rose from Finlay's laptop, which was sitting on her bed.

Finlay stood at the threshold of her closet Friday evening, hands on hips, trying to figure out just that.

"He needs a target," Isabel said. "So I'm thinking crotchless panties are a must."

"Izzy!" Finlay laughed, though she blushed a red streak.

"What? It seems like the right thing for a *Bullet train*."

"No, just *no*. Please be serious. I'm so nervous. Something sexy but not too sexy?" Finlay suggested. "After the kisses we shared, I don't want him to think I'll just give it up, you know? But I also don't want him to think I won't *ever* give it up."

"I've got it!" Isabel waved her hands, her hazel eyes wide with amusement. "You need one of those light-up T-shirts that has two big yellow traffic lights, one on each boob. That will give him the message *don't stop, but don't speed through. Just take it nice and slow.*"

Finlay rolled her eyes. "That's really helpful. Do you *know* how nervous I am?"

"I think the fact that I had to hear about you changing your lingerie four times gave me a pretty good idea of how nervous you are. I'm glad you went with the white lace, though. That's totally you, and I think even badass Brutus would wonder what other sexy secrets you were keeping if he found edible underwear on the first date."

"He's not going to find white lace, either!"

"Penny's there," Isabel said matter-of-factly. She lifted her dark hair into an updo and sucked in her cheeks. "Do you think I should start eating healthier so I can look like those ridiculously skinny models who eat air for dinner?"

"What? No! And what did you say about Penny?"

"She's there. Three, two, one…"

There was a knock at Finlay's door. "You did not call her!"

"Okay, let's go with that. Answer your door, please."

"I don't need Penny pressuring me tonight!" She stalked out of the bedroom and answered the door.

"Hey, sis. Nice outfit. Are you going for the June Cleaver look?" Penny walked right past her, carrying an armful of clothes, an enormous bag slung over her shoulder. "Where's Iz?"

"Bedroom." Finlay followed her down the hall. "What's wrong with my bathrobe?"

"Nothing if it's 1950 or you're eighty-two years old with a dusty cootie and hangnails."

"I hate you right now," Finlay said as she followed Penny into the bedroom. "What are you two, anyway? Plot bunnies, secretly scheming behind my back?"

"Hey, Iz." Penny blew a kiss toward the laptop and tossed the clothes on the bed. She set her bag on the floor and said, "We are your saviors. Now, take off that boner killer bathrobe and let's see if we can find an outfit that might incite some boob-touching action."

"Cock-knockin' action," Isabel said with a laugh.

"Oh, yeah, even better. A little hide the handlebar? Smoke the muffler?" Penny dug through the pile and held up a black T-shirt with GOOD GIRLS SIT, BAD BITCHES RIDE emblazoned across the front. "Huh? What do you think? If you go with that, I got you this to give to him." She picked up an enormous men's shirt and showed them the back, which had two red and white targets and read, PRESS 'EM HERE 'N' HANG ON TIGHT.

Isabel fell onto her side laughing.

"What is wrong with you people?" Finlay said as she laughed and yanked the shirt from Penny's hand. She tossed it on the chair in the corner of the room and said, "No, no, and no. Do you have anything reasonable in here?" She picked up a little black dress that looked like it would fit a seven-year-old. "How can you wear this? You're five inches taller than me."

Penny, who looked like Zooey Deschanel with her blue eyes and walnut-brown hair, took after their father. She was tall and lean and about as carefree as a girl could be. She smoothed her hands over her jeans-clad hips and said, "It's all in the stretch of the material."

"This thing couldn't stretch to cover my cooch. How on earth does it cover yours?"

"Try it," Isabel suggested.

"Yeah, put it on and see." Penny reached for the tie on Finlay's robe. "Give me Grandma's robe. Let's sex you up."

As Finlay stripped off her robe, Isabel whistled and cheered and Penny lowered her voice and started singing, "Come on, girl, strip off the robe. That's it, girl. Show those globes."

Finlay gave her a deadpan look.

"I liked it," Isabel said. "It made creative sense."

"Nice lace, sis." Penny picked up the black dress and handed it to her. "Now, let's cover up that innocent lingerie with some sluttiness."

"Aren't I supposed to wear the sluttiness *underneath* the innocence?"

Penny set a hand on her hip and said, "Only if you never want to touch his drive shaft."

"I feel like a stuffed sausage in this dress."

"Stuffed sausages are *good*," Isabel said. "And you look hot, like take-me-from-behind hot."

Finlay ripped the dress over her head and tossed it on the bed. "Nope. Not going there."

"Dark blue shift?" Penny picked up a midnight-blue dress that was almost as small as the black one.

"No."

"Leather miniskirt?" She plucked it out from beneath the pile. "I've got my lace-up fuck-me boots in the car."

"Leather goes well with a motorcycle," Isabel said. "And that one is cute!"

"No leather. Why can't you guys just help me be *me*, only better?"

Isabel made a kissing noise. "I love you, Finny, and you know I'm only giving you a hard time."

Penny flopped onto the bed on her side and began picking up each outfit. "It's our job to try to get you sexed up, no matter how hard you fight it."

"Why?"

"Because one day you might want to get sexed up and be too embarrassed to ask," Penny said.

"We know how nervous you are about going out with Bullet," Isabel added. "We just wanted to lighten the mood."

"With leather and slut boots?" Finlay flopped onto her back beside Penny. "Why don't I just wear one of my sundresses?"

Penny's face appeared over hers. "Because your sister would never leave you hanging, and neither would Izzy. We shopped today and found something we think you'll love."

"You shopped?" Finlay turned toward the computer, and Isabel held up her phone.

"FaceTime shopping. We found you the *best* outfit! Pen took me to Chelsea's Boutique. Oh my God, Fin, when I move there we are going to spend hours in that shop. *Days.* We may never leave!"

Finlay's hopes rose. Isabel and Penny had great taste when they weren't trying to be too wild. She sat up, and Penny reached into her red bag and withdrew a gift box, complete with a big pink ribbon. Finlay's throat thickened with emotion. Before their father had died, he'd celebrated each of their milestones with a gift, wrapped up with a big pink bow. The milestones were never things they wanted to celebrate with their father—their first bras, first periods, first kisses—but now they were some of their most cherished moments.

"Penny..."

"Take it." Penny handed her the box and hugged her. "I wasn't there when you got all googly-eyed over Aaron, and I'm glad you let me be a part of this first date."

Tears welled in Finlay's eyes. She glanced at the laptop, and Isabel blew her a kiss. Her heart was so full, she couldn't imagine how the night could get any better. "Thank you both so much. I know I'll love it, as long as it's not made for a sex romp."

"No promises there," Isabel said with a smile.

She untied the ribbon and opened the top, gasping at the

pretty rose-beige material. "You guys, this is gorgeous."

She lifted the dress out of the box and moved across the room to hold it up in front of the mirror, but she couldn't wait, and turned her back to the girls. She removed her bra, then slipped the beautiful dress over her head. Soft cotton dusted the tops of her feet.

"Let me." Penny gathered Finlay's hair over one shoulder and tied the halter.

Finlay turned around, overwhelmed by how well they knew her. She stood before the mirror unable to believe how pretty she looked, how perfect the dress fit. The halter-style top was trimmed with lace, and a crocheted pattern covered her midriff. The long skirt had a thick crocheted stripe above her knees, giving it just the right amount of sexiness without looking like she was trying too hard.

"Finny," Isabel said, "you look gorgeous. Bullet, and every other man out there, is going to fall at your feet."

Finlay looked at Penny and said, "I thought you were really trying to get me to wear something I never would."

"Nope. I love my big sister just the way she is. But when you're ready for Tramp City, we're your girls." Penny hugged her. "I'm glad you're back home again. You look lovely, and very fuckable."

"Bullet will appreciate both," Isabel chimed in. "Let's accessorize!"

For the next twenty minutes, Finlay modeled sandals, earrings, bangles, and necklaces, her nervousness increasing with each rendition. She finally settled on a pair of cute beige sandals, rose-gold dangling earrings, and a simple Alex and Ani red kindred cord heart bracelet. With the outfit accessorized, Penny left to meet friends for dinner and Finlay ended the video call with Isabel and was left alone to pick apart her thoughts. She had gone on a few dates over the past couple of years, but they were typical guys and typical dates. She had been nervous before them, as anyone would be on a first date, but those guys hadn't picked her up when she'd been drinking and driven her home. They hadn't seen her *uncorked*, singing silly songs like a ridiculous teenager and screaming at the sight of a dog. They hadn't carried her through the very living room in which she now sat, nervously fidgeting with the soft fabric of her dress. She definitely hadn't wanted to see them naked or touch their bare chests, and not one of them made her knees weak with a single kiss.

Geez, Bullet had really gotten a show from her the other night. Why on earth did he still want to go out with her after all that?

She rose to her feet and paced. It was seven thirty on the dot, and with every tick of the clock, her heartbeat quickened. She didn't even know where he was taking her. What if she was overdressed? Did Bullet ever wear anything other than jeans and T-shirts? Maybe *she* should wear jeans. She went into the bedroom, but the thought of wearing jeans made her even more nervous. Penny was the jeans girl in their family. Like their mother, Finlay had always preferred more feminine outfits. Some girls felt sexier when they showed everything in tight jeans, but Finlay felt prettiest in dresses, and this dress made her feel extra sexy, because of the crocheted midriff. Nope, jeans would not make her any less nervous.

She headed back toward the living room, trying to imagine what Bullet had planned for their date, but every time his face appeared in her mind it was accompanied by pieces of their conversation. *Don't fight it, lollipop. Tonight's our night.*

She stopped cold in the middle of the living room. What was he expecting to happen tonight? Had she given him the impression they would sleep together? What if their kisses, which had felt magical and special to her, were *just* kisses to him? *He must have a lot of experience with women. Maybe he kisses them all like that.*

The thought made her feel a little queasy.

She walked out onto the deck and crossed her arms against the cool September air, gazing out at the wooded expanse buffering her backyard from outsiders. She didn't want to be just another kiss for anyone, but did she want to be intimate with Bullet? A quick and electric pulse radiated through her.

Placing her hands on the railing, she inhaled the salty harbor air and closed her eyes, enjoying the fluttering of her heart at the thought of going out with Bullet. She'd forgotten how exciting it was to *want* to go out with someone. Then again, her nerves were probably equally as heightened by not knowing what going out with Bullet really meant.

She was surprised to see that it was nearing eight o'clock when she finally went inside, and she wondered if she was being stood up. She checked her phone, but she didn't have any messages. Assuming Bullet got held up at the bar, she tried to cut him a little slack. Not everyone was as punctual as she was. She sat on the couch, paced the floor, then sat down again, all the while watching the clock. Her insides hurt a little more with each quarter hour that passed.

*I definitely enjoy pushing your buttons, and I'm pretty much an asshole.*

Her thoughts went from forgiving to irritation.

As it neared eight thirty a warning voice sounded in her head. Her face grew hot with humiliation. If he thought this was acceptable, he was dead wrong, and if he'd done it to piss her off, then he'd succeeded. She went outside again, needing cool air to calm herself down. She didn't want to believe he would stand her up. Not after the glorious connection they'd had when they'd kissed and the sweet things he'd said to her when Dixie had left the room. *I'd never in a million years try to hurt you.*

She went back inside and turned on the television to distract herself, only to turn it off a few minutes later and stare at her phone, debating calling him. If he had purposefully stood her up, it would be embarrassing to chase after him. Plus, she'd likely give him a harsh piece of her mind, and she would *not* want to finish the job at the bar, which wouldn't be fair to Dixie and the rest of their family. But was this fair to her? To get all dressed up and then be forgotten?

The idea that he would purposefully do that to her didn't sit right. It didn't fit what she knew of him. It didn't fit what her heart felt, and her heart had never led her astray before. If something happened to him, wouldn't he have called if he could?

A cold knot formed in the pit of her stomach. He and Dixie seemed to think their outlook on protecting the town was normal, but to Finlay it was unfathomable. Her father had been a tough man. He'd worked long, hard hours, and he'd never put up with disrespect from others, but she couldn't imagine him actually fighting with anyone. Could the things Bullet and Dixie had told her about turf wars really happen anywhere other than in novels? Were there territories and turfs all over the world secretly protected by groups like the Dark Knights? Did she want to be involved with Bullet if it were true? If there had been an incident, wouldn't it be on the news?

What if this was typical for him because of the club?

Could she deal with this much worry on an ongoing basis?

She flipped on the local television station, crossed her arms, her legs bouncing nervously. Fifteen minutes later, after hearing about the upcoming fall festival and other community news, she turned it off.

This was ridiculous. Clutching her phone, she forced herself to call Bullet. It rang endlessly, and when his voicemail kicked in, his deep, raspy voice brought rise to goose bumps, despite that he may very well have stood her up. She'd leave a quick message, hoping she didn't sound as confused, irritated, and hurt as she felt.

*Hi, Bullet; it's Finlay…* Now she felt stupid. What was she supposed to say? *Remember we had a date? I hope you're okay? Call me?* If he'd stood her up, she didn't want him to call, and if he hadn't…

Her heart hurt with the idea that something could have happened to him. She found her voice, and the truth came out. "I was worried that something happened, or maybe you changed your mind." That was all she could manage, because if he'd changed his mind and not called, then he was a big jerk.

She debated calling her sister, or Isabel, but they'd been so happy for her, she'd only feel worse talking to them. Maybe she should call Dixie. *How embarrassing would that be?*

*Ugh!* She'd never been in this situation before. What did women do when faced with this? It felt wrong, and it made her angry. No man should have the power to make her wonder if he thought she wasn't worth a phone call. She set her phone on the coffee table, kicked off her sandals, and curled up on the couch. But curling up on the couch had never been her way of dealing with a hard situation. Sixty seconds later she was in the kitchen, loading her counter up with ingredients and flipping through her favorite recipes. She put on an apron like a boxer donned his gloves, her mind instantly turning to familiar, safe territory, which came in measurements and degrees, not black leather biker boots.

STREETLAMPS SHIMMERED OVER dark hollows on the lifeless residential street where Bullet sat alone in his truck. Meanwhile, on the main drag, traffic lights blinked on endless timers and empty cars lined the streets like soldiers awaiting their next missions while their owners slept safely tucked away from the elements, blissfully unaware of the tragedies and crimes around every corner. Trees swayed in the breeze along the quiet road, reminding Bullet that fall was bearing down on the last of the lingering summer heat. He'd walked these roads as a teenager, driven them in the middle of the night in search of answers. Answers that had come years later, when the military had sent him overseas, the perfect place to unleash his demons. He'd come home a different man, and now traveled these same city streets with the sole purpose of eradicating trouble.

But tonight, for the first time in his life, he hadn't been searching for a damn thing. He wasn't looking for answers, or meaning, or fucking trouble. He gripped the steering wheel with bloodstained fingers, swallowing the metallic taste that lingered like an unwanted ghost. His chest constricted, and his breathing quickened as memories came at him like a hurricane, fast and unrelenting. His eyes slammed against the sounds of the babies crying, the mother screaming, and her brother gurgling, struggling to get to his family. Drawing upon the grounding techniques he'd learned to manage the rare and horrific occurrences when events triggered flashbacks to the war and they crept up on him like demons out of the darkness, he fumbled for the radio, turning it up loud enough to give him something to focus on before they could take hold. He let the music pound through him, obliterating the rage, the fear, and the goddamn taste and smell of death.

Minutes passed like hours, elongated and painful in the wake of the trigger, but the music and his mental fortitude did the trick, keeping the flashback at bay. *This time*. If only he'd been in the right frame of mind to have halted it earlier.

He turned the radio down and grabbed his phone from the seat beside him. The message light blinked like a beacon, as it had been doing since he'd gone back to the scene of the accident to retrieve it. He didn't have to look to know sweet Finlay had tried to track him down. He didn't need to hear her voice to know she was probably furious and hurt. He owed her an explanation, and an apology, but giving it would mean risking another flashback. Finlay didn't need a man with demons he couldn't slay.

He set the phone on the seat beside the flowers he'd brought for her and started the truck, taking one last look at Finlay's house. His heart thundered wildly, memories of the hurt in her eyes from earlier clawing at him like an animal burrowing into his soul. He punched the dashboard, furious at his vulnerability. How many times had he driven away from a woman and never looked back? *Once and done*, that was the motto he lived by when it came to women. Hell, it'd be easier to count the number of times he'd given a shit about them.

*Once.*

The goddamn angel in that little house was the only one

that mattered, and he'd fucking screwed her over again. He knew he should walk away, knew she didn't need the weight of his past hanging around them like a noose waiting to tighten. But he couldn't leave without giving her an explanation. He couldn't take the hurt he'd caused and drive it deeper.

At least that's what he told himself as he cut the engine, grabbed the flowers, and climbed from the car at too-long-after midnight. He strode through the darkness, telling himself to take every bit of shit she handed him, because he fucking deserved it.

# Chapter Seven

BEYOND LOSING HIS family, there wasn't much Bullet was afraid of, but as he stood on Finlay's front porch, fear gathered in his gut, which was fucking ridiculous. He'd suffered through wars, looked down the barrel of more guns than he cared to remember, seen more death than any man should. Yet the idea of seeing the hurt he'd caused in Finlay's beautiful eyes *again* had him tied in knots. What was worse was that he had no idea if telling her the truth would cause another flashback.

He eyed the steps. He could just fucking leave, lock himself away behind the steel walls he'd erected practically since the day he was born. Brush her off tomorrow so coldly she'd never look at him again. His hands fisted, nearly crushing the bouquet.

He wasn't a goddamn coward.

He knocked much harder than he meant to, and leaned his hand against the doorframe, staring at his boots, which were speckled with blood.

"Bullet?" he heard through the door, then the rattle of the chain, the click of the dead bolt.

Finlay opened the door, blinking sleepily. His gaze swept down her pretty dress, and his heart stumbled.

The color drained from her face, and she pulled the door open wider, bracing it against her hip. "Oh my gosh. You're bleeding. Are you okay? What happened?"

"Nothing," he mumbled. "I just came by to apologize—"

"Nothing? Bullet, your shirt is torn, your arm is cut, and it looks like you have blood all over your clothes. Were you in an accident?"

"No, please, let's not do this. I'm sorry I—"

Her eyes went cold. "Let's not *do* this? You stand me up after hounding me to go out with you. Then you show up looking like you've been in a fight, and you don't want to explain? I don't know what other girls consider okay, but this is *not* all right with me."

"Goddamn it." He gritted his teeth. He'd gone through enough shit tonight. He didn't have the energy for any more.

"Is this part of your *club*, or whatever? Because if it is, I don't want any part of it. I can't sit around worrying about if you've been hurt or killed, or if you just decided to blow me off."

"Forget it. I'm sorry I fucked up your night." He handed her the flowers and headed down the steps.

"That's it?" she called after him. "You're leaving? Without any explanation or anything?"

He turned, his gut twisting and tightening like it was being wrung out, and he stalked back up the steps, chest tight, every muscle constricted. "You just told me that you want nothing to do with me. Fuck me for saving a family's life. I'm sorry I messed up your evening. I'm sorry I didn't call you, but I was tending to more urgent matters."

Her mouth opened, then closed. "I'm…You saved…Oh my gosh, Bullet. I'm sorry. I had no idea."

"Would it have mattered? Because it could just as easily have been club business that called me away. I'm not Prince Charming. Hell, lollipop, I'm not even the fucking toad. But I always do the right thing. And it just so happened that the right thing meant staying at the hospital with the woman whose babies and brother are in fucking critical condition until her goddamn sister could be there with her. Should I have called? Yes. Could I have? No. I dropped my phone after calling nine-one-one so I could get the family out of the fucking car before it went up in flames. But the truth is, I wouldn't have left that woman to make the call. Not for anything. Her babies' and her brother's lives were hanging on by a thread. You don't leave someone alone in that situation, even if it means losing something you want. This..." He pointed to the space between them, shaking his head. "This either will or won't happen, but either way, we'll see each other around town. That woman— Sarah Beckley—may never see one of her children breathe again."

Fear and regret filled her damp eyes. "I'm sorry. That poor family. That's awful."

"Yeah. It was. And so was leaving you hanging. But you're right. You don't need a guy like me messing up your life." He headed for the steps again.

"Wait!" She ran after him, snagging the back of his shirt as he descended the steps. "Please don't go. I'm sorry. I was hurt and worried about you, and..." His forward momentum sent her tipping forward.

With his heart in his throat, he circled her waist with his arms so she wouldn't fall from her precarious position. In her bare feet, she was even more petite, reminding him of just how delicate and fragile she was, despite her confidence and demands for respect. She was a mighty force of good, pure and kind in ways that made him want to be closer to her, to find a way to be a better man for her. But he wasn't a dreamer, and when he gazed into her eyes, he knew what he had to do.

"Finlay, you just told me you didn't want any part of my lifestyle, and I don't blame you. Look at you, all dressed up like a princess, more beautiful than any woman I've ever seen, and *this* is what I am." He waved at his bloody, torn T-shirt and jeans. "You're warm sunshine, and I'm a winter storm. That's not going to change. Trouble happens, and I go. Even if I could change it, I wouldn't, sweetheart. I can't watch others suffer, or know someone's in trouble and not do something."

She looked down at her feet, and this time he didn't lift her chin, didn't try to change her mind, because this was his reality. And probably the end of the line for them.

FINLAY HAD ALWAYS considered herself a selfless, giving person, but Bullet Whiskey brought new meaning to the word *selfless* and to the saying *double-edged sword.* There was so much goodness about him, as everyone had told her, but to be with a man like Bullet meant being okay with coming not *second*, or even third or fourth, in his life. It meant taking a backseat not just to a career, like most men, but to an entire town full of people, and it clearly didn't end there. She thought she'd never met anyone like him because he was so gruff, but she'd witnessed enough of his softer side to know it existed. And now she was starting to understand where all that hardness came from. Carrying the weight of his family, their business, and the safety of the town on his shoulders had to take its toll. Did anyone have Bullet's back the way he had everyone else's?

"Bullet, as I've said, I don't know much about guys like you, and honestly, I'm not sure there are other guys like you. But you make me question who I am, which is something I thought I've known forever."

A deep V formed between his brows. "Trust me, Fins, there's nothing wrong with you. I'm pretty fucked up. But don't worry. I won't get in your way at the bar. I'll take a step back while you finish your work. Go on, lollipop. Get inside so I know you're safe."

With a pang, she realized he'd misunderstood her intent. She stepped closer, her hand hovering around his waist, but there were so many bloodstains, and the magnitude of what he'd faced hit her with greater force, bringing rise to tears—for him and for the family he'd helped.

"Finlay," he said in that gravelly voice that made her stomach dip.

She blinked away the tears and lowered her hand to his. His fingers curled around it, holding tight.

"I don't want you to take a step back," she said tentatively, unsure if he was purposefully trying to push her away because he wanted to, or doing so to protect her. She had a feeling it was the latter. "I don't know what will happen between us, but you say I'm sunshine and you're a winter storm. For me, knowing winter is on the horizon makes the oppressive days of long hot summers more bearable. And on the coldest of winter nights, I have summer to look forward to. They kind of complement each other."

"I can't change, lollipop. And I have a feeling you're used to guys who can."

"But that's just it. I don't want to change you, but I do want to *understand* you. To know what you've gone through and what has led you to become the man you are."

He squeezed her hand, but his gaze shifted over her shoulder. His features were tight, as if he was struggling to keep a raw emotion in check.

Taking a cue from his way of doing things, she stepped into his line of sight and personal space. When their eyes connected, a different type of electricity sizzled between them. It was stronger, louder, and somehow also softer and more pliable than before. "If that makes you uncomfortable, then I don't know. Maybe we can meet halfway? I'm an over-communicator. I know that."

His mustache lifted with an *almost* smile.

There was no denying that they were on the opposite end of the communication spectrum, but her curiosity had grown to something much stronger, and she wanted to try to get to know him better. Though she wasn't sure he'd ever really open up to her. But she'd been trying to ignore something that had been nagging at her, and she didn't want to wonder about it anymore.

Swallowing hard, because she was a little afraid the answer might only be sexual, she asked, "Why do you like me, Bullet? I see you with someone much tougher."

He was quiet for so long, she didn't think he'd answer. When he finally spoke, his tone was warm and certain. "I'm not going to lie to you. At first it was purely physical. Your sweet little body and that smile knocked my boots right off, and your eyes. *Jesus*, Fins, your eyes fucking kill me. And then you were all ballsy and pushy, which totally turned me on."

Heat spread across her cheeks, and she lowered her gaze.

He lifted her chin with his finger and said, "But then I saw you around town, and I swear you lit up the streets. You lit *me* up inside, and it's been a damn long time since I've felt anything but darkness." He shrugged. "How could I ignore the glow of an angel?"

"Bullet," she whispered, completely taken with his honesty. "How can you be so hard one minute and so romantic the next?"

"I don't know a damn thing about romance. I just say what I feel. I can't explain it, and I'm no wordsmith, but when you stood up to me in the bar and you didn't care how big I was or what I could do for you, like most people, you demanded my respect. I'm sure this isn't what you want to hear, but I'm not used to women giving a shit about why I do things or what I really want, and honestly, I don't usually have to talk at all. One look is enough to…" He shrugged, his gaze sliding up to the sky. When he looked at her again, he said, "I've unknowingly hurt you twice, Finlay. That's not the man you deserve, or the man I want to be."

"Well, not that it's okay to hurt me, but you did tell me this afternoon that I'd misinterpreted what you'd said. That you weren't calling me stupid, and tonight it sounds like you were a hero, so how can I not forgive you?"

"I'm nobody's hero. I told you that."

He was frustratingly modest, and that was another thing she wanted to understand, but for now she set that aside. She needed him to understand where she was coming from. "I don't know if I'll be okay with coming second, or seventeenth, or last in a long line of people who need you. That's a hard concept to grasp, a little like accidentally putting salt in whipping cream instead of sugar. It could be a deal breaker, but that would be on me, not you. And I won't know unless we try. But on the other hand, you might not want to be with a woman who is afraid of dogs and motorcycles." Disquieting thoughts whispered in her mind. "We don't make much sense."

His arms came around her and he lowered his lips to hers, kissing her so tenderly, it felt like a dream.

"Nothing in my life makes sense, Finlay, but you fucking wreck me. I don't know if I can give you the answers you need, but that's on me," he said, throwing her words back at her with a coy smile that warmed her all over. "And I'd rather try with you than walk away."

They stared at each other for a long moment, quieting her troubled spirits enough for her to realize they were still standing in her front yard—and that in the space of an evening, everything had changed. She took his hand and led him up the porch steps. "Let's get you cleaned up, and maybe we can salvage our first date."

He stepped over the threshold, and she felt his hesitation, saw a mask of discomfort come over him like a veil. Her table and counters were covered with cookies, cupcakes, and tarts. "I cook when I'm having a hard time," she explained as she carried the flowers he'd brought her toward the kitchen. She filled a vase with water, and as she put the flowers in it, she realized he hadn't moved from the doorway. He was gripping the doorknob like a lifeline. "What's wrong?"

He cleared his throat, his eyes darting around the room. "I can't be in here, Finlay. I'm sorry, but I can't breathe. I need space."

Her heart pitched, but could she blame him? After everything he'd been through? "Okay, then—"

He strode past her, opened the doors to the deck, and stepped outside. He gripped the railing as she had earlier, and his head fell between his shoulders. His silhouette looked even more imposing against the bluish hue of the moonlight, and at the same time, she sensed something subdued within him, like an injured wild animal.

"Are you all right?" she asked as she came outside. "Listen, Bullet, if what you said out there isn't true, or you just said it so I wouldn't be pissed, I get it. You don't have to lead me on if I'm not what you want. You can walk away without any hard feelings."

Without a word he pulled her into his arms, folding them around her like a vise, and held her. He didn't speak, resting his cheek on top of her head. She didn't know what to make of him, but she knew in her heart this was his way of saying he meant what he'd said. He held her there, with light spilling out the glass doors, rough decking beneath her bare feet, and the cool air sweeping over her back. But she wasn't cold or uncomfortable, because after the initial awareness of those things, they fell away, overshadowed by the sound of his heart beating, the potent scent of his body, and the strength of his arms embracing her.

"Nothing in my life has ever felt real," he said, holding her so tight it was as if he thought she might run away if he didn't. "You do."

"Then let me in," she said softly.

Silence stretched between them. She tried to lean back so she could see his face, but he kept her there against him, cradled within his arms, beneath his cheek.

"I want to," he said gruffly, "but it's going to fuck with my head. I can't be confined."

"Confined as in, by me, or…?"

"Not *you*. I need space, but not from you. I need *air*, room to breathe, to *deal*."

She tried to push from his arms again and his grip tightened. "Let me see you, Bullet," she said firmly, and he reluctantly eased his hold. She gazed up at his stormy eyes. "Are you okay here on the deck?"

His fingers curled around her waist. "You should probably tell me to leave."

"Your words say I should, but you're holding me so tight that I don't believe you want me to."

"Because I don't. But you fucking should."

She couldn't help but smile. "You're so rough and demanding. How about you let me make the decisions about who I spend my time with? Take that bloody shirt off. I'll throw it in the wash and get something so we can clean you up, because I'm pretty sure if you can't handle my living room, then you can't handle my tiny bathroom."

His gaze dropped to her dress, and he uttered a curse. "I got dried blood all over your dress. I'll buy you a new one."

She'd forgotten she was even wearing it, and as important as it had felt earlier, now it seemed almost insignificant. She could buy a new dress, but he could never erase the tragedy he'd witnessed tonight. "It's okay. Give me your shirt."

He flashed a cocky smile.

"Is there ever a time you don't think about sex?" she teased as he tugged off his shirt and leaned his butt against the railing.

His eyes locked on hers, instantly dark and serious. *Tortured?* She didn't have time to decide as she was riveted by the ink covering his body and the scars that lay beneath. She gasped at the fresh gashes on his abdomen and upper arm.

"Why didn't you...?" She couldn't finish her sentence, and didn't need to ask why he hadn't had his wounds tended to at the hospital. She instinctively knew he'd been too focused on the family he'd saved and the woman he was trying to console to worry about himself.

Even through his chest hair, it was like his tattoos screamed for her attention and tried to scare her away simultaneously. His left pec was covered with writing. What looked like hundreds of names ran together, overlapping, crisscrossing, some completely unreadable. Two sets of unseeing eyes came out of billowing smoke on the right side of his chest, obscuring two Mardi Gras–like masks, complete with a single black ribbon on either side. Behind each one were darker shades of gray, as if the rest of their heads were missing from the tortured men's masklike faces. She followed a halo of birds from behind the masks to his collarbone, where the word *Blessed* was tattooed in script along one side and *Destroyed* on the other. Each image sent a spear of pain rattling through her like chains being dragged beneath her skin.

She didn't think as she touched a dark tattooed cave at the juncture of his rib cage. The sun's rays radiated from his shoulders and the outer edges of his chest, beneath the other tattoos, leading into the darkness. A hulking figure stood like a pillar of strength before the lower edge of the cave, arms extended, its back covered with an evil face. Dark eyes, fanglike teeth, and sharp brows disappeared into wispy drawers hanging low on its hips. Two broken angel wings hung from the shoulder blades.

Her shaky fingers moved down his body to the image of an eagle flying across his stomach, over water and land, a limp body suspended by its talons. On the opposite side, she touched birdcages with people crouched down low inside them, spanning the breadth of his rib cage. She traced indiscernible patterns below his belly button and above the waist of his jeans, where the word *Family* was surrounded by shields and guns, hearts—broken and whole—and surprisingly, a bed of flowers. The only colors on his torso were red roses and green vines winding around the tail of the *F* and *Y* in *Family.*

The heat of Bullet's stare burrowed beneath her skin, chasing the pain the images had brought. She was too captivated by the frightening canvas before her to look away. Swallowing hard, she forced her attention to the puckered scars just below his right shoulder and near his ribs. Her gaze trailed lower, to more scars peppering his side.

Her insides ached for what he must have gone through. Not just tonight, which must have been horrific, but for whatever had led to the mural of agony before her. She tried to mask her expression but knew from the worry in his eyes she looked as pained as the images emblazoned on his body.

"I'll go throw this in the wash." She reached for his shirt and he reached for her, tossing his shirt onto a lounge chair.

"My shirt's history."

His warm hand pushed gently beneath her hair to the nape of her neck, drawing her closer. He widened his stance, bringing her between his legs, and touched his forehead to hers.

"I'm a lot to take in," he said.

"It's fine," she said quickly, although it *wasn't* fine.

"Finlay, it scares you. I see it in your eyes."

"Okay," she relented. "It's not fine. Nothing about this is fine. It's *terrifying,* but I'm not scared of *you.* I'm scared *for* you, for whatever you went through to cause so much pain to be permanently inked on your body. I hurt in here." She put her hand over her heart.

"Don't be scared for me," he said sternly. "There's *nothing* I can't survive."

That only made her hurt for him more. She gazed into his eyes, which were colder now. His walls were going back up. "Surviving and *living*, being happy, are two totally different things."

BULLET FELT THE weight of his and Finlay's worlds colliding as she disappeared into the house. He pushed from the railing and paced, trying to wrap his head around the look he'd seen in her eyes and the things she'd said when she'd seen his scars and tattoos. He'd never given a thought to his tats around women, but Finlay wore her heart on her sleeve, and he'd seen all the conflicting emotions as she experienced them. The shock, fear, and worry had coalesced when she'd gazed into his eyes, and for the first time, he'd considered what the mass of demons on his torso looked like. It was bad enough that he'd had to bolt out the back door because he'd hit enough triggers tonight to be on edge, and being confined added the likelihood of a flashback if, or when, he told her about the accident.

He didn't want to chance adding to the darkness she'd already seen, and hoped he wouldn't need to go there.

Finlay came outside wearing a pink crewneck sweatshirt with FINLAY'S emblazoned across the chest in white script and gray shorts that were made of the same soft material, a matching logo across her left thigh. He'd rather that sweatshirt said WHISKEY'S—or that it was black without the girly script and he could wear it. Because damn, being hers would be amazing.

She set a plate of cookies and cupcakes down on the table and held up one finger, looking deliciously sweet herself. What miracle had occurred for him to deserve this chance with her? He wasn't the kind of guy who found himself unworthy of a damn thing, but he couldn't help worrying about burdening her with his baggage.

"I just have to grab the stuff to clean you up, but I thought you might be hungry, and I have a house full of goodies, thanks to you." She took a step toward the glass doors and turned back, flashing a bright smile. "What can I get you to drink? I don't have beer, but I have wine coolers."

"Whatever you're drinking is fine, but I can get it." He took a step toward the house and she held up a hand, stopping him.

"No. You stay put and eat some of the *hip plumpers* you caused me to make."

He watched her gorgeous hips sway in those sexy shorts on her way back inside, feeling a little lighter than he had just moments earlier. He eyed the treats, but the only thing he wanted to get his hands on was currently carrying a bowl of soapy water outside, a roll of paper towels tucked under one arm, cloth towels tucked under the other. He grabbed the bowl and paper towels and set them on the table.

"I can clean up in your bathroom, Fin. You don't have to go to any more trouble. I'm doing better now."

She rolled her eyes. "No way. I just got all this stuff ready. Now you're going to sit your butt down and let me clean that mess up."

"Damn, babe. I like this side of you."

With a shy smile that conflicted with her bossiness, she held up a finger again and darted inside one more time, returning with two wine coolers. He'd never had a wine cooler in his life, but when she handed it to him with that sexy smile, he was so mesmerized by her, so grateful for her, she could have handed him lighter fluid and he would have sucked it down.

She set her drink on the table and pointed to the chair. "Sit down and let someone take care of *you* for a change."

He gritted his teeth. As much as he wanted her to touch him, he hadn't needed to be taken care of in so many years, it went against every fiber of his being to let her do it. She tilted her head with a sweet smile as she dunked a washcloth in the bowl, and his insides turned to frigging mush. He lowered himself to the chair.

She wrung out the cloth and moved so she was standing between his legs. "You have to tell me if it hurts, okay?"

"You can't hurt me." Even as he said the words he knew they weren't true. If she'd let him leave tonight, it would have hurt like a motherfucker.

"Okay, tough guy." She leaned in close as she gently washed the area around the wound on his arm. Her eyes flicked to his face, then back to the wound. She rinsed the cloth, carefully cleaning the gash. "You okay?"

He nodded.

"But you're really tense. Are you sure I'm not hurting you? This cut's pretty deep."

"I don't even feel it."

"Then why are you all knotted up?" She paused her caretaking and looked at him. "Your hands are fisted. Is the water too warm?"

He looked at his fisted hands and made a conscious effort to unfurl them. "No, but you're perfectly hot in those little shorts." He ran his hand up her thigh. Her skin was warm and soft, the perfect distraction from her efforts.

She smiled and continued cleaning out the cut, stealing glimpses at the left side of his chest. "What happened to you?"

"I told you. There was an accident and I had to get the family out of danger."

"No, not the accident. What happened to *you*? How did you get all those scars?" She put the washcloth down and patted his arm dry with a paper towel. When he didn't answer, she said, "Bullet?"

He lifted a shoulder. "Military."

"Bullet…" She sighed, her shoulders dropping.

"You don't want to hear this, Finlay." He looked away from her pleading eyes.

"I do," she said so earnestly, he was drawn to her eyes again. "I want to understand what you went through. Why you can't be inside the house without feeling confined. How else can I know what other things might bother you, or help you move past it? How can *you* move past it if you keep it all bottled up inside?"

He pressed his hands to his thighs, channeling all the dark energy there.

She set the washcloth down and placed her delicate hands over his. "Do you never talk about it?"

He didn't respond, and he knew by her empathetic expression he didn't need to. Her fingers curled around his hands.

"Have you ever?"

He swallowed against the acidic taste moving up his throat. "Bones knows a good deal of it, but nobody needs to hear the details about the hell that goes on over there."

"How long were you in the service?" she asked carefully.

"Too long, and not long enough."

"Bullet," she whispered for what felt like the hundredth time. "How long have you been out?"

"Seven years."

"And you've never shared the hard parts with anyone other than Bones?"

"Finlay...You don't want to go there."

"But the things you must have seen. The death and destruction, it will eat you alive if you don't get it out, won't it?" She squeezed his hands. "You should talk about it to someone. It doesn't have to be me, but you shouldn't carry the weight of the world around like that."

"I'm doing a pretty damn good job of it."

"No, you're not. You couldn't be inside my house, Bullet. I don't know if that was from the shock of the accident and all that happened, or..." Her eyes found the scar on his chest.

The scar that peppered his nightmares.

He blew out a breath. "What do you want from me, Finlay? What do you want to hear?" He pushed past her and stalked across the deck. "That I have fucking flashbacks sometimes? That I'm fucking invincible until they hit? That they make me want to get the hell away from everyone I know so I don't ruin their lives? That while I was laser focused on saving those babies, knowing I had to get to the people in the other vehicles before they blew up and the mother's bloodcurdling screams threw me right back to the battlefield? That part of me wished the accident had happened on the other side of the bridge instead of at the end of my goddamn street? Or that it took every ounce of my strength to get back in that car and get them to safety without shutting down completely?" He paced the deck, unable to keep his voice from rising. "That I was afraid I was going to fail and someone would die because of my fucking head?"

She lowered herself to the chair, and only then did he see the tears streaming down her cheeks. He rushed over to her and sank to his knees. "Shit. I'm sorry, Finlay. I didn't mean to yell and take that out on you."

She closed her eyes, rivers streaming down her cheeks as he gathered her in his arms. "I'm sorry. *Fuck.* I'm so sorry."

"It's not you," she choked out. "It's war. It's…"

Sobs stole her voice, and he pressed his hand to the back of her head, holding her against him. "Shh. It's okay. It's okay, baby."

"No, it's not *okay.*"

"I never should have said a word. You don't need darkness in your life."

She drew back, the pain in her eyes as tangible as the ghosts inside him.

"It's already there. I had a serious boyfriend when I was younger. He was in the military and was killed during his second tour. It was awful."

He pulled her against him again. "I'm sorry. I wish I could take that pain away."

"It was a long time ago. Now it only hurts when I think of him out there alone when he died." She inhaled a ragged breath and blew it out shakily. "War sucks."

"Yeah."

"But you survived," she said softly, and leaned up, wiping her tears. "Don't let the war steal *more* of your life. Aren't there things you can do to help ward off flashbacks?"

"Bones hooked me up with a buddy of his who taught me some strategies to use, and it helps, but sometimes, like tonight, if I'm not focused on triggers, they can hit like I've stepped on a mine."

"I thought you and I were so different when I saw you at Tru and Gemma's wedding. But we aren't that different after all."

It pissed him off that she'd been touched by the ugliness of war. "We're different, lollipop. You're as precious as they come."

"I know you'll dispute it, but so are you."

He raised his brows. "I don't think anyone has ever used that word in connection with me before."

She smiled and ran her finger along his collarbone. "That's because most people look at you and see big, bad, tattooed *Brutus*, the intimidating guy who doesn't let anyone get too close. I was almost one of them."

"Almost?"

"When you walked down the aisle holding Lincoln's hand at Tru and Gemma's wedding, he looked up at you like you were his world, and I remember thinking that babies had an innate ability to judge good people from bad people, like animals do. I've always believed that, as children, we have this sense of clarity that gets clouded as we get older and we're influenced by society."

"Are you telling me that when you came into Whiskey's that first day to meet with Dixie, you didn't see me as a badass? Because I might have to work on my intimidation skills."

"Oh no, you were definitely badass. But no matter how hard you were, somewhere in my mind I still had the image of you and Lincoln walking down that aisle. And there were other moments I've been thinking about, like when you were dancing with Kennedy and then with your mother. And the way you continually scanned the yard, as if you had to make sure your chicks were all in the pen."

"Something like that," he admitted.

"They're lucky to have you, and I think I'm pretty lucky, too." Her gaze moved to the gash on his stomach. "We'd better get you cleaned up. I forgot the ointment and bandages. Hold on."

She pushed to her feet and took a step toward the door.

Gratitude pooled inside him. Bullet grabbed her sweatshirt, drawing her back. "Thank you."

"For what?"

"For giving a shit."

Her lips curved up and her smile reached her beautiful eyes. "I'm sure anyone who knows you would do the same if you'd let them." She turned and walked inside.

She had no idea how wrong she was. The last time he'd been taken care of like this was when he was lying flat on his back beside a dying man, staring up at a dark sky crackling with crossfire, sure he was going to die.

He sank down to a chair, leaned his elbows on his knees and his face in his hands, willing the memories to remain at bay.

# Chapter Eight

BULLET FELT FINLAY'S hand on his shoulder and sat up, breathing deeply as she applied the ointment and bandaged the wound in silence.

"Is this hard for you? Letting me take care of you?" she asked as she used the washcloth to cleanse the dried blood that had seeped through his shirt onto his torso.

"A little."

"Because you're the protector?" She didn't wait for an answer as she lifted the washcloth and said, "Lift your chin. There's some blood on your neck."

The longer she cared for him, gently bathing his arms, hands, chest, and torso, the easier it became for Bullet to relax. Her touch became the salve to his emotional wounds, her sweet, caring nature, the sutures to the fissures tonight's flashbacks had caused.

"When my dad would get a cold, or sick, which wasn't very often, he'd do everything he could to keep from resting," she said as she rinsed the washcloth. "And my mom would tell him that it took a stronger man to let someone take care of him than it did to be the caretaker." She gazed into his eyes and said, "I think that goes for you, too, Mr. Whiskey."

"I'm not feeling very strong at the moment," he mumbled more to himself than to her.

"Strength of character is stronger than power of muscle. That's another of my mom's sayings. You have both, and what you did tonight proves how strong you really are."

He pulled her closer, wanting to kiss her, to soak in her goodness, but he didn't want her to feel like he was taking advantage of her generosity. "Are you close to your parents?"

"Yes. But we lost my father a few years ago, and then my mom moved to Montana, where she was from. She said she saw my dad everywhere, which I understand, because I still feel him around sometimes. Then she remarried. I'm happy for her, and it wasn't like she was running away from me and Penny. She just needed to move on and couldn't do it here."

"I'm sorry you lost your father." He brushed his thumb over her cheek. "That must have been awful for you."

"It was. My biggest regret was that I was living in Boston at the time. He worked at the power plant and there was an electrical misfire or something. They classified it as an industrial accident. I guess they were lucky no one else was hurt."

He pulled her into an embrace, wishing he could have been there for her when she'd lost him. "Are you okay here? Being back in town?"

"Yes. I needed to be here, closer to Penny." She pushed away, busying herself with the washcloth again, but as she washed him, her touch changed.

No longer was she washing him with a corner of the cloth. She spread it over her hand, bathing him from shoulder to shoulder, slowly and sensually, furtively glancing up as she moved over his chest and down his ribs. Her eyelids grew heavier, and he wasn't sure she realized it, but she moved closer, until the space between them was barely big enough for her hand. Desire filled the space between them, growing hotter with every stroke, but the conflict in her eyes told him she was struggling—to decide if she should go for it or ignore it, he wasn't sure, but he couldn't take his eyes off her, either. And when he rested his fingers on her hips, she trapped her lower lip between her teeth, inching even closer.

That subtle, telling move brought their mouths a whisper apart. Their gazes locked, lust pulsing between them like a drum. He wanted to tell her it was okay. *Just let go. Surrender to me.* The urge to *take* was strong, but his desire not to screw this up was even stronger.

The tip of her tongue swept along her lips, and he gritted his teeth.

"We should..." She nibbled on her lip again. "Um. Let's check out the cut on your stomach."

She crouched before him, and holy mother of God, seeing his blond angel crouched in front of his cock shoved all the ugly thoughts of war and flashbacks aside. The therapists had never shared *this* tactic with him. Wanting Finlay Wilson was *magic*. When she put one hand on his stomach, the other on his thigh, balancing as she inspected his wound, he clenched his teeth harder.

She squinted, her lips twisting in contemplation. "That definitely needs some attention."

*Fuck yeah.* She had no idea how dirty his thoughts could be.

She reached for the washcloth, and he caught her hand. Their eyes connected and the temperature spiked. Her eyes turned midnight blue, and the pulse at the base of her neck throbbed erratically. The hell with the cuts. He wanted to seal his mouth over that frantic pulse and drive it up even higher.

She licked her lips again, and he placed his other hand on the back of her thigh, bringing her closer. Sparks showered around them, sizzling and popping, but neither one said a word. He fought the need to kiss her, wanting to stay on this emotional high with her, suspended from the rest of the world forever.

She didn't say a word as she reached for the washcloth and carefully cleaned the cut. The energy between them shifted again, spiking hotter, delving deeper, as if their confessions had bound them, creating a pulse all their own. Every swipe of the cloth against his skin brought more awareness—of her stilted breathing, stolen glances, her legs brushing against his inner thighs. He wanted to feel her legs against his bare skin, to have her hot little hands all over his body, healing his fractured soul.

"Okay," she whispered, and set the cloth down. She patted the area dry with a paper towel, her face a mask of attentive sweetness.

She reached for the ointment, and he ran his fingers along her arm from elbow to wrist. She stilled, her hand inches from the ointment, her soft exhalations filling the silence. He pressed his thighs tighter against her legs and traced the curve of her hip with his other hand. She tensed at the first stroke down her thigh, but she didn't look away, a whirlwind of emotions passing between them. Wordlessly, she reached for the ointment again.

He wanted her to reach for him, but he knew that wasn't her way. She was like a scared rabbit coming out of its hole, then retreating, only to return and sniff the air, inching closer until she trusted him completely.

He watched as she applied the ointment to his wound,

admiring her for so many reasons. She wasn't living her life angry at the world for stealing her father and her man away, or walling herself off for fear of being hurt again.

"How do you do it?" The question came unbidden.

She picked up a bandage. "Clean out your cuts?"

"No, Fins. How'd you move past the hurt? You're so happy."

"Now? Sure, but back then? I cried a lot, talked my friend Izzy's and Penny's ears off. I cooked and baked enough food for a small army, and I prayed a lot. I'm not religious, but I thought if I sent positive, loving thoughts into the universe they would somehow make it back to Aaron and my dad. And you know, I was so young. Twenty-one when Aaron died, and then we lost my dad a couple years later. Time may not heal wounds, but it allows for perspective. I'm thankful I had them in my life."

She put the bandage down and said, "I'm afraid to put that on your cut."

She was as adept at changing subjects as he was. He understood that. Sometimes enough was enough. Beating things into the ground wouldn't bring people back.

"It'll stick to the hair on your stomach and hurt like crazy when you take it off." Her eyes widened. "I could shave a path around the cut."

"Real men only shave for tattoos and blow jobs. Get up here." He motioned to his lap.

"Why, Mr. Whiskey, are you getting frisky with me?"

He lifted her onto his lap, guiding her legs around his hips, and ran his hands along her outer thighs. Her cheeks heated, and he loved that about her. The women he'd been with had never blushed. They'd never felt real either. They were a means to an escape, a release, while Finlay...She was the only reality he didn't want to escape.

"Don't worry, lollipop." He wound his fingers through her hair and pulled her closer, speaking directly into her ear. "I'm not asking you to blow the whistle or ride the train." He slicked his tongue along the shell of her ear, earning a lusty moan. "I just want to taste you, get a little sugar rush to hold us over."

He sealed his mouth over the sensitive skin at the base of her neck, and a sexy little gasp slipped from her lips as he took a long, sensual *suck*. She inhaled a series of sharp breaths as he loved his way along the column of her neck to the other side.

"You're so sweet," he said between tastes. "So perfect, lollipop, but I need your mouth on me." He told himself to slow down, but she whispered, "Yes," silencing his thoughts altogether.

She bowed toward him, pressing her sweet center against his hard shaft. He pushed one hand up her thigh, and when she ground harder, he slipped his long fingers beneath her shorts. The scratch of lace pulled a groan from his lungs as he filled his palm with her tempting bottom. His emotions reeled, as he groped and kissed, sucked and nipped, and the real world failed to exist. His hands were everywhere at once, caught up in the spiral of desire, on a mission to feel as much of her as he could. He pushed under her sweatshirt, palming her breasts as they rose with her heavy breaths. Her sexy moans and whimpers drove him out of his fucking mind. He rocked his hips, and she pushed her hands into his hair, grinding harder, kissing him deeper. She was too much, too good, too *willing*, filling him with all that sweetness.

He tore his mouth from hers, needing to see her beautiful face, to make sure he wasn't imagining her eagerness, wasn't *forcing* and *taking*, too caught up in her to catch her signals. Her lips were swollen from their kisses, her cheeks pink and scratched from his beard. It probably made him an asshole, but he loved knowing she'd feel his mouth on hers tomorrow.

"Kiss me," she pleaded, and lowered her face toward his again.

The kiss started out soft, sweet, but within seconds they were eating at each other's mouths, ravenously taking and giving in equal measure. Greedy sounds slipped between them like they'd both been waiting years for this connection—and in his case, he'd waited a lifetime. He claimed her neck again, loving the way she quivered and shook with each stroke of his tongue.

"I've got to feel you against me, Fins." He rose to his feet with her in his arms and laid her on the lounge chair, coming down over her.

She was so small, so feminine, his protective urges surged, and he was getting too carried away. He forced himself to move beside her. They lay facing each other, kissing and smiling. Jesus, he couldn't remember the last time he'd smiled when he'd kissed a woman. The last time he'd *cared*.

He ran his hand down her leg, and words poured out. "I love your legs. Your soft skin."

He hooked his hand beneath her knee, bringing her leg over his, her knee resting by his hip. *Oh yeah*, that was nice. All her softness pressed against him. She arched forward, rubbing against his cock, and he lowered her onto her back and gazed into her eyes, overwhelmed by the trust and emotions staring back at him—*for* him.

He wanted to be the man she counted on, to see that trust in her eyes always. To be the man who would be there for her when she hurt and when she celebrated. And he had a feeling Finlay's life would be full of celebrations, because she didn't wallow, didn't let the darkness overtake her. She was open and caring, and that trust just about did him in. Bullet knew all about trust. It was the very foundation of his being. His brothers at arms had an unbreakable trust, and the club brotherhood and his blood family lived and breathed by that bond. He wanted that with Finlay, and he knew it all started now.

"Tell me to stop, Fins, and I'll back off. You own tonight."

She craned up and touched her lips to his. "I don't want you to stop, and I don't want to own it. I want to share it with you," she said earnestly, unleashing his desires.

He explored the dips and curves of her body as they made out like they'd waited their entire lives for each other and they may never get another chance. She arched and moaned, pressing her whole body against his. He pushed his hand up the leg of her shorts, beneath her panties, seeking her slick heat. She bent her knee, letting it fall to the side, giving him better access to tease her silken flesh. Emotions bubbled up inside his chest, mounting and throbbing as he discovered just how badly she wanted him. She was so wet, felt so incredibly warm and sweet. He dipped his fingers inside her, gently taking her where they both needed her to go as he kissed her deeply.

He crooked his finger and her head fell back with a long, surrendering moan. Her hips rose to greet him, and he tugged up her shirt and unclasped the front of her bra, freeing her magnificent breasts. He stole a glance at her closed eyes, the flush of her skin, wanting to remember this moment forever. The closeness, her openness. He dragged his tongue over her taut nipple as she met each of his probes with a thrust of her hips, her breathing coming in shallow, needful gasps. She clung to his shoulders, her nails digging into his skin, probably carving scars he'd proudly wear.

When he lowered his mouth over her breast and sucked, she cried out, "Ah! So good!" Her hips rose up, up, *up*, and when he sucked harder, she bucked and cried out again, her sex pulsing tight and hot around his fingers.

"That's it, baby. Jesus, *fuck*, you're beautiful."

He reclaimed her mouth, circling her clit with this thumb, keeping her at the height of her orgasm. She whimpered and mewled, panting into his mouth. When another orgasm slammed into her, sending her into a wild, rocking frenzy, his name flew from her lips like a demand, again and again, until it was nothing but a whisper. And when she collapsed back to the chair and he withdrew from between her legs, she was shaking all over.

He gathered her against him, kissing every spec of flesh he could reach.

"Bullet," she pleaded. "Good Lord. You were heaven sent."

"More like the devil. I'm thinking very *sinful* thoughts about you, lollipop." He lowered his lips to hers. God, he loved her mouth.

He drew back for only an instant, to look at her beautiful face, and then he returned to her delicious mouth, loving it thoroughly, pushing his tongue in and out, deep and insistent like he wanted to do with his cock. He cupped her jaw, holding her cheeks so he could feel their tongues moving inside. More sinful sounds bubbled up from inside her. He kissed his way down her body, slowing to love each breast with his hands and mouth. He wiped her arousal from his fingers on her nipple and licked it off, tantalizingly slowly, reveling in his first taste of her.

"Bullet—" she said desperately.

Good Lord, she was his undoing. Her eyes were closed, her

breathing shallow. Her hair was tousled around her trusting face. She was the most beautiful creature he'd ever seen, the purest, kindest, and perhaps one of the strongest women he'd ever known. He wanted to stay right there, loving her until the sun came up.

But he knew he couldn't, and because of that, he said, "Open your eyes, sweet girl."

FINLAY OPENED HER eyes, her body still tingling from head to toe. Bullet was looking at her with the most tortured, and somehow also contented, expression. He slid his tongue along her lower lip and drew up quickly, as if he wasn't sure he should have done it. She couldn't stifle another greedy noise from slipping from her lungs. She'd never felt so needy in all her life, but there was an energy, a *hunger* in Bullet that fed the empty parts of her. He was so visceral, so intense and closed off most of the time, but in the moments when those barriers lifted, he was warm and passionate. Tonight he'd allowed her to peek beneath his complex layers, deepening their connection well beyond the physical. There was no doubt in her mind that he'd revealed a side of himself that had been long ago sealed shut. And the more she learned about him, the more layers she peeled back, the more complex and *real* he became.

He cradled her face between both hands and gazed deeply into her eyes. "Hi, beautiful."

"Hi."

"It's nearing the witching hour, when guys like me turn into werewolves."

An uneasy feeling floated through her. "You're leaving right now? Seconds after…?"

"Not on your life," he said in a raspy voice full of so much emotion it calmed the worry that had crept up on her.

He kissed her neck and carefully hooked her bra and righted her sweatshirt, which was so unexpectedly sweet, it felt intimate and special. Then he gathered her in his strong arms, and she snuggled into the curve of his body, feeling safe, even though she didn't really know where they were heading or what a night like this meant to a guy like him. For the first time since she'd been with Aaron, her heart was beating for something more than her job, and it felt too good to dissect the meaning of it.

He tipped up her chin and pressed his lips to hers. "I just need to put on the brakes so that *doesn't* happen."

"I didn't know the *Bullet train* had brakes," she teased.

"That makes two of us," he mumbled.

A pang of discomfort trampled through her. "You mean you don't *ever* stop before going all the way?"

He kissed the top of her head, but no answer came. She pushed back so she could see his face, and wasn't surprised to see his go-to serious expression. The one that told her—and everyone else—to back off. But they'd just been more intimate than she'd been with any other man in forever, and she didn't feel comfortable backing off.

"Seriously?"

He sat up and said, "You don't want to go there, Finlay."

"I shouldn't *want* to go there, but I do."

"Why would you put yourself through that? Why does it fucking matter what I did with anyone else if I don't do it with you?" He stood up, and his boots *thump*ed across the deck as he paced, his massive frame looming in the darkness.

She pushed to her feet, her mind spinning. Her cognitive

brain knew it shouldn't matter what he did with anyone else. They weren't even a couple, but she wanted to know. Needed to know, needed to understand him.

"I don't know," she admitted. "I feel like I should understand what you're usually like so I know if you're different with me. I mean, you *stopped*, so that's obviously *epically* different for you, right? But what about diseases?"

"I don't ride bareback, and I've never had a damn disease," came barreling out of him. "I've got a handful of women I screw when the urge hits. They're clean. They know me. They don't give a shit if I leave afterward." He threw his arms out to the sides, an annoyed expression on his face. "What else do you want to know? I don't fuck them naked. I don't even give a shit if they come. It's quick and dirty." He stared back at her, his jaw clenched tight. "It's not like it is with you. Nothing in my life has been like it is with you. Not even close."

Finlay crossed her arms and sank back down to the chair, trying to grasp how she could be so attracted to a guy who could say, much less *do*, those things. *A handful of women? Quick and dirty?* "So, you *use* them?"

He stopped pacing and shoved his hands in his pockets and shrugged. "We use each other."

He let out a long, steady breath, watching her as she processed the information. His features softened as he knelt before her. "Finlay, nothing about me will fit the mold of who you see yourself with. We talked about this."

"I know, and I don't really care about that, because when I'm with you, I want to be with you. But it's one thing to think you've done those things and another to have confirmation. I don't want to be a one-night stand, or one of the girls you use."

"Don't even fucking say that." His eyes narrowed angrily.

"I'd never do that to you. I *stopped* before we went further. Doesn't that tell you everything you need to know? Do you think I'm proud of the fact that I can't have a normal relationship? That I can't sleep without my fucking dog for fear of nightmares? That it took every ounce of strength I had not to walk away instead of coming over to apologize to you?"

"You can't sleep without Tinkerbell?" Oh, how he made her heart hurt.

"Tink can't sleep without me, either. She'll be clawing at the window whining until I get home." He huffed out a laugh. "She hasn't slept alone since I found her. Some asshole threw her out of his car with a load of trash on the highway. She was in a green garbage bag, rail-thin, scared to death. I took her directly to my buddy, a vet and a member of our club, and spent weeks nursing her back to health. She's been by my side ever since. She gets me. On the rare occasion when I have a nightmare, she wakes me up before it pulls me too far under."

Finlay swelled with love for both of them. It was no wonder he didn't want to leave her.

"We're both messed up," he said, "but we work. I need her and she needs me."

The love in his eyes was tangible. "And you debated not coming over at all? Just leaving me hanging?"

He took her hand in his, his gaze as apologetic as it was honest. "I debated saving you the grief of having a guy like me in your life. I was coming down from major flashbacks. That scene unearthed all sorts of shit. Fin, everyone's got baggage, and I know I've got a whole cargo load of it. I know what I am, and I'm not ashamed of it. I'm a survivor. My life is what it has had to be in order for me to make it through each day. I'm good at protecting others. I suck at"—he lifted their joint hands—

"this. Even as a kid I didn't go on dates. I'd nod at a girl and we'd hook up. That's all I've ever known or wanted. And then you came into my life like a star falling from the night sky, and all I wanted was to catch you."

His honesty was like a drug, soothing the harshness of his confession. "It was all physical at first," she reminded him.

"Absolutely. You're gorgeous."

"So if I had accepted a ride on the *Bullet train*, that would have been it?" The thought made her uneasy.

"We'll never know for sure, but I can't believe for a second that I would have fu—gone through with it, or that I would have let you walk away afterward. Not if we had spent ten minutes having a real conversation. You're too special. You said there was a difference between surviving and living, and I know you're right. It's evident in who you are and how you live your life. When I'm around you, you lift me up, make me see and *feel*. Because of who you are and who I want to be for you, I brought you flowers from my garden, showered, and shaved before our date—"

She glanced at his beard. "Shaved?"

He looked down at his privates.

"Oh my gosh. You *did* think we'd sleep together!" As she said it she realized she'd been thinking about what he'd be like in bed for far longer than just one day.

"I don't recall saying real men shaved for *sex*."

She gasped. "You thought I'd...on the first date? I mean, I let you touch me, and I've never done *that* on a first date before, but I wouldn't have..." *Would I? Oh gosh! I might have!*

His brows lifted, and they both laughed softly.

"Clearly whatever this is between us is new and different for both of us," he said, a spark of hope glimmering in his eyes. "I just found you, Finlay. Please don't let my messed-up life scare you away. For the first time in as long as I can remember, I don't want to just survive. I want to *live*."

"Bullet," she said breathlessly, trying to solidify her melting heart. "I haven't been really living either. I know it looks like I am, but I didn't move back only because I missed Penny. I moved back because I was lonely. I tried to feel something toward a man after Aaron died. I went out on a few dates and I tried to be intimate, but I was too broken to feel anything, even as recently as last winter. I moved back home because I figured I might not be able to love or be loved by a man, but at least I could love and be loved by Penny. And sisterly love is better than no love at all."

"That breaks my heart. You're too sweet to be alone forever."

"But I felt something tonight," she admitted. "I felt a *lot*. So much, it's a little scary."

"Don't be scared. Just be with me. Give us a chance."

She wanted that now more than ever, despite their differences. She'd never met anyone as honest, or as selfless, but at the end of the day, there was a certain level of respect she needed from others, and for herself. She gathered her courage like a cloak and said, "I can't if you're going to be with other women. I don't have it in me to share you. Protecting others is one thing, but giving your body to them is another."

"I won't share you," he said with the demanding tone that for some crazy reason endeared her toward him. "And I'd never expect you to share me."

"Okay."

His breath rushed from his lungs with a long, "Ah, lollipop," as he hauled her onto his lap and kissed her breathless.

"Tomorrow," he said against her neck, "I'm making up for tonight and taking you out on a proper date."

"You are?" She couldn't wait to see him again.

"What are your plans during the day? I have to work at four, and I want to stop by the hospital in the morning and see how the Beckleys are doing, but I could pick you up afterward."

Her heart filled at his thoughtfulness. "How about you pick me up in the morning and I'll go with you? I have to order the appliances for the bar, and I was going to work on the menus, but I can do that after four, when you're at work. I think I'll also bring some of the goodies I made tonight to the bar. The customers really liked the cookies."

"Just what I need, more guys going apeshit over *your* goodies." He groaned, smiling, though she was pretty sure he wasn't teasing. Then his tone turned serious again, and he said, "But you don't need to be around that sad stuff in the hospital. I'll swing by afterward."

She wound her arms around his neck and said, "Mr. Whiskey, let me give you a little lesson in relationships. It's okay to let people who care about you be there *for* you. That's how coupledom works. You might not *need* me there, but if you'll let me, I'd like to be there anyway. Just in case you need a hug, because even big, tough protectors need hugs sometimes."

"What if I need to be kissed?" His eyes smoldered, and he pressed his lips to her neck.

Shivers ticked over her skin. "Mm. That could be arranged."

"And touched?" He nipped at her jaw.

"Maybe in private," she said coyly.

He brushed his lips over hers and said, "*Ah*, so you do want to touch my privates."

# Chapter Nine

FOR THE SECOND time in less than twenty-four hours, Bullet found himself sitting in front of Finlay's house in his truck with a handful of flowers from his garden. Only this time there wasn't a damn thing that could make him contemplate walking away. And just to be sure, last night he'd called Bones to talk about the flashbacks he'd had when he'd been dealing with the accident. Bones had reminded him of what he'd learned from his buddy, the therapist. And now, as he cut the engine, he was on the phone with his younger brother again. Bones had called to make sure he was still cool.

"I'm good, buddy. I'm sorry I called at such a crazy hour last night."

Bones was fifteen months younger than Bullet, and to an observer they were about as different as two brothers could be. Not only was Bones a clean-cut professional to Bullet's scruffy appearance and blue-collar job, but he also kept his ink carefully hidden from the eyes of his patients and peers, limiting his tats to his shoulders, torso, and above the knee, while Bullet's body was a testament to all the hell he'd seen. But while they looked and acted different, the foundation of what they believed in and the creed by which they lived were the same.

"No worries," Bones said. "I was just getting in from a party out in Pleasant Hill. I know last night you said you didn't want to talk about Finlay, but B, if you're going to be with her, you've got to clue her in about your past."

"Dude, she's more clued in than you are now," Bullet admitted.

"This is me you're talking to, B. Just tell me to shut my mouth. Don't give me a load of horseshit."

Bullet glanced up at Finlay's house, his chest constricting with the memory of her expression when she'd seen his body and the hurt and confusion in her voice when he'd been honest about his personal life. "It's true, bro. I have no idea what compelled me to be honest with her about all the shit in my head, but she didn't run, and she didn't tell me I was too fucked up for her."

Bones was quiet for a beat too long.

"Spit it out, Bones," Bullet said angrily. "You think when I go to pick her up today she'll blow me off now that she's had time to think about it?" He'd been worrying about the same thing since he'd gotten up that morning.

"No, man. Just the opposite. You've never let anyone into your head. Hell, B, it took you almost dying to reach out to me, and you still haven't come clean to the rest of the family about what really happened with your medical discharge."

Bullet mindlessly rubbed his hand over his chest and side, where scars marked the end of his military career. "Your point?"

"My point is, you must feel a hell of a lot for Finlay for you to let her in. You're an incredibly smart, capable, bighearted guy, and it sounds like you found someone who sees those qualities in you, the way the rest of us do."

"You make me sound like a pussy."

"No. I just make you sound human, and you hate that." Bones laughed and added, "What are you going to do about the whole sleeping with Tink thing?"

Last night Tinkerbell had been a whiny mess of love when Bullet had gotten home, and he'd taken her for a long walk around his property while he'd talked with Bones on the phone. "Tink is as much a part of my life as you are. She's not going anywhere."

"That's no answer."

Bullet laughed. Leave it to his younger brother to push him into a corner. But this was a corner Bullet was ready for. "Well, she doesn't know it yet, but I plan to bring Fin home with me this afternoon to get to know Tink. I figure she's not *terrified* of dogs, since she could sit in the truck and sing herself silly with Tink in the backseat. She's scared, and if there's one thing I know how to do, it's ease into something that scares you."

"Good luck with that. Maybe you can go to joint therapy—you for your flashbacks and nightmares and Finlay for her fear of dogs."

"Fuck you," Bullet said with a smile. "If we're going, then so are you."

"For…?"

"Needing to go out of town to find a woman to fuck." While Bullet had a host of women he could call day or night and never cared who knew it—*until now*—Bones was discreet with his extracurricular activities. As a well-respected oncologist, Bullet knew he had to be, but that didn't stop him from giving his brother shit.

"Asshole."

"Fuckhead." Bullet glanced at the house again and saw

Finlay walking through the living room. "I gotta run, bro. Love you."

"Love you, too, B. And for what it's worth, I really liked Finlay when I met her at the wedding, and Mom said the guys at the bar were crazy about her. Don't fuck her over."

"*Jesus...*"

"Just giving you shit. She said they couldn't stop talking about how personable and upbeat she was—*and* about her cookies. I'm happy for you, bro. I'm heading out for a run."

On his way up to the porch, Bullet caught another glimpse of Finlay through the living room window, causing a strange fluttery sensation in his chest. He froze, fearing the accident had opened a vortex that lumped Finlay into some sort of trigger. He drew in a deep breath as she set the vase of flowers he'd given her the night before on the end table. She turned, and their eyes caught, turning that flutter into brain-numbing desire. A wide smile lifted her cheeks, and she hurried toward the door, her short green dress whisking around her thighs. She wore a pair of tan lace-up ankle boots that did amazing things to her gorgeous legs. Damn, her smile and those legs would be the death of him.

The door flew open, and a gust of cinnamon seeped into his senses. His gut seized as he remembered what she'd said about cooking when she was upset. But her eyes danced with delight, and like the sun had finally come out, his whole world brightened.

"Hi," she said joyfully.

"Hey there, lollipop." He stepped forward as she went up on her toes, greeting him with an enthusiastic press of her lips.

She tasted like cinnamon and sugar and a whole lot of happiness, shattering any lingering worries he might have had about her turning tail and running scared. He wanted to forget their visit to the hospital, carry her into the bedroom, and spend the day worshipping her naked body.

As their lips parted, he said, "I might have to come over every morning." He kissed her again, deeper this time, slow and sensual, until she exhaled one of those dreamy sighs he loved.

"Damn, I missed you." When he realized what he'd said, he rose to his full height, startled by the revelation.

"I missed you, too," she admitted with a shy smile. "But you were stuck in my head. I dreamed about you all night long."

That made his insides all warm and mushy. "Naked, I hope."

"No!" Her cheeks flushed. "*Maybe*."

"Good." He leaned closer and spoke directly into her ear. "Just be sure you dream big enough."

"Bullet!" she whispered. "I think you like embarrassing me."

"I think I'm going to like breaking you of that embarrassment even more." She visibly shivered, and he handed her the flowers. "For you, beautiful."

"More flowers? They're gorgeous, thank you. Are these from your garden, too?"

"Mm-hm."

"You'll make your garden bare if you keep bringing me flowers from it."

"I'm not worried." He had more gardens than he could ever deplete. Gardening had been a form of therapy when he'd first returned home, plagued with severe PTSD.

He followed her into the kitchen, where she'd set a table for two, complete with fancy cloth napkins, wineglasses filled with ice water, and a pitcher of orange juice, and was glad to see the anxiousness of last night was gone. "Expecting company?"

"Only you," she said with a quick tap on his chest. She leaned on the counter and went up on her toes to grab a vase from a top shelf in a cabinet, and he retrieved it for her.

His body brushed against hers, and the Finlay radar detector in his pants awoke with the alarm. Finlay inhaled, just faint enough to kick up his heart rate.

"You didn't have to go to this much trouble," he said as he set the vase on the counter.

She picked up the vase but didn't face him. "It was no trouble. You had a hard night last night, and we got so close, I wanted to make you something special."

He sensed her arousal in the shakiness of her voice. She turned on the sink and he reached around her, keeping her close as he filled the vase with water and placed the flowers in it. Then he lowered his mouth to her neck and kissed her tenderly, but tenderly wasn't enough, and he opened his mouth so he could taste her better. She shuddered against him, and he turned her in his arms.

"You're my something special." He brushed his lips over hers and said, "You're all the breakfast I need."

"Bullet," came out breathless.

He tipped her chin up and took her in another passionate kiss. His hips ground against her belly, and he knew she could feel how hard he was. "I don't want you to think I came over expecting this."

"*This* is good," she whispered.

"Christ, Fins. I can't get enough of you." He lifted her up onto the counter and wedged himself between her legs, devouring her mouth like a starving refugee.

She pushed her hands into his hair and guided his mouth to her neck again. Man, he loved that she wasn't too shy to show him what she liked. He sealed his mouth over her warm skin, sinking his teeth in just enough to earn a sinful sound that sizzled through him. He pulled her to the edge of the counter, aligning her center with the steel spike in his jeans, and pulsed his hips against her.

"Oh gosh, Bullet," she pleaded, and pushed on the back of his hips, keeping their bodies flush.

"If you keep saying my name like that, I'm not going to stop, baby." He pushed his hands along her outer thighs and clutched her ass through her silky panties. "You feel so damn good."

"*Bullet, Bullet, Bullet,*" she whispered greedily.

His mouth crashed over hers, rough and demanding. She arched against him and...

*Beep! Beep! Beep!*

Bullet snapped upright at the sharp sound, his eyes darting around the kitchen.

"It's the oven timer," Finlay said quickly. "The Wicked Sticky Buns are ready."

An unstoppable guttural noise rumbled in his throat. He grabbed her ass and said, "Trust me, babe. I can get your buns *wicked sticky* real fast."

Finlay giggled as she wiggled off the counter, landing on her toes before him as the alarm sounded again.

"Your kisses make other parts of me sticky, too," she said quietly as she slipped an oven mitt over her hand and bent to remove a tray from the oven.

Like metal to magnet, he splayed a hand on the back of her thigh, gathered her hair over one shoulder, and kissed her neck again. "Christ, lollipop. You're killing me."

She took off the oven mitt, still facing away from him, and

steeled herself against the counter with both hands, leaning back against him with a sigh. He moved his hands to the front of her thighs, his fingers creeping up between her legs. The scent of warm cinnamon assaulted him, and he caught a glimpse of the freshly washed bowls and measuring cups drying beside the sink, bringing rise to a spear of guilt. She'd gone to all this trouble to make him something special, and all he could think about was eating *her* for breakfast.

He made room for that organ in his chest to lead the way, kissed her cheek, and said, "What can I do to help?"

AFTER A BREAKFAST filled with enough heat and stolen kisses to catch Finlay's Wicked Sticky Buns on fire—and a quick covert panty change, which Finlay assumed she'd be doing a lot of with Bullet around—they headed over to the hospital to see how the Beckleys were doing. Bullet hauled her across the bench seat in his truck so she was sitting beside him, and no part of her wanted to put space between them. She'd been honest about missing him in the few hours they were apart, and it had shocked her as much as it had thrilled her.

She'd been so wired last night after Bullet left, she'd packaged up all the desserts she'd made into pretty boxes, including a gift for Mrs. Beckley, and she'd finally fallen into bed around three thirty. She had no idea how she'd fallen asleep, because her mind had been reeling from everything they'd done and all that they'd revealed to each other, but somehow she had, and she'd slept like a rock. Her dreams had been nothing short of erotic. One second Bullet was perched above her, his thick shaft moving inside her, and in the next she was on her knees with his cock in her mouth. Finlay had been intimate with only four men in her life. Sex had always been missionary, and pleasurable enough. Until that last guy, after Aaron died, when she hadn't enjoyed it at all. She'd had oral sex before, but it was more out of duty than desire, and she hadn't gotten *on her knees* for *any* man. With Bullet, she didn't just desire him in her dreams, but she craved him in the light of day, when she was wide-awake and he was miles away. Even more so when he had his mouth on her.

When they arrived at the hospital, he put an arm around her waist and lifted her out of the truck, keeping her pressed against him. Her insides heated up as she slid down his body and her heels touched the ground. It had never been like this before, where just a touch, a look, a single kiss turned her into a pulse-pounding, tingling mess of desire. If there had been a thought bubble over her head when he'd picked her up, they never would have left her foyer. Bullet was one hot dessert, and the man knew how to fill out a pair of Levi's. She had embarrassingly noticed every bulge, from the thickness of his thighs to the fullness of his formidable package. And his chest? She wanted to run her tongue from belly button to nipple. Okay, she wanted to start *much* lower.

*Don't even get me started on his beard.* The scratch of pleasure and pain was beyond tantalizing, and she couldn't wait to feel it on her thighs.

Bullet gazed into her eyes, searching for she had no idea what. "You okay? You zoned out."

*Oh, geez!* "Yes, sorry. I was just thinking." If she didn't stop fantasizing, she'd need to carry extra underwear in her purse!

"Would you mind carrying this?" He handed her the gift box she'd packaged for Mrs. Beckley. "I have to grab a few things from behind the passenger seat."

He went around the truck and withdrew two enormous teddy bears, one with a blue ribbon tied around its neck and one with a pink ribbon. She fell a little harder for him right then and there.

On their way inside, she asked, "Are you worried at all that seeing the family again will trigger flashbacks?" She'd wanted to ask more about them last night, but he'd shared so much of himself, she didn't want to trigger any worse feelings. She'd already started doing some research online to see if there were any strategies she could use to help him if he got a flashback when they were together.

He stopped walking, and his expression went dark. "Finlay, I'm not a walking time bomb."

"I don't think you are. I just want to be prepared so I can help if something happens."

Something intense flared in his eyes. It wasn't anger, but it wasn't pleasure either.

"Come here." He cocooned her between the giant stuffed bears, and his gaze softened. "They don't happen often anymore. Before last night, it had been almost a year since the last one. Last night was like the perfect storm. I had just pulled onto the main drag. It was dark, and the sounds, the smells, the sparks caused by the collision struck all the right chords. And then I saw gasoline leaking from the truck, and that's when the panic happened. But I don't want you to think for one minute that I can't protect you. No matter what happens around us."

She realized that her concern for him had somehow morphed into something altogether different in his head. "I don't doubt that for one second. You saved an entire family despite having flashbacks. You're the strongest man I have ever met.

But it's okay to let someone have *your* back. Just in case. If I were there last night, I might have been able to help you in some way."

He shook his head. "I wouldn't ever want you in danger like that, and my family always has my back."

She tried not to let the sting of his words affect her expression, but she must have failed, because he squeezed those cuddly bears around her and said, "By 'family' I mean my club members and my brothers. I didn't mean that I don't want you to care about me. It's a knee-jerk reaction."

She let out a relieved breath. "You're not used to having a woman care about you."

"Not besides Red and Dixie."

"Well, then, it's time you added 'Finlay' to that list. I'm pretty sure you missed some other names, too, like Gemma, Crystal, Penny—"

"Let's not get carried away," he said sternly, then lighter, "How about I work on adding *you* to that list and you work on laying your lips on me before we get inside and I have to stare down every man who leers at you."

She went up on her toes, puckered and ready for him to make her belly flip with one of his decadent kisses. And flip it *did*.

As they walked into the hospital, Bullet squared his shoulders, scanning the surroundings as if he were looking for signs of trouble. Several people looked their way. Some even went so far as to stare, eyes locked on him. A tiny voice inside Finlay's head wondered if they were judging or intrigued by him. She felt both jealous and protective and debated giving the women who were looking at him the stink eye. But that wasn't Finlay. Instead, she proudly slipped her hand into his, earning a rare—

and beautiful—smile from Bullet.

In the elevator she said, "You were wrong. Everyone was looking at you, not me. Like, *everyone.*"

He shrugged. "People stare at me all the time, babe. No big deal. But trust me, there were guys checking you out. I just shut them down before they could take too long a look."

"Aren't you chivalrous?" She smiled up at him as the doors to the elevator opened, and a doctor stepped in, wearing a white lab coat, focused on reading the chart in his hands.

"Hey, bro," Bullet said.

When he lifted his face, surprise filling his dark eyes, Finlay realized it was Bones.

"Hey, B." His dark eyes swept over Finlay as she read the embroidered name on his chest, Wayne Whiskey, MD. An appreciative smile curved his lips. "Nice to see you again, Finlay."

"You, too. I didn't recognize you with your lab coat and your nose buried in that chart." The last time she'd seen him was in town a few weeks ago, when she was at Penny's ice cream shop and Bullet, Bones, and three other guys on motorcycles had stopped at a store down the block. Bones had been wearing a black tank top, which had revealed the tattoos on his shoulders and back, and his hair had been messy from his helmet, not styled as it was now.

"I get that a lot." He nodded at the bears in Bullet's hands. "Going to see the Beckleys?"

Bullet nodded.

"I thought you might. I checked on them this morning. Sarah's being really brave. Bradley, her three-year-old is doing well. Lila, the baby, is still in critical care. They're watching her closely because of her head injury. And Sarah's brother, Scott, is still in ICU, but the prognosis is good." The elevator stopped on the next floor, and Bones held the door open, hesitating before he stepped out. "B, have you seen today's paper?"

"No. What's up?"

Bones grinned, and the mischief in his smile reached all the way to his eyes. "Nothing. I'll catch up with you later. Finlay, our mother said the cookies you made were a big hit. Save me some next time, will you?" He winked.

Bullet glowered at him as the elevator doors closed.

On the pediatric ward, a thick-waisted brunette nurse who looked to be in her late fifties or early sixties came around the desk as they approached. "Well, if it isn't our local hero."

Bullet turned and looked behind them.

"Oh, now, don't do that, Bullet." The nurse moved right in and hugged him. "Your mama must be very proud."

"I have no idea what you're talking about, Cindy. Can you please just point me in the direction of the little Beckley boy's room?"

"You always were modest." Cindy smiled at Finlay and said, "But we know the truth, don't we? This brave soldier saved that family." She reached over the desk and picked up a newspaper. She pointed to the front-page article. "Says right here, LOCAL HERO SAVES FAMILY FROM THREE-CAR PILE."

Finlay's stomach pitched. She grabbed Bullet's arm to keep her weakened legs from collapsing over the photograph of the accident. A truck lay on its side, the front bashed in. A dark, nearly unrecognizable heap of metal lay upside down, its side crushed, tires askew. Smoke plumed from the mangled juncture of that car and another. She looked up at the brave man beside her, his expression detached, almost cold, and she knew she was witnessing what was probably one of his many coping mechanisms.

She wanted to wrap her arms around him and find a way to be with him in that dark place so she could help him deal with the emotions that were clearly eating away at him.

"It says in the article that you got them out before the car went up in flames," Cindy pointed out. "So you take that hero crown and wear it proudly."

Bullet visibly cringed at her words. "Cindy, cut the crap. Where's the boy's room?"

"Bullet," Finlay chided him softly. Even though she knew he was protecting himself, she was embarrassed that he was rude to a woman who clearly respected him. Would it be so bad to admit to being the hero so many believed him to be? Would it bring on more flashbacks, or would it be cathartic to talk about the things he'd seen and experienced?

"It's okay, darlin'," Cindy said. "He's got a big bark, but he's one big love muffin. I've known Brandon since he was a smart-talking little boy. His mother and I were in nursing school together." She pointed down the hall to a patient room. "Bradley's in room 412. That boy's poor mother has been running between floors all night. I don't think she's eaten a thing."

"Thanks, Cindy. Burn that paper, will you?" With a stuffed bear at her back, he guided Finlay down the hall.

"Bullet, you were mentioned in the *paper*. That's *huge*, and it's obviously why so many people were staring at you in the lobby. I know you don't like to hear it, but you should be proud of how you helped those people."

"It's the media trying to sell papers. It's bullshit. I'm not what matters in that equation." He eyed her as they approached the little boy's room.

"Well, I still think it's a very big deal, and I'm proud of you." She went for levity. "*Brandon.*"

He scowled as he reached for the door.

Little Bradley Beckley looked up from his hospital bed, his tiny body made even smaller by the stark-white sheets surrounding him. He had a bandage on the left side of his forehead and bruises on his neck. Sarah, his mother, had long sandy-colored hair, scared brown eyes underscored with dark crescents, and a tiny bruise on her cheek. She sat on the edge of the bed, fidgeting with a plastic dinosaur.

"Bullet," she said, slowly rising to her feet.

Only then did Finlay realize she was pregnant. Her fingers slipped from Bullet's arm as he moved closer to the bed. Recognition rose in the sweet little boy's eyes.

"Sarah, I hope it's okay that I came by," he said in a rough voice, which Finlay knew was another mask for his emotions. He glanced at her and said, "This is my girl, Finlay."

*His girl.* Was it wrong for Finlay to melt at that when there was so much pain around them? She tucked those tender feelings away for now.

Sarah smiled with tears in her eyes. "I'm glad you're both here."

"I know you," Bradley said in a scratchy voice. "You saved my baby sister and my uncle."

"He saved us all," Sarah said.

Bullet's gaze rolled over the little boy, his chest expanding with the long inhalation. This was hard for all of them, including Finlay, as she bore witness to the emotion in Sarah's and her son's eyes and rolling off Bullet in waves. She noticed that Sarah wasn't wearing a wedding band and wondered where the children's father was. But she knew better than to ask.

Bullet set the bear with the blue ribbon by the little boy's legs. "Hey, Buddy. How's my brave boy?"

Bradley stuck his thumb up in the air and smiled, earning a sigh of relief from Bullet.

"Is that bear for me? And the pink one for Sissy?"

"It sure is. You heal up and get better, you hear?"

Bradley reached for the bear, and Bullet tucked it beside him. The happy boy wrapped his arms around it, grinning from ear to ear, and pointed to the box Finlay had forgotten she was holding. "What's that? For Mommy?"

"Yes. Just a few goodies," Finlay said as Sarah came around the bed. She handed her the box of treats, feeling like it was the most insignificant thing in the world and wishing she had thought to bring a meal or something more meaningful. "I am so sorry for what your family is going through. The nurses said you hadn't eaten much. I'd be happy to go down to the cafeteria and get you something."

"You're too sweet. Thank you, but I have so many food allergies I'm afraid to eat here."

"Mommy's allergic to everything," Bradley said. "Milk, eggs, peanuts…"

Finlay eyed the box of goodies, mentally ticking off all the potential allergens in it. "I would hate for you to eat those treats and have a reaction. Why don't I take them out to the nurses' station and bring you something you can eat instead," Finlay offered. "What else are you allergic to?"

"You don't have to do that for me." Sarah put her hand on her belly and said, "I've been drinking protein drinks. That helps."

"Please," Finlay said. "I'd like to help, and your baby needs more than protein drinks."

Bullet set the other teddy bear on a chair and put an arm around Finlay. "She's right, Sarah. You need your strength, especially now."

After a little more coaxing, Sarah gave her a list of the things she was allergic to, and Finlay began mentally preparing an allergen-free menu. Bullet asked about the baby and Sarah's brother.

"They're watching Lila because she's been lethargic, but they keep telling me not to worry, that it's not uncommon and it could resolve on its own. But telling me not to worry about my baby is like telling me not to breathe. And Scott developed an embolism from the breaks in his legs, or rather, from one of his broken bones, so add that to the collapsed lung and he's just a mess. But they keep telling me things look good, so I'm trying to focus on that."

Finlay's heart broke for her.

"I ran into my brother, Dr. Whiskey, in the elevator. He couldn't give us details because we're not family, but he said the prognosis was good for both Scott and Lila."

"Yes. When he stopped in he said he was your brother. He's got such a nice bedside manner. He helped me to understand what was happening with the embolism, which I guess was a fatty clot of some sort."

The door opened and a slender gentleman walked in. "Sarah? I'm Arnie Carmichael, from the finance department. We spoke briefly when you checked in last night?"

"Yes, I remember."

"I've checked on the insurance issues and deductibles. When you have a moment, I'd like to go over them with you."

"Thank you." Sarah turned to Bullet, the color draining a bit from her face. "My ex never let me work, and it turns out he let the kids' insurance lapse. It's like we have a gray cloud over us. We just moved to the harbor last week. We were on our way home from dinner celebrating Scott's new job when the truck hit us. It doesn't look like he'll be able to take the job after all. They said his collapsed lung could take several weeks to heal, and with one broken leg and his other in pins from the shattered femur, they're talking about more surgery down the road, weeks of casts, and physical therapy. I think we'll be mired in medical bills forever, but thanks to you, we still have each other." She sighed, blinking against tears. "I don't know how I can ever repay you."

Bullet looked her square in the eyes and said, "Repay me by taking care of your family and future baby. Rest. Eat. And if you need anything, day or night, call me."

On their way out of the hospital, Finlay said, "We have to help her," at the very moment Bullet said, "I'll pay for the food if you can bring her meals until her family is out of the hospital."

"I was going to suggest we spend our first real date grocery shopping and cooking so Sarah doesn't starve."

He leaned down and pressed his lips to hers. "Lollipop, I think I love you."

# Chapter Ten

BULLET WAS QUICKLY coming to believe that Finlay Wilson was truly capable of magic. All she needed was a cell phone, a big-ass shopping cart, and a fully functioning kitchen. She'd flicked and touched and navigated her way through so many websites he got dizzy watching her. Then she infiltrated the grocery store like an army of ten, buying all new cookware to be sure they were allergen free, checking ingredients and prices and consulting her phone as if it were a mandate from the president himself. He hadn't even known there was such thing as rice milk. After a trip to the organic market and another to the bookstore, because she *needed to study up for Sarah*, they finally landed back at her place with eight grocery bags and a fire in her belly. She scrubbed her counters *just in case*, slowing down only long enough to read the article about the accident before setting it aside and getting to work. She was on a bighearted mission, creating a notebook with three weeks' worth of recipes for the Beckleys, and Bullet was falling harder for her by the minute.

She hustled around the kitchen like she was on speed, looking sinfully sexy in that little green dress and lace-up boots with a pink apron over her dress that said FINLAY'S across her chest. She put Bullet to work cutting up chicken and vegetables while she filled a Crock-Pot with meat, onions, brown sugar, and other seasonings.

"What's your plan here, Fin?" he asked as she moved from the Crock-Pot to mashing up bananas. "I figured we'd whip up a few sandwiches and dinner for tonight, then bring a few more tomorrow..."

She scrunched up her face like he'd insulted her. "Are you kidding? Sarah is sitting in the hospital with her entire family in various states of peril. She needs *comfort* food, and lots of it. And she's pregnant. How could you leave out that little detail?"

"I didn't notice last night. I was too focused on trying to calm her down. I figured she was just pudgy until you said something about her baby."

Finlay leaned her hip against the counter, studying him for a long moment. "You also didn't tell me the accident was so hellacious, or that you were interviewed by a reporter."

"Every accident is hellacious, and I wasn't interviewed."

"They quoted you in the paper. The writer's name was Walt Norsden."

"Walt? He was the dorky guy in the waiting room annoying me while I was with Sarah. He kept getting in our faces, and I finally told him to bug off or I'd break his legs."

"Bullet." She laughed. "That explains why he said tensions were running hot."

"It's all media hype, lollipop. The article is bullshit put out there to sell papers."

She took the knife from his hand and wound her arms around his middle, gazing up at him with a sugary-sweet smile. "Or maybe it's community reporting to keep residents in-the-know about local happenings so they can come together and help. Like we are."

"Did you see other people rallying around Sarah today?"

"No, but at least we are." She went up on her toes, and he met her halfway in a startlingly quick kiss, because she turned around mumbling something about needing to get everything in the ovens at the same time.

"She's allergic to so much. Are you sure this is all okay? You've got so many platters out."

"I'm going to freeze some for other nights, but I'm sure. I triple-checked to make certain everything would be gluten-, soy-, dairy-, and nut-free." She pointed to the chicken he was cutting up. "That's for creamy Tuscan chicken. I even found a great recipe for mac and cheese that's allergen free. Most kids love mac and cheese, so I'm hoping Bradley will like it. And this"—she pointed to the mashed bananas—"is for banana bread, because banana bread is one of the best comfort foods around."

"How did you get into cooking?" he asked as he cut the chicken and vegetables.

"My mom is an amazing cook, and she was always making something delicious. Our house smelled like fresh-baked hugs *all* the time. That's where Penny learned to make homemade ice cream. She was the dessert girl, but I've always loved cooking and baking and seeing smiles on people's faces when they take that first bite. This is going to sound really bad, but one of my favorite events to cater is funerals. They're the hardest events to attend, because people are hurting so deeply they don't know how they'll ever breathe right again, and that's difficult to take in. But then, when they get a nice, warm dollop of mashed potatoes, or hearty chicken soup with dumplings, or rich, flaky biscuits, it's like a hug from the inside, and you can see their spirits lift—even if only for a moment. The warmth and scent of a creamy casserole, fresh-baked cake, or the memory-inducing aroma of brisket or stew can make all the difference in the world for someone who has suffered a great loss. It can transport them back to a happier time and help them get through a few hours or days."

"That's..." He didn't know the word he was looking for, and "beautiful" just came out.

"Thanks. I think it is, too."

"So, you went to school for cooking?"

She nodded. "College first, because my father insisted, and then I went to a culinary school, first to become a professional chef and then as a pastry chef, because I wanted to know it all. I worked for a restaurant for a while and then started Finlay's Catering. My friend Izzy, back in Boston, helped me run it."

She finished mixing the banana bread and set it by the other trays beside the oven. Then she collected the vegetables and chicken he'd cut up and worked her magic on those, too. They cut up potatoes and sausage and put them in a second slow cooker with a host of other ingredients for some sort of soup. He'd never seen anyone cook so many things at once.

"Would you mind draining the pasta for me?" she asked, and set a large colander in the sink. As he poured the spiral pasta into it, she said, "What about you? When did you join the military?"

"Right before my twentieth birthday."

She retrieved a large bowl from beneath the counter, and he helped her transfer the pasta into it. As she added other ingredients, she said, "Did you always know you wanted to join the military?"

"Definitely. Special Forces was the ultimate show of power and loyalty to our country. I wanted to make my mark."

"Then why did you wait to enlist?" She handed him a big wooden spoon and said, "Can you please mix that up while I get the chicken ready for the oven?"

"I stuck around to help my parents, to be with my family," he said as he mixed. "It was a confusing time." Bullet had a great deal of respect for his father, but when he was younger, he'd harbored a good amount of resentment, too. Although Bullet knew it wasn't his father's fault he hadn't known how to fill out the armor his father wore so easily.

Finlay dipped the chicken into a marinade she'd whipped up, then coated them with a seasoning mixture. "How so?"

"For as long as I can remember, there was a lot of pressure on me to protect my brothers and Dixie, to prepare to be the man of the family in case anything happened to our father. I watched over them, taught them all how to defend themselves, manned up Bones and Bear and toughened up Dixie, because in my head, if something could happen to my old man, something could happen to me. Then what? Bones graduated high school early and went off to college, as he should have. He's the smartest guy I know. But all I could think about was how Bear and Dixie needed me. There was this thin line I felt like I was always toeing. On the one hand, we were taught not to take shit from anyone, and on the other, we were taught not to cause trouble, start fights, or go out carousing. As a kid full of piss and vinegar, it was hard to understand why we didn't just pound the hell out of anyone who caused trouble."

"I can see how that would be confusing." She set the chicken on a tray, then placed the tray in the oven.

"I've never been good at communicating. I'm not like you,

Fins. Even back then I couldn't voice what was going on in my head. I went out looking for trouble so I could shut it down before it found my family. The problem was, I couldn't get my arms around it all, and I *became* trouble."

"That kind of makes sense. You were under so much pressure you didn't know how to handle it."

She put the rest of the trays in the ovens and turned on the cock-blocking timer. He realized with a start that he was more interested in sharing his past with Finlay than in sex.

"I was always locked and loaded, ready to fire. I was a *bullet* looking for a target. Bones is the one who finally said to get the hell out of here and enlist. He pushed me so hard, I remember fighting with him over it. He was off at college, and I was blinded by loyalty but heading down a shit path. He finally laid it all out on the line for me. He said if I didn't get out of there, I'd fuck up our family or my life. I owe him a hell of a lot."

"It sounds to me like your siblings owe a heck of a lot to you, too."

She washed her hands, and he pulled her into his arms. "I've never told anyone this stuff before. Why does it seem so easy to share with you?"

"Because you know I care about you. Or maybe you're just tired of holding it in? Everyone needs an outlet sometime. And for the record, you may not *usually* be a man of many words, but you get your point across quite clearly."

"You've got me under your spell, lollipop, and I hope like hell you never break it, because I sure do like you, and it's not just physical anymore. Although…" He felt himself grinning as he pressed his lips to hers and slipped his hand beneath her dress, groping her ass and earning a surprised *squeak.*

"What is it about my butt that you love so much?"

"I'm not sure," he said as he lowered his mouth to her neck and nipped at it. "Why don't you turn around and let me explore. Maybe I can come up with an answer."

Her skin flamed against his mouth.

"You talk *very* dirty," she whispered as he dragged his tongue up to her ear. She wound her arms around his neck and said, "Why don't you show me what that dirty mouth is capable of?"

"Mm, baby, get ready for a wild ride." He swept her into his arms.

As he lowered his mouth to hers, she said, "Timer! Get the timer from that counter. We can't burn all the food."

Timer in hand, he carried her down the hall to her bedroom. He set the timer on her dresser and said, "We need to have a talk about you and timers." He tore down her pretty blankets and laid her in the center of the bed.

She laughed and pulled him down over her. "We have forty minutes. Do you want to talk, or do you want to—"

FINLAY'S WORDS WERE smothered by the hard press of Bullet's lips, the delving of his tongue, and the thrusting of his powerful hips against her. All day long she'd been thinking of the way he'd kissed her when she was on the counter that morning, when he'd been ready to *take* her and she'd been ready to surrender to him. All afternoon she'd fought the overwhelming urge to be closer to him, his rugged scent and the slow caress of his hands over her hips each time he walked by taunted her. She felt like a boiling pot ready to blow, and it had taken all her concentration to focus on cooking, but now, with his glorious mouth wreaking havoc with her senses and his hard body grinding in a dizzying rhythm, she was *done* holding back.

He moved straight down her body, his big hands sliding along the length of her legs to the edge of her high-heeled boot. His mouth curved up in a wicked grin. "We're leaving those on, but this has got to go."

He pushed her dress up over her hips, and she stopped him from lifting it higher. "Wait," she said quickly, and he held his hands up, confusion filling his eyes. "I have scars, too."

"Baby, you could be covered in them and it wouldn't make a difference."

She swallowed hard and slowly lifted her dress a few inches higher, waiting for the shocked look she'd seen in the eyes of most of the other men she'd been with. Aaron was the only one who hadn't reacted with shock. That was how she'd known Aaron really liked her. It was a silly thing, letting a scar gauge the depth of attraction, but that's how she'd seen it. And now, as Bullet's eyes found the scars, they brimmed with compassion.

"Oh, my beautiful girl. We really were made for each other." He pressed his lips to the divot in her lower belly and proceeded to kiss each of the puncture scars along her side. "What happened to my girl?"

"I was fifteen. Penny and I were at the mall. We were waiting for the bus, when this dog came out of nowhere, running across the street. I thought it was running toward its owner because it was charging so fast. By the time I realized it was coming at me, it was too late. Penny tried to push me out of the way, but the dog had already gotten ahold of me."

"Baby," he said in a low, pained voice. He rested his cheek on the scars and splayed one hand across her belly. He pressed his lips to her belly again in a series of the lightest kisses she'd ever felt, his beard tickling her side, and whispered, "No wonder you were afraid of Tinkerbell. I wish I had known."

"She's an important part of your life. I was okay, just startled. And I'm even better now."

She ran her fingers through his thick hair as he loved his way along her belly more tenderly than she could ever imagine a man of his size being. His rough hands moved over her skin, hot and strong, caressing her sides as he moved her dress up and over her breasts, carefully stripping it from her body. He went up on his knees, his eyes boldly raking over every inch of her. She felt herself go damp and was vaguely aware of the ticking timer a few feet away as he reached behind his back and tugged off his shirt, bringing his glorious body into view. How differently she saw him now. All that ink was no longer a scary mural of his life. It was the very foundation that made him the admirable man he was.

He perched above her and slanted his mouth over hers in a rough, insistent *possession* that she matched perfectly. His large hand cupped her jaw as he'd done before, making love to her mouth with his tongue until she was moaning and rocking against his hard length, desperate for more.

"That's what I'm going to do to you, baby. I'm going to taste you so deep, you'll never forget how good it feels."

"Yes," she said as he blazed a path lower, slowing to suck and nip, driving her out of her flipping mind.

His hands played over her body, clutching her ribs as he feasted on first one breast, then the other, taking each nipple between his teeth and tugging, sending shocks of lust between her legs. She cried out, and he cupped her breasts, pressing them together between both hands, kissing and licking the tender spots he'd caused. She clawed at the sheets, every swipe of his tongue taking her higher. Then his hot mouth was on the move again, tasting every bit of her flesh from rib cage to belly, delving in and around her belly button, and lavishing her scars with openmouthed kisses.

Cool air swept over the wet trails he'd left, making her shiver and shake. He hooked his fingers into the hips of her panties, and she lifted off the mattress as he slipped them off. She should feel self-conscious, lying naked save for her ankle boots while he still had on his jeans, but there was no room for embarrassment when her body was thundering from the inside out, begging for his touch, his mouth, his naked body all over hers.

He came down over her again, rough denim rubbing against her sensitive, swollen sex as he recaptured her lips in a punishingly intense kiss, sending spirals of ecstasy careening through her. Her world tilted on its axis as tingling sensations climbed up her thighs. He tore his mouth away in one swift yank, and she craned up off the mattress, reaching for him, pleading for more, but he was already moving lower. His hands splayed over her inner thighs, spreading her wide as he lowered his face to within an inch of her sex and inhaled deeply. Flames ignited in his eyes, and his mouth came down over her sex as soft as a caress. His tongue slid along the very heart of her, tasting and teasing. His beard scratched her sex, her thighs, and when he sucked her most sensitive nerves into his mouth, the scratch turned *erotic*, drawing long, pleading sounds from her lungs.

"*Bullet—*"

Her hips struggled against his strong grip, pinned to the mattress as he sealed his mouth over her, thrusting his tongue in an act of raw, unbridled passion. She clawed at the sheets, but she wanted *him*. She grabbed his hands, which was all she could reach, and dug her fingers into his hot skin. Her heels pushed at the mattress and her head rose off the mattress with the intensity of the sensations engulfing her. His tongue plunged deeper, and *holy moly*. She tried to throttle the dizzying currents racing through her, shattering her ability to hold on to any one thought, but the feel of his tongue invading her, the tension of his hands and body caging her in, and the guttural, appreciative sounds he made as he loved her collided, exploding inside her in a series of hip-bucking, brain-numbing convulsions.

Just when she started to come down from the peak, he eased his grip, lifting her hips, and like a lion who had just slayed his prey, his eyes turned coal black, and he plunged his fingers inside her while simultaneously taking her clit between his teeth, sending her reeling once again.

Long after she came down from the clouds, as she lay panting beneath him, Bullet brushed kiss after tender kiss on her inner thighs, and then he brought his mouth between her legs again, licking and kissing as if he were savoring every ounce of her arousal. As he moved up her body, kissing her scars again, her ribs, the skin between her breasts, she wanted to memorize the feel of him, the slow, sensual slide of his tongue, the tenderness of his touch. He wasn't in a hurry. He didn't try to whip off his pants and take what he must be dying for. He ran his hands along her sides, up the underside of her arms, pushing them above her head. Then he was kissing her neck, his beard tickling her skin, her arousal clinging to him like cologne.

The timer sounded, and he stilled, his eyes closing for a beat. She didn't want to move, didn't want their closeness to end, and when he moved beside her, pulling her sated body against him, and kissed her softly, she said, "Let's stay right here."

His gaze was so soft, his features so appealing and happy,

she wanted to see *that look* more often. She wanted to know he was at peace in his heart, which was precisely how his entrancing smile appeared, and it brought her lips to his in another slow, loving kiss.

He ran his hand through her hair, and the faint sound of the oven timer floated down the hall as he kissed her forehead, cheeks, chin, and finally, her mouth.

"I want to stay, Fins, but I've got to get home and clean up before going to work, and you put so much effort into those meals, I'd feel horrible if they were ruined."

She tucked her face beside his neck and breathed a kiss there. "'Kay."

"Can I see you tomorrow?"

She nodded, wishing she could close her eyes and that when she opened them it would magically be morning and she'd still be right there, wrapped in Bullet's arms.

# Chapter Eleven

THE PIERCING REBELLION of an electric guitar echoed off the walls of Whiskey Bro's, grating against Bullet's nerves for the first time that he could remember. He loved the Rebels, a local band made up of members of the Dark Knights. They were one of the best bands around, and their renditions of legendary classic rock bands were the best he'd ever heard. Their music was ragged and raw. The pitches and riffs played deep, hollow, or shrill, always too loud and overly dramatic, which normally was right in line with Bullet's emotions. But he'd been messed up ever since leaving Finlay. As he'd helped her put back on that sexy little dress, she was so damn sweet and understanding about his leaving, but he'd seen longing in her eyes that mirrored the new emotions tearing him up inside. What was fucking wrong with him? She had plans anyway. She was bringing food to Sarah, ordering the appliances for the bar, working out the renovation schedule with Dixie. But as the evening wore on, he couldn't stop seeing her lying naked in his arms, was unable to quell the memory of her breath warm on his neck, and those addicting sounds she'd made played in his ears, competing with the band.

Torment coursed through his veins. Every chord yanked him toward an angry edge he didn't want to approach. For the first time since he'd come out from under his PTSD and started working at Whiskey Bro's, he didn't *want* to be there. And every second he was made him want to slam something against a wall.

"What do you think, B?" Bones took a swig of his beer, looking expectantly at Bullet. He and Bear had been hanging out at the bar for the past hour. "Sunday ride? Head out to Riker's?"

Riker's Point was a solid two hours from the harbor, and a hell of a nice ride. But Sunday was Bullet's only day off work, and he'd be damned if he wasn't going to spend it with Finlay. After learning why she was afraid of dogs, he was already rethinking his idea of bringing her over to meet Tink. He hadn't even asked why she was afraid of motorcycles, but he had a feeling that navigating her fears was going to be a minefield in and of itself.

"Can't," Bullet said, and went to the other end of the bar to take an order, ignoring Bear's and Bones's comments. After filling the order and wiping up a spilled beer, he returned to answer his brothers' curious gazes.

"You never miss a Sunday ride," Bear said. "What's up?"

A guy down the bar raised his empty glass. Bullet said, "Busy," to Bear and took care of the customer. He didn't know why he wasn't telling his brothers about wanting to see Finlay, but figured it went hand in hand with not wanting to work tonight. They'd just gone through a family upheaval about the bar when Bear had backed out of working there. They didn't need to go through another one, and that fed the guilt eating away at him.

"With what?" Bear pushed, his eyes narrowing. "What's more important than going for a ride?"

"Let it go," Bullet warned.

"What's got your balls in a sling?" Bear asked. "You're even more of a prick than usual. Not getting any lately?"

"Fuck off. I just don't want to be here tonight," he admitted.

Bear and Bones exchanged a confused glance, which irritated him even more. That passive-aggressive glance alone showed the difference between Bullet and his brothers. Had one of them said to him what he'd just said to them, he'd tell them to get it off their chest or shut the fuck up.

"Why not?" Bones asked. He was the most even-keeled of them all, smart, careful, methodical in his thinking. While he'd be there in a heartbeat to back up his brothers if there was trouble, his gut instincts led him to figure things out mentally before acting physically.

He was surprised Bones hadn't put two and two together, but then again, there had never been a woman Bullet would rather be with more than he wanted to spend time at the bar.

"Doesn't matter," Bullet said. It wasn't like he wouldn't see Finlay tomorrow, and he didn't understand why it was messing with his head to have left her tonight and come to the place that had been his safe haven for all these years. Until Finlay, Bullet's life had been easy. Black and white. Things were either *fine*, or they were ass backward and needed to be fixed. But Finlay brought a world of emotions and middle grounds he didn't know what to do with.

"Well, who were you with?" Bear asked. "What were you doing before you came here? Maybe we can figure it out."

Bear was as much of an overcommunicator as Finlay. If

others hurt, Bear hurt, whereas with Bullet, if someone within his circle was hurting, he stepped in and applied whatever muscle was necessary to remove that hurt from their lives.

Bones took another drink, and a slow grin spread across his lips. "A certain blonde with a knack for baking delicious cookies."

"Ah, Finlay," Bear teased. "Everyone's wondering when she's coming back with more."

*More like wondering when she's coming back so they can leer at her.* Bullet ground his teeth together.

"That's it, isn't it?" Bear asked. "You were fucking Finlay and you didn't want to leave."

Bullet reached a hand across the bar and grabbed Bear by the collar, hauling him up to eye level and sending drinks crashing to the floor. Customers casually stepped back. They knew better than to get in between Bullet and *anyone.*

"B!" Bones sprang to his feet, throwing an arm awkwardly between them.

"Don't you ever talk about her that way again," Bullet seethed through gritted teeth. "Got it?" Before Bear could respond, he tossed him backward.

Bear stumbled, laughing as he found his footing. "Dude, you've got it bad, and you'd better get it under control."

The music came back into focus, and Bullet saw Red making a beeline for them. She looked like hell on wheels, her eyes narrow, her black boots clomping with each determined step. She was the epitome of a biker's old lady. Tough as balls and unafraid of stepping into the line of fire. But her lips were tipped up at the edges, making Bullet laugh softly. She'd raised them and was used to the ups and downs of brotherhood. Like Bear, she was a talker. She knew most of their demons—but only Bones knew the truth of Bullet's.

He slid his gaze back to the brother who had been there for him when he was hanging on to life by a thread. When he'd hidden out from the rest of his family, too ashamed to face them.

"What the hell, Bullet?" Bones stood between Bullet and Bear, staring him down in the way only he could.

He was looking so deeply into Bullet's eyes, Bullet knew he was searching to see if the demons had returned, or if this was the normal shit that went on between brothers. Bullet shifted his gaze to Bear and said, "You a'right?"

"Always, but what the hell?" Bear picked up a few pieces of glass from the floor and set them on the bar.

"Didn't get milk in your Cheerios this morning?" Red asked as Bullet came around the bar with a broom to clean up the mess. She shook her head at Bear, who was circling the bar, and began mopping up the counter. Her eyes found Bullet again, and she said, "Or did your baby brother open his yap about the article in the paper? I told him not to give you a hard time about that."

"It's all good, Red." He eyed Bear, who made kissing sounds. Bullet cocked his arm back, feigning prepping for a fight, and they both laughed.

"For what it's worth, I'm proud of you for helping that family, honey." Her green eyes coasted over Bones, who was crouched on the floor, holding the dustpan for Bullet, and then they moved up to Bear, who was busy talking to a customer. By the time she looked at Bullet again, her gaze was soft and worried. "I love you guys, but my heart stops every time I see your hands fisted."

Bullet finished sweeping the mess into the dustpan and

handed the broom to Bones, who carried the broom and dustpan behind the bar. When he was out of earshot, Bullet stepped closer to Red, lowering his voice. "Leading with your heart? Is it supposed to confuse the hell out of you?"

A warm smile lit up her eyes. "Only if you're doing it right, honey."

Several hours later, after closing the bar and telling himself to drive home, he found himself parked in front of Finlay's house, staring at his cell phone. The curtains were drawn, and the house was quiet as the night. He knew he should turn around and bide his time, see her tomorrow, as he'd asked to. But he craved her in his arms, needed to see her sweet face, to hear how her evening had gone.

He lowered his hand to his leg, wondering when he'd become so pussy-whipped. But the thought sent another fiery gust through his core. He wasn't pussy-whipped. This wasn't like that. This was bigger than anything he'd ever felt before. Bigger than life itself, and he didn't know what to do with all the emotions blustering inside him.

*Fuck it.* He needed to hear her voice. He put the call through and lifted the phone to his ear.

"Hi," she said in a sleepy voice.

"Hey, lollipop."

He listened to her breathing, could practically see her sleepy blue eyes gazing up at him, a smile curving her lips, could almost feel her cheek against his chest...

FINLAY LAY ON her back, staring up at the ceiling in the darkness of her bedroom and waiting for Bullet to say more.

She'd kept herself distracted all evening. When she'd taken food to the hospital, she'd also brought more goodies for the nurses, who were happy to let Finlay stock their freezer with a few meals for Sarah. She'd gone straight from there to meet Dixie at Penny's ice cream shop, where they'd gobbled down sundaes and made the final decisions on the kitchen renovations. Dixie had arranged for Crow to handle the appliance installations and counter modifications this week, which meant Finlay was free to work on menus and start the interviewing and hiring process. She'd *almost* gone to the bar to see Bullet afterward, but she didn't want to appear too needy. Instead she'd spent the rest of the night trying to distract herself from thoughts of him. A long, hot bath hadn't done the trick, and sitting out back had only reminded her of how close they'd become when they were there. She'd lain in her bed for the past hour, trying to sleep, but she missed him too much, and now, as silence filled the airwaves, she worried about what that silence meant.

"Aren't you going to talk to me?" she asked, smiling to herself because Bullet was a man of very few words in person. She imagined it was even more difficult for him over the phone, since most of his communication was visual. When she could see his face, she knew in a hot second if he was sad, angry, worried, or horny.

"Just wanted to hear your voice," he finally said. "Did I wake you?"

"No. I was lying here thinking of you." She was met with silence again, and she closed her eyes, her pulse racing like never before. "Maybe you should come over. I can't read your eyes over the phone."

The line went dead, and she stared at the phone, confused. Had she upset him?

Seconds later her answer came as a knock at her front door, and she leapt from the bed, grinning like a fool as she padded down the hall in her bare feet and peered through the peephole. Bullet had one hand on the back of his neck, his eyes downcast. She couldn't open the door fast enough. She flung it open, her heart jolting as his gaze moved swiftly up her bare legs to the words emblazoned across her chest. GOOD GIRLS SIT, BAD BITCHES RIDE. She felt her cheeks burn.

His lips curved up as he took her in his arms. "Thought you were afraid of motorcycles," he said, pressing an enticing kiss on her cheek, his beard tickling her skin.

"I am." She wound her arms around his neck as he drove her crazy with his insistent lips all over her neck and jaw. "Penny gave it to me," she managed. "It reminds me of you."

"Christ, Fins," he said in a gravelly voice.

Crushing her to him, he claimed her with his lips, rousing a burning need, an aching desire within her. His hand moved roughly down her hip, meeting her bare thigh, pulling a greedy moan from both of them. He intensified his efforts, kissing her so deeply, pleasure radiated all the way to her fingertips. A hungry groan rumbled through them, a heady invitation to a world she so desperately wanted to explore. His large hand splayed across her butt, and more greedy noises erupted between them.

"*Lace*," he ground out against her lips.

With his hand covering her whole bottom, he lifted her easily while burying his other hand in her hair, making her scalp burn. He stepped into the house and pushed the door closed with his back.

"I can't get you out of my head," he said between rough kisses. "And I don't want to."

His words pounded through her, hot and explosive. She took in the anguish and seductive emotions warring in his dark eyes, and in the next breath, his mouth was on hers, taking and exploring. The hardness of his body, the fierce possession of his kisses, electrified her. Desire flooded her veins as she clung to him, rocking against his body, loving the feel of his hands all over her, as if he couldn't get enough.

"Bedroom," she panted out.

His boots sounded on the hardwood, every step bringing another throb of anticipation. Their kisses turned wilder, and their hungry noises echoed in her head, obliterating the rest of the world. She pushed her hands into his hair, holding on as she arched against him, urging him to take more of her. He lowered her to the bed and followed her down, one hand still clutching her ass as he devoured her mouth. His broad chest pinned her to the mattress. Every swipe of their tongues sent titillating sensations skittering through her, heightening her arousal to epic proportions. She tugged at his shirt, and he broke their connection only long enough to pull it over his head and toss it to the floor. He fiercely reclaimed her mouth, and she reached for his thick leather belt, but his body was too heavy, trapping her hands between them.

"I need you naked," she said, surprising herself with her eagerness. But no part of her wanted to deny her desires.

There were no more words, only swiftness, as he withdrew his wallet from his back pocket and tossed it on the bed, then removed his heavy boots and socks. He pushed to his feet as he unfastened his belt, and his jeans puddled at his ankles. He stepped from them, revealing powerful thighs and muscular calves covered in colorful ink and marred with scars. Forty-eight hours ago, she might have been shocked, but now she was enthralled, wanting to study each and every tattoo and scar, to hear the stories she knew he might never tell, to understand the quiet storm that was Bullet Whiskey.

They focused on each other as the silence wound around them, and she went to the edge of the bed so she could watch her beautiful man. And he was *beautiful*. Finlay no longer saw only his size and once-intimidating appearance. His harnessed power and commanding presence would always remain, but now she also saw the soft-hearted man who used the pain of his past to help those around him.

Her gaze traveled to the juncture of his massive thighs and his thick arousal straining against dark cotton. Rivers of heat flowed through her as he came down on his knees before her, wedged his broad body between her thighs, and took her face between both hands. An inferno raged in his eyes as he visibly struggled with the emotions burning between them.

"I need you, Fins," he said in a husky voice. "I can't fucking breathe without you in my arms."

She gathered the hem of her shirt in her hands and drew it over her head, wanting to jump into his fire with both feet. She knew he'd never let her get burned. "Then let me fill you up so you never run out of air."

His lips descended slowly and powerfully upon hers, hypnotizing her with his demanding mastery. She felt transported to a higher plane. The needy pulses inside her beat faster, throbbed harder, and at the same time, she felt lighter, lost in him. He shifted them to the center of the bed. His hips rocked between her thighs, spreading them wider, and pressed his girth against her center, hard and persistent. Her insides tightened and pulled, wanting *all* of him. When his hands moved to the swell of her hips, she lifted for him, and he held her firmly as his cock, sheathed in his briefs, teased and rubbed against her damp panties. His mouth left hers, claiming her neck with savage intensity.

"Bullet, I can't—" *Wait*—

She gasped, pushing at the back of his briefs as he sucked and licked, his beard and teeth sending *need* careening through her.

He blazed a path down her body, rougher than before, biting and sucking like nothing would ever be enough. Every sharp bite, every lick and stroke, made her writhe and beg for more. She never imagined roughness could be so hot, but her body was on fire, shaking with desire. She didn't want to be taken and lavished. She wanted to *give*—everything she had. A fleeting worry zipped through her with the newness and shock of her loss of inhibitions, but everything about Bullet, from his intensity to the caring man beneath the armor, made her want to climb into his world and explore the carnal side of herself that was vibrating beneath her skin.

Feeling breathless and bold, she pushed at his shoulders as he tasted every inch of her skin. "Bullet," she pleaded, but he just moaned and continued driving her out of her mind. "Bullet," she said harsher, and he lifted his head, brows pulled together. God, she loved his intensity. "I want to..." She pushed at his chest again, and he rolled to his side, clutching the swell of her hip.

She brazenly moved down his body, kissing and touching, trembling with the newness of taking control. She kissed his stomach, his body hair tickling her cheeks. His manly scent amped up her arousal. She slicked her tongue along the hot flesh just above his briefs, earning another gratuitous groan. She lifted the waistband of his briefs, her heart thundering against her ribs, as his shaft came into focus. She slicked her tongue over the broad head, slow and determined, causing his entire body to flex.

He uttered a curse and grabbed her by the hair, tilting her head up so she had no choice but to look into his eyes. She knew she wasn't as experienced as him, but the *need*, and undeniable deeper emotions, she saw swimming in his eyes told her none of that mattered.

She quickly tugged down his briefs, freeing his eager erection, and he made quick work of kicking them off. Still lying on his side, he fisted his hand in her hair. The heat of his gaze burned through her as she dragged her tongue along the length of his shaft. He let out a hiss that slithered beneath her skin.

Spurred on by his reaction, she did it again, earning a darker, sexier noise.

Those sounds were like a drug, and she needed her next hit. She wrapped her fingers around him and teased over the crown again, then dragged her tongue from base to tip, getting him nice and wet. When she fisted his cock, his hips bucked, and his thick arousal pushed through her hand with such power her sex clenched in anticipation. She lowered her mouth around him, earning a long, appreciative *growl*. Her heart pounded out an erratic rhythm as she surrendered to her desires, consuming every inch of him and sucking for all she was worth. His cock swelled in her hand, and she worked him faster, took him in deeper, until his every muscle was corded so tight she knew he was on the verge of exploding. A mild panic bloomed inside her. She wanted *this*—to drive him wild, to taste the very essence of him—but more than that, she *longed* to be in his arms, to feel him inside her, as close as two people could be.

She gazed up at him, and his hands slid from her hair to her cheeks, the warmth in his eyes melting her from the inside out. He carefully brought her up beside him so they were face-to-face and kissed her once, twice, three times. Her feelings intensified with every single touch of his lips.

Her eyes fluttered open, and he whispered, "I need you."

The way he said it, emphatic and impassioned, made his meaning unclear. But it didn't matter if he meant sexually or emotionally, because as he carefully lowered her to her back and took off her panties, she knew in her heart the two were tightly intertwined.

He went up on his knees, a glorious, solid man, so thick and powerful all over, his body a map of fears, tragedies, and hope. Her pulse quickened as he reached for his wallet and withdrew a condom. His gaze never left hers as he tore it open and rolled it on. A sensuous wave passed between them as he came down over her and gazed deeply into her eyes. He felt different without clothes on. Heavier, warmer, *closer*.

"Say you're mine," he whispered before lowering his mouth to hers.

He was so demanding *and* confident, he hadn't given her time to respond. She smiled into their kiss. Their connection was too solid, too *real*, for him not to know that she would have said, *I'm yours, Bullet. Truly yours.*

Their bodies came together slowly, his girth spreading her wider, his arms holding her tighter as he filled her so completely she could barely breathe. She pressed her hands on the back of his hips, not wanting him to move until she'd had a chance to know the feel of him by heart. But the pressure of him inside her, the feel of his fingers curling around her shoulders and their tongues dancing to an urgent, exploratory beat, was too much, and *she* had to move. Trapped beneath his weight, it was all she could do to press deeper into the mattress, then rock upward. They quickly fell into sync, every thrust striking that magical chord. Bullet pushed his hands beneath her bottom, angling her up so he could love her deeper—and Lord Almighty, the man was a sexual master. He thrust and pumped, ground and pulsed, until she was clawing at his back. Her legs lifted and shifted, trying to wrap around his waist, but he was too big, the angle too severe. In one fell swoop he rose and trapped her knees beneath his torso, driving into her hard and fast. She cried out with the intensity of the pleasures, the visceral greed coursing through her. His chest came down over hers, her knees pushed out to the sides of his hips, and he grabbed hold of her bottom again, spreading her cheeks to a painful distance apart. She whimpered with the shock of what felt like her skin tearing, but then he pistoned his hips, sending turbulent tides of passion crashing over her. She gasped, and he did it again, until pain and pleasure shattered like glass inside her, and she lost all control, bucking and crying out, thrashing as her sex convulsed.

"*Don'tstopdon'tstopdon'tstop,*" she begged, but she needn't have worried.

He was so lost in the moment, he buried his face in her neck and sank his teeth into her skin, sending her careening once again. Indiscernible sounds flew from her lungs, as unstoppable as their emotions. Their flesh was slick and heated, their breathing choppy and hindered. Bullet intensified his efforts, and suddenly he released her bottom and his arms pushed beneath her back, cradling her so tightly against him that she felt his heart thundering against hers. Her skin was on fire. Her body tingled from head to toe, like a thousand needles prickling at once, as another orgasm built up inside her. Bullet sealed his mouth over hers, their bodies moving in exquisite harmony.

The heat of his desire seared down the length of her as his entire body tensed up, and he thrust deeper, grinding out her name as they found their mutual release.

As Bullet took care of the condom, Finlay got her first look at his bare back, and a sinking feeling moved through her stomach. While the front of his torso was covered with multiple images and scenes, his back was one giant mask of darkness. The face she'd seen tattooed on the hulking figure standing guard at the cave on his sternum looked back at her. Dark voids—sunglasses—covered both shoulder blades, sightlessly staring back at her below coiled and pointed brows. A skeletal nose and jaw and a mouth full of jagged fangs were surrounded by the kind of decorative swirls she'd seen on iron rails. Crosses, Jewish stars, and other religious symbols covered the backs of his arms and elbows.

When he climbed back into bed, gathering Finlay in his arms, the world came back into focus. His body was as tightly wound as a mattress coil, and her full heart chipped away. She didn't want to bring up the image that was more terrifying than the others, but she couldn't help herself, even though she knew it would take a lifetime to fully understand the man beneath the ink.

"Your back?" she whispered. "It scares me."

He kissed her forehead, holding her tighter. "Don't let it. It's the Dark Knights emblem. It's such a big part of me…When I was young, it was my strength and my undoing. Now it's only strength, baby."

She breathed a little easier. "And your elbows and arms?"

An unexpected smile lifted his lips. "There's so much baseless hate in the world. I wear all the symbols proudly and will protect the people who follow them equally. It's just a way for me to honor the human race. It's like getting in haters' faces and saying, 'Go ahead, try to fuck with someone around me.'"

"You're amazing," she whispered, curling into his warmth, wishing they could stay like that until morning, though she knew he would eventually have to leave.

"No. Just doing the right thing."

He seemed to always do the right thing, which made her wonder more about his teenage years, when he'd been so confused about toeing the line with his family and the motorcycle club. But he seemed at peace with that line now, and she was glad for it.

"I hate that I can't stay the night," he said, and kissed her forehead. She closed her eyes, knowing he was just as unhappy about his having to leave as she was.

"Do you think Tink would be okay for just one night?" she asked, and immediately regretted it. "I'm sorry. I don't mean that. I don't want you to leave her alone. I know how much you two need each other."

"That's only part of it, babe." He crushed her to him and put his thigh over her hip, cocooning her against his solid frame.

"Nightmares?" she asked softly.

He didn't respond, which made her want to be with him even more. But how could she ever ask him to leave Tinkerbell for a night? To some people a dog was simply a pet, but it was clear that Tinkerbell was as integral a part of Bullet's healing as the scars were daily reminders.

They lay together for a long while, each lost in their own thoughts in the silence of her bedroom. When they finally, reluctantly, gave in to the end of their evening, Bullet stood on her front porch with her face in his hands and a tortured look in his eyes and said, "You deserve more than a broken soldier, but I can't give you up. I know that's selfish, but I can't, Fins. Not even after only a few days."

"My mother used to say that the best parts of cobbler weren't the big pieces that everyone gobbled down, but the broken ones left behind. Those were drenched in sweetness, but only some people were lucky enough to realize it. I realize it, Bullet. I want only you."

He pressed his lips to hers with a disbelieving expression and said, "Lock up tight tonight, lollipop."

Finlay watched the taillights of his truck disappear in the darkness, wishing things could be different. And as she locked the door and followed the scent he'd left in his wake back to her bedroom, she wondered if it was possible for her heart to feel full and torn at the same time.

She'd been broken, too. She hadn't thought she was capable of feeling anything toward a man after losing Aaron. But as she crawled back into bed, resting her head on the pillow where Bullet had just lain, she realized she hadn't been *broken* after all. She simply hadn't been with the right person until now. She closed her eyes, images of Bullet swimming in her mind, and wondered if he wasn't quite as broken as he thought, either.

# Chapter Twelve

AFTER A QUICK call to Penny, Finlay packed up the doggy treats she'd made at the crack of dawn Sunday morning and followed the directions on the GPS down a long, windy rural road not far from Whiskey Bro's to a narrow driveway. Long, unkempt grass gave the property an abandoned feel. An old, dilapidated red barn came into focus, and the overgrown meadows disappeared, as if swallowed up by gorgeous rock gardens interspersed with trees and lush bushes, fall flowers, and greenery. The gardens, though beautiful, contrasted with the disrepair of the chipped and weathered red barn. A peaked metal roof hung over the edge of the building, as if it belonged to a larger structure and had been mistakenly put on this one. A newish double window was centered above two rustic garage doors, framed with unpainted wood. The garage doors were the old type, like she'd seen in Western movies, comprised of vertical weathered wood planks. Two planks formed an $X$ on each door, giving them an off-limits aura. Beside the right garage door was what appeared to be a scuffed and marred front door, above which was a lower-pitched roof that slanted toward the ground, ending at the same height as the door. A single lightbulb hung from a black iron fixture beside the door.

Finlay put her Suburban in park and looked down at the GPS, wondering if Penny had given her the wrong address. The deep *woof* of a dog sent her heart into her throat. She gasped, and the phone tumbled to the floor. Clinging to the steering wheel, she peered out her windows. *This is definitely the right house.* Thank goodness she sat up high in the van. She did not want to be eye-to-eye with the rottweiler pacing beside the driver's door. Finlay had forgotten how big Bullet's dog was, though Dixie had since told her Tinkerbell was only a puppy. *Liar. Cujo* had a head the size of a watermelon and beady dark eyes.

She fished around at her feet for her phone as she reprimanded herself. "It's just a dog. *Bullet's* dog." She felt the phone between her fingertips. "He *sleeps* with her, for goodness' sakes. How vicious can she be?"

*"Woof!"*

She shrieked, sending the phone flying again, and pressed her forehead to the steering wheel, fighting the urge to flee. The sound of motorcycles roared up the driveway, and she shot a look in her rearview mirror, catching sight of two motorcycles.

*Flipping perfect.*

UNABLE TO SLEEP past sunrise, which had always been pretty much the norm for Bullet, he was dicking around with one of his bikes in the garage when he heard motorcycles approaching. Tinkerbell *woof*ed again. Bullet wiped his hands on a rag, raised the garage door, and stopped cold at the sight of Finlay's pink chick mobile in the driveway. His brothers' bikes sped up the driveway behind her. It was the perfect day for a ride, and he itched to feel the raw power between his legs, the gust of the world rushing by, and the exhilaration of his entire being on high alert in a numbing combination of anxiety and thrill. The only thing that had ever come close to mirroring that all-consuming pleasure was last night when he was buried deep inside Finlay.

He strode across the driveway toward her van, and her gorgeous, panicked face came into focus. A single sharp whistle and hand motion sent Tinkerbell down on her belly, panting excitedly about a new person to play with.

*Fat chance, girl.*

As Bear and Bones climbed off their bikes and whipped off their helmets, their cocky smiles eased the knot that had formed in his chest as he'd paced the floor for hours last night, keeping him *and* Tinkerbell awake.

Bear helped Crystal off the back of his bike and said, "You look like hell," to Bullet before dropping to his knees and loving up Tinkerbell.

Bullet gritted his teeth against the memory of how much it had sucked to leave Finlay last night and tried to calm the crazy shit going on in his stomach as he approached the van. Finlay white-knuckled the steering wheel with both hands, her eyes as wide as saucers.

"Hey, babe. How about you roll down the window?"

Her eyes shot to Tinkerbell, who was lying on her back with her feet up in the air while Bear scratched her belly. Finlay rolled the window down an inch as Crystal came to Bullet's side. He put an arm around Crystal and said, "How're you feeling, sweetheart?"

"Better. My stomach's been quirky for the last week or so,

but I'm good." She smiled at Finlay. "How's it going, Fin? Are you going to stay in that big spoon of Pepto-Bismol all day, or come out and say hi?"

"How about you give us a minute," Bullet said, releasing Crystal.

"Hey, bro." Bones slapped Bullet on the shoulder as he walked by on his way to join the others.

Bullet grabbed the door handle, and renewed panic filled Finlay's eyes. He opened the door and blocked the opening with his body. "Hey, sweet girl. What are you doing here?"

"I was thinking, you came to see me after that accident when you said everything inside you told you to walk away. That was hard for you, so I pulled up my big-girl panties and thought if I could get to know Cuj—*Tinkerbell*, that maybe we could spend more time together."

His heart swelled to near bursting.

She leaned closer and whispered, "But I didn't know you had plans, and I might have overshot my abilities. I'm not sure I can go anywhere near her."

"I know one way to help you get past that fear." He leaned into the van, wrapped her in his arms, and kissed her. He felt the tension drain from her body and continued kissing her, until her hands left the steering wheel to embrace him. And then he deepened the kiss, because nothing—*nothing*—was better than this.

"Better?" He pressed a softer kiss to her lips.

"Now I'm turned on *and* scared."

He chuckled. "Do you trust me?"

She nodded.

"I know a thing or two about overcoming fears. Can you give me a few minutes? Promise me you won't take off?"

"If you guys have plans, I can come back." She glanced at Bear and Crystal, both crouched beside Tinkerbell. Bones had his back to the van, his phone pressed to his ear.

"We don't. Give me a sec." He closed the door, relief pushing through him like a gale-force wind as he headed into the barn, returning with one of Tinkerbell's leashes.

As he hooked it on her collar, Bear said, "What's up with Finlay?"

"She's afraid of dogs."

Crystal went to the van and said, "Tinkerbell's really sweet. She just looks mean. Like Bullet."

*Christ.*

Finlay made a pleading face.

"She won't hurt you," Crystal urged.

Finlay rolled down the window a little further and said, "I'm sure she won't, but I'm still scared of dogs. *Any* dogs. Chihuahuas scare me, which I know is silly. But I'm trying, because…" She glanced at Bullet again, and his gut went funky again.

"We came by to see if you were sure you didn't want to join us on our ride," Bear explained. "Finlay can come along. Make a day of it?"

"She doesn't ride," Bullet said.

"You don't ride?" Crystal asked Finlay.

Finlay shook her head with an apologetic expression.

"Neither did I when I met Bear," Crystal said. "Maybe after you conquer Tink you can learn to ride."

"That would be a big *if,* and I don't know if I can handle two things at once. First let me get through this," Finlay said.

Bullet handed the leash to Bear. "Fin was attacked by a dog when she was younger. Think you can stick around long enough for me to get her out of the van?"

"Whatever you need." Bear took the leash. He crouched with an arm around Tinkerbell again and said, "You need to be sweet, Tink." Then to Crystal he said, "Come here, sugar. Let's give Bullet some room to work his magic."

*Magic.* If only he had one-tenth as much as Finlay did.

Bullet opened the door to the van and turned Finlay so she was facing him. Holy hell, where did his girl shop? Turnonyourman.com? She wore a flimsy, short pink dress and brown leather boots that laced up to her knees, beneath which were some sort of frilly socks that went halfway up her thighs. Her outfit was completed with a wrist full of bracelets and a flowery ring on her right hand.

"Sweet baby Jesus, lollipop. Did you dress to make me want to lay you down in the back of the van on purpose?"

"What?" She gasped and looked down at her outfit. "No! I wore tall boots so Tink couldn't get at my legs, and this is one of my favorite dresses. I figured I should be as comfortable as possible."

"Well," he said as he adjusted himself. "At least one of us will be."

She giggled. "Sorry."

He put his hands on her hips and tugged her against him, trying not to think about what type of panties she had on under that slinky little dress. *Fuck.* Now that was *all* he could think about.

"What's going on?" Bones asked, jerking Bullet's mind back into submission.

"Fin's afraid of dogs," Bear explained.

As his brothers talked, Bullet gazed into Finlay's eyes and said, "Tink will listen to everything I say, but she's a puppy.

She's going to get excited, and she might bark or wiggle around because she's straining not to jump up and kiss your face, okay?"

She gulped and nodded. Her eyes shifted in Tinkerbell's direction. Tinkerbell was licking Bear's face. "Has she ever bitten anyone?"

"Never. And she isn't trained to attack. She's trained to behave, babe. She's my girl. I'd never put her in danger, any more than I'd put you in danger, and she knows it."

Finlay's gaze softened, and a genuine smile appeared. "I love how much you love her."

"I take care of the things I love." *And I want to take care of you.* "She's docile enough to let Lincoln crawl all over her and Kennedy hug her up. But before I bring you over to meet her, I want you to know how much it means to me that you're here. I don't know big enough words to say it, but thank you."

"I take care of the things I care about, too," she said softly.

# Chapter Thirteen

FINLAY STEPPED FROM the van, remaining glued to Bullet's side. Her pulse was sprinting even though Tinkerbell was leashed. Bear and Bones flanked her. In their dark jeans and leather jackets, they looked like biker bodyguards. Bullet was a wall of concentration, watching her and his pup intently. What must it feel like to be him right now, with a girlfriend who was petrified of the animal that made him feel safe?

Finlay reached for his hand, and he glanced down at her with concern in his eyes. "I brought her treats that I made. Will that help?"

His lips tipped up. "Only if you want my eighty-pound girl trying to snarf food out of your hands." He glanced at Tinkerbell and then back at Finlay. "You *made* her treats?"

She nodded. "I couldn't sleep, so I looked up the healthiest treats for puppies. I made them shaped like bones." Her eyes flicked up to Bones and she said, "The doggy kind."

His brothers chuckled.

Crystal tucked her dark hair behind her ear and said, "Aw, it might have been fun to see Tink gobbling down little *Bones*."

Tinkerbell's head popped up, and she took a step toward

Bullet. Bear held tight to the leash and said, "Stay, Tink."

Finlay exhaled a long breath.

"Here's how this is going to go." Bullet lifted her hand and pressed a kiss to the back of it. "You're scared, and she's going to sense that. When Kennedy gets scared, Tink rallies around her. She might whimper, she might try to lick you, but she will *not* try to bite you, okay?"

Finlay nodded. "I can't help being scared."

"I know. It's okay, but you need to know that she has feelings, too. She hurts when people she loves hurt. See how she's watching you? Watching us? She sees your hand in mine. She senses that you're important to me. She'll act on that."

"Okay," came out in a whisper.

"When we walk over, I'm going to have her lie down, and then I want you to offer your hand to her, let her smell you." He lifted her hand to his nose and inhaled deeply. "She'll smell your sweetness and will probably lick your hand. When you feel comfortable, you can pet her, okay? No pressure, but if you can keep from screaming and running away, that would be best."

Finlay smiled, remembering how she'd freaked out in the parking lot at Whispers. "I'm not going to do that again. I think I can handle this. I mean, look how she is with you guys. I already feel like a loser for needing an army of protection from your dog."

"Everyone needs support," Bones said.

A comforting glance passed between him and Bullet. She could only imagine how the rest of Bullet's family would have rallied around him had he shared the worst of his experiences with them. She wondered if he'd still have nightmares and flashbacks if he'd gotten it out of his system.

"You can totally do this," Crystal said. "By the way, that

outfit is the bomb!" She whipped out her phone and took a picture. "I'm going to make one like it, but black."

Crystal made many of her own clothes, as well as costumes for Gemma's princess boutique. Finlay's thoughts shifted to clothes, and the distraction took her nervousness down a notch.

"Ready?" Bullet asked.

"No." She smiled and said, "But let's do it anyway."

Holding her hand tight, he motioned with his other hand and said, "Tink, lie down."

Tinkerbell lowered herself to her belly again, her long paws stretched out before her. Her head was perched high, her tongue hanging out, like she couldn't wait for them to come over. Tinkerbell had a broad head and body, a black face, and brown fur around her snout and down her chest, which made her look like she was wearing a dark mask. But lying there, with her ears twitching and front paws stretched out, she looked concerned, excited, and a little confused.

*Join the party. I'll be sweet if you will,* Finlay thought nervously.

Bear crouched, one arm around Tinkerbell, and nodded at Bullet. Finlay loved the way they stuck together in everything. Even something as silly as helping his fearful girlfriend get to know his dog.

"Okay, babe. Go nice and slow."

Her heart beat frantically as she stepped forward, clinging to Bullet's hand. She offered her other hand to Tinkerbell, trembling as the pup stretched her neck toward her hand. It took all of Finlay's focus not to pull back when Tinkerbell's nose touched her hand and her tongue tickled over it. Nervous laughter fell from Finlay's lips. Bullet stepped behind her, his big body like a wall of strength for her to borrow from.

"Kneel down, sweetheart," he said in her ear.

She was suddenly engulfed by memories of their bodies tangled together last night and his hot breath on her neck. Her knees weakened, and kneeling wasn't so difficult anymore. He went down with her, one arm around her back, the other reaching out to pet Tinkerbell. What was wrong with her that she was thinking about how close they'd been when five minutes ago she'd been scared out of her mind?

"That's my girl," he said coaxingly.

She wasn't sure which of them he was talking to, but she had a feeling it was both, and it made her appreciate his big heart even more. Bullet knew only one way to love, and that was to love hard. Knowing he'd never put either one of them in danger eased the knots inside her.

"You okay?" he asked.

"Yes," she answered, breathing deeply. "Actually, I'm doing pretty well."

Tinkerbell crept forward, still lying on her belly, her pleading eyes tugging at Finlay's heartstrings as she weaseled between her and Bullet and nosed at Bullet's belly. Bullet used his free hand to love her up, then pressed a kiss to the top of her snout.

"That's my girl."

Finlay reached over and petted her, too. Her fur was short but soft, and she felt solid, like Bullet. Tinkerbell lifted her face and Finlay pulled back.

"It's okay. She just wants to kiss you," Bullet assured her.

Finlay closed her eyes. Tinkerbell's scratchy tongue licked up her cheek, making all of them laugh. She sank down to her butt beside Tinkerbell, the cold concrete prickling the backs of her thighs as Tinkerbell lay her big head on Finlay's leg and sighed. Finlay petted her, growing more comfortable. When she stopped petting her, the pup whimpered and licked her leg.

They sat on the driveway for a long while, getting to know each other, Finlay and the dog who had become Bullet's security blanket. Her love for the pup grew as she thought about how much Tinkerbell meant to Bullet, how much she helped him, and how much Bullet had helped her. Soon everyone was talking and laughing, and Tinkerbell was sitting pressed against Finlay's side. And for the first time in years, she was okay around a dog.

The joy in Bullet's eyes, the laughter he so rarely shared, and that sexy smile that she didn't see often enough, was worth every second of the trepidation she'd experienced and the sleepless night she'd spent gathering the courage to drive out there and try to overcome her fears.

Finlay took a long look at the three big men sitting on the pavement like they didn't mind at all. Bear's arm was around Crystal, and they were both smiling as he stole kisses after every word she said. Bones and Bullet were reminiscing about when Bullet had first found Tinkerbell. The love between them was so rich and real, she felt buffered from the rest of the world and blessed to be welcomed into their world.

"Thank you all for helping me through this. I'm sure you had better things to do than play babysitter this morning."

Bear pushed to his feet, bringing Crystal up beside him. "We're heading out for a ride. How about we break that motorcycle cherry of yours next?"

"Bear!" Crystal elbowed him. "One major life event at a time."

"Watch it, bro," Bullet warned as the rest of them rose to their feet.

Bear shrugged. "Just trying to help."

Tinkerbell leaned against Finlay's side as they said their goodbyes and Bullet's brothers and Crystal took off for their ride. Finlay couldn't believe she'd actually gone through with overcoming a fear she'd lived with for more than a decade.

Bullet gathered her in his arms and said, "How're you really holding up?"

As she soaked in the warmth of his embrace, she knew she might never have done it if it weren't for him. "Surprisingly well. I can't promise I won't be fearful of other dogs, but at least this is a step in the right direction."

"A huge step." He brushed his thumb over her cheek and said, "I know how hard it is to face your fears, and I'm really proud of you."

"Thank you. I knew Tink took after her papa with those dark eyes and that intimidating stance, but I didn't realize she had your big heart, too."

"Thanks, babe." Worry washed over his features. "Were you afraid of me when you first saw me?"

"No. I just didn't know what to make of you. You looked like a bully, all big and bad, and you spoke too roughly. I mean, come on. The first thing you ever said to me was offering me a ride on the *Bullet train*." She laughed, and he silenced her with a kiss.

It didn't surprise her that he didn't try to refute it, or give her an explanation. Bullet made no excuses for who he was, and that was only one of the reasons she was so drawn to him.

"Think you can stay for a while? I have something I want to show you."

"Is it anything like what you showed me last night?" she asked playfully.

A deep, seductive noise sounded in his throat as his lips

came down over hers in a kiss so warm and wonderful, so *perfect*, she never wanted it to end. But Tinkerbell had other ideas, and nudged her big head between them, making them both laugh.

He took Finlay by the hand and led her toward the back-yard with Tinkerbell trotting happily along beside them. More elaborate gardens came into view, with slate paths snaking between them. One path led to a small patio with a stone fireplace, and another weaved toward the far side of the yard, where a pond glistened in the late-morning sun. There were acres of greenspace as far as she could see, so picturesque she couldn't look away.

"Can you stay long enough for a walk? Tink loves to walk around the pond."

"My only plans for today have been accomplished. I'm yours for as long as you'd like."

"Careful, lollipop. I might never let you go."

"YOU THINK THAT'S some kind of threat?" Finlay bumped her hip against Bullet as they walked along his property, tossing a ball for Tinkerbell.

"Most women would think so." He took the ball from Tinkerbell's mouth and threw it across the yard. The pup bolted after it.

"Maybe if you said you were going to tie them up and chain them to a bed…"

"Christ, lollipop, you can't walk around in that outfit and talk like that, or *you* might end up chained to my bed."

She spun around, facing him with a radiant smile and sunlight glittering in her eyes. "I think getting to know your dog is enough of a challenge for one day."

He hauled her against him. "Don't worry, babe. I'm not into feeling trapped, and I'd never want you to feel that way, either."

He lowered his lips to hers, and then Tink's snout pushed between them. He reluctantly pulled back and took the ball from her mouth, tossing it away again—farther this time. "I think my girl's jealous."

"I would be too, if you had your lips on someone else." She took his hand, and they continued to walk around the gardens. "How long have you lived here?"

"A few years. I stayed in the apartment above the auto shop for the first few months while I pulled my shit together. Quincy and Jed live there now, and Tru stayed there before them. It was too confining for me, and sleeping out on the balcony got old real fast. I spent a lot of time at the bar instead of going home. Then one day I was out for a ride and I saw this place. It was in foreclosure, and I got it for a song. There's lots of room for my bikes. Room to *breathe*."

She glanced up at the house.

"It's not what you're used to lollipop. That dollhouse you live in is mighty nice, but I'm a barebones kind of guy. Give me a mattress and some fresh air and I'm good."

She pressed herself against his side as Tinkerbell barreled toward them with the ball in her mouth. "Do you sleep outside?"

"On occasion, but my place is so open, I don't usually feel too closed in."

She seemed to think about that as he tossed the ball again.

"Well, you sure lucked out with the gardens. I've never seen a yard like this."

"It was pretty much all dirt when I moved in." He steered her across the yard toward the pond, hoping to avoid talking about why he had such elaborate gardens.

"Then you must have an amazing gardener."

"My father was, before his stroke." Biggs had suffered the stroke while Bullet was away on tour, which added to the guilt Bullet wore like a lead coat.

"So, *he* did this? Dixie told me he suffered his stroke while you were in the military, but you said you bought this place afterward. Does he still garden? I know he walks with a cane and the stroke hindered his speech."

As much as he didn't want to appear weak in Finlay's eyes, he wanted her in his life, and he knew that meant he had to be completely honest. His chest constricted with the thought of exposing so much of himself, but he'd already ripped open so many wounds in her presence, he told himself this was just giving her a birds'-eye view of the wreckage.

"Not really. Even though I didn't come home until months after I was discharged, I was still pretty messed up when I got back to the harbor. I hate labels, but there's no escaping PTSD. It really screwed with my head." He filled his lungs with crisp air, watching Tinkerbell roll around in the grass. "Back then flashbacks hit hard and nightmares came often. I was with my parents one afternoon, and my father asked me to clean up my mother's gardens. I was a mess, Fin. I was angry and out of control, and it didn't matter that I'd served my country; I felt like a fucking failure. I told you I'd waited to enlist because I had to watch over my brothers and sister, and then I had the crushing weight of trying to figure out what that really meant. By the time I enlisted, I had gotten into trouble and brought some bad shit down on my father and the motorcycle club by infiltrating the wrong territory outside of the harbor. I was young and stupid, but I knew I had to get my act together. Being away when my old man suffered his stroke messed me up even more. There I was, overseas, years later, still torn over where I really belonged, and…"

He swallowed the confession that he'd only shared with Bones. The event that had led to his medical discharge. But when he gazed into Finlay's compassionate eyes, he couldn't keep from sharing his innermost secret with her.

"You already know about the terrible shit that goes on in wars. I was in the middle of my third tour, and when you're in the thick of it, you don't question or sit around and wonder how to get out from under the shadow of it. Your only focus is surviving and making sure your brothers in arms make it out alive. Even the fact that you're doing it for a bigger purpose gets lost when you see men you've fought with, laughed with, given shit to go down." A bead of sweat formed on his brow, and he swiped at it with his forearm.

"You don't have to share this with me. I don't want to ruin your afternoon."

"Babe, you're here. Nothing can ruin today."

She leaned her head against his arm, and it eased the tension in his chest.

"Anyway, one of the guys went down. He was bleedin' real bad. Like, so much I knew he didn't have time to wait for the medics to come to him. I threw him over my shoulders." He motioned to each side. "I held one leg over my left shoulder and his chest pressed to my right, and I hauled ass trying to find a medic. I didn't feel the bullets when they hit me. When I finally went down, I twisted so the guy I was carrying landed on my chest. There was blood everywhere, and I was pumped with adrenaline. I didn't know I'd been hit. My only thought was to save the other soldier. I spotted a medic and pushed to my knees, threw the injured guy over my shoulder, and made it a few more steps before collapsing. He had blood pouring out of his wounds, and when I laid him down, that's when I saw the new wound in his chest. I was leaning over him, holding his hand, telling him we'd get him out of there, to hang on. *Jesus*, I would have given my own life to save his. That's when I realized blood was pouring from my chest, where the bullets had gone through me, and hit him. He said all sorts of things while I tried like hell to stop the bleeding in his gut and legs, his chest. He was so fucking brave all the way to the end, telling me to save myself. I held him against me as he took his last breath. I'll never forget the feel of that, and then everything went black."

His heart hammered against his ribs with the memories, and he steeled himself for a flashback, but the words still came, and the flashback remained at bay. "I woke up in a military hospital, thrashing and trying to get back to the field. In my head, that's where I belonged. That's all that mattered. But I had taken a lot of fire, and they wanted to notify my family because they weren't sure I'd make it. I told them I'd sue their asses if they contacted anyone before I was dead. My family had been through enough with my dad's stroke, and we had lost my uncle, who ran the auto shop, after that. By the time I was hit, Bear had been running both for a few years, and Dixie was helping him. My father had gone through physical therapy, and their lives were finally stable again. They didn't need the stress of not knowing if I'd survive, or of caring for me if I ended up too fucked up to function."

"But what if you'd died? They wouldn't have been able to

say goodbye." Tears slid down Finlay's cheeks.

"I know my family loves me. I wanted them to remember me strong, not in a hospital bed, riddled with bullet holes."

"But you were alone through all of that?"

"Yeah, but it was no big deal." He wiped her tears and pressed his lips to hers.

"It was a very big deal." She wrapped her arms around him, holding him so tight he shut his eyes against his own emotions. "I hate knowing you went through that alone."

He remembered what she'd said about her late boyfriend, and guilt consumed him. He shouldn't have told her, shouldn't have made her sad.

"Hey." He tipped up her chin and kissed her again. "I was fine, Fins. Fucked up, slammed with PTSD, but I was okay. And I wasn't alone the whole time."

He took her hand as they walked beside the pond, needing to move. "Once I healed enough, I called Bones, who hooked me up with a buddy of his, that therapist I mentioned the other night. And a few months later, when I felt like I had my head on straighter, I came home. All my family knows is that I took a few bullets and suffered from PTSD. They didn't need to be saddled with the rest. But being home was hard. It stirred up all those old confusing feelings, and I learned firsthand that PTSD was a damn nasty competitor. It came out of nowhere at times and sucked the life out of me, which is why I have these gardens."

He glanced across the yard at the burgeoning gardens and paths, remembering how cathartic working with his hands had been, and after he felt more like himself, how focusing on the bar had also helped him heal.

"My old man had me out in his gardens day and night,

teaching me everything he knew. He told me it was to help out my mother since he could no longer use both hands well enough to do the things her garden needed. Bear would show up, and he'd spend hours with us." He laughed with the memory of the two of them out there on their knees, shooting the shit while they weeded and mulched flowerbeds. "I was too messed up to realize it until later, but Biggs used gardening to get me out of my own head enough to help me heal. And Bear? He's so damn empathetic, he couldn't heal from my wounds until I did. Talk about a reason to get past my shit..."

"And you still don't call yourself a hero," Finlay said, watching as Tinkerbell trotted toward them with the ball in her mouth.

The pup plopped down on her butt in front of Finlay and dropped the ball. Finlay picked it up, holding the slobbery ball by her fingertips. Bullet put out his hand.

"No, I can do it. I'm not afraid of dog slobber, just dog bites." She pulled her arm back, and as she released the ball— and Tink took off running after it—Bullet realized it was flying directly toward the pond.

"Tink!" he hollered, but the dog was already in the air, front and back legs extended as she dove for the ball. Bullet hauled ass into the water, vaguely aware of Finlay calling after him.

# Chapter Fourteen

"I'M SORRY. I didn't know she couldn't swim," Finlay said as Bullet trudged from the pond with Tinkerbell in his arms, his clothing and boots drenched.

"She can swim just fine," he said as the pup lavished him with kisses. "But she freaks out in the water and cries, paddling around in circles. She only goes in after a ball or a stick." He set Tinkerbell down on the grass, and she immediately shook off the water, showering Finlay with stinky pond water.

She gasped as the dog did it again, and she couldn't help but laugh.

"Tink," Bullet said harshly.

Tinkerbell barked and leaned against Finlay, soaking the skirt of her dress. "It's okay," Finlay reassured him. "I'm the reason you're all wet, so it's only fair that I'm wet, too."

The pooch went paws-up on Bullet's stomach, panting happily.

"I think she had fun," Finlay offered as Bullet huffed out a breath and Tinkerbell dropped to all fours.

"I'm sure she thinks it's a game, but we're all going to stink. I need to bathe her." He whistled and pointed to the house.

"Tink. Home."

The dog took off running.

"Can I help?" Finlay asked.

Bullet tugged off his boots, dumped out the remaining water, and pulled off his socks. "You sure? While she freaks out in bodies of water, she loves showers and baths, but you're going to get soaked."

She looked down at her wet dress. "I think I already am."

"Then you won't mind if I do this." He began pulling off his shirt.

Finlay saw it as if in slow motion. The drenched cotton slid up his slick skin, revealing ripped abs and sticking to his muscular pecs. He shifted and his lats flared as he tugged it over his head, leaving him in only a drenched, form-fitting pair of Levi's and bare feet. Gosh, she loved a man with bare feet. Bullet's feet were big and masculine, like the rest of him. He held the shirt and his wet boots in one arm and reached for her with the other.

His cool, hard chest pressed against her as he captured her lips in a passionate kiss. His body slid against her, getting her wet from the inside out. He made one of those appreciative sounds that sent sparks through her veins, and when their lips parted, the air rushed from her lungs.

He pressed a firm kiss beside her ear and said, "Come on, sweet thing. Let's get my other girl cleaned up, so we can get nice and dirty."

His arm circled her waist, but her legs had forgotten how to function. He gave her an inquisitive glance, and understanding dawned on him, as evident in the slight narrowing of his dark eyes. His hand moved lower, squeezing her bottom, wreaking more havoc with her, and for some crazy reason, her mind reeled back to last night, when she'd heard the *clink* of his heavy belt buckle—which was now gleaming just below his navel—on the hardwood floor.

He chuckled and bent at the knees, lifting her up with one arm around her thighs.

"Bullet!" She shrieked with laughter.

Tinkerbell bolted toward them, barking, making her heart beat even harder. She didn't look like she was going to stop. Bullet took off running toward the house with Finlay over his shoulder, and Tinkerbell was right beside him, her dark eyes locked on Finlay. When they reached the back of the house, Tinkerbell went down on her front paws, her butt up in the air, wiggling excitedly, and Bullet lowered Finlay into his cradled arms. He pressed his lips to hers, laughing right along with her, and it was the most wonderful sound she'd ever heard.

"I *really* like your laugh," she said as he set her on her feet.

Bullet turned away, but not before she saw a flicker of something that looked like embarrassment flash in his eyes. Tinkerbell licked Finlay's leg. She reached down to love her up as they followed Bullet to an enormous outdoor washroom behind the garage. It had three walls made of the same type of weathered wide planks as the rest of the house, and a wooden deck for a floor. There were two showerheads, one up very high, obviously installed just for Bullet, and one about a foot to the left of it, much lower, clearly made for Tinkerbell. Two tree stumps served as tables, atop which sat two bottles of shampoo, one for dogs and one for humans, along with a bottle of body wash. There was a utility sink and a deep counter just inside the wall to the right and, she noticed, there was no door. The washroom overlooked more gardens and vast grassy lawn.

Tinkerbell ran around the room whimpering and pawing at

the faucet.

"See?" Bullet said. "She loves this part." He opened a door above the sink to a cabinet built into the wall and pulled out a couple of towels. He set them on the counter, eyeing Finlay with a seductive leer. "You might want to take those sexy boots off."

"Good idea." She sat down on the edge of one of the stumps and began unlacing her boots.

Tinkerbell plopped down beside her, and Bullet knelt before Finlay, silently taking over. He set her foot on his leg, holding her gaze as he unlaced the boot. After unlacing each hook, he slid his hands along her thigh, making her breathe a little harder. She wasn't used to being with such a virile, sexual man, and as he touched her slowly and purposefully, like they had all the time in the world, and looked at her like nothing else existed, his desire invaded her, making her wish *she* was touching *him*. He removed that boot and her long, frilly sock and pressed a kiss to the top of her foot, then gently set it on the floor.

Tinkerbell whimpered, and in her peripheral vision, Finlay saw her cock her head, her ears perking up.

Bullet lifted Finlay's other foot and repeated his sensual efforts. She clutched the edge of the stump. The gnarled bark dug into her fingers, which was good, because he was making her so tingly she was afraid she'd go numb.

He set the boot and her sock aside and scooted forward, between her legs, gripping her outer thighs. His strong hands pressed into her flesh, making her acutely aware of how close his thumbs were to her very needy privates. Finlay's pulse skyrocketed as he went up on his knees and leaned forward, his beard tickling her skin as his lips touched her cheek.

Tinkerbell's head tilted the other way, and she pawed at Bullet's arm. But Bullet's eyes never left Finlay's. Her mouth watered for another taste of him.

"Ready to get wet, sweet thing?" he asked in the gravelly voice that sent heat between her legs.

"Yes" fell from her lips as she leaned forward and took the kiss she'd been dying for.

Her arms circled his neck as he pulled her legs around his waist and sank back on his heels. Passion stormed through her, releasing all her inhibitions. She kissed him rougher, fisted her hands in his hair, her tongue delving deeper into his mouth, and he was right there with her. She tore her mouth away to taste more of him, kissing his cheeks, his beard, his neck. Then she lowered her mouth to his shoulder. His skin was hot and cold at once. It tasted salty and rugged. Bullet grabbed her bottom, holding her tight as she ground against his arousal.

Tinkerbell's paw swiped at them, catching Finlay's arm and startling her back to reality. They both drew back, a hot current running between them as Tinkerbell pawed at Bullet.

"You've turned me into a nympho," she whispered, as if Tinkerbell might understand.

"No, babe. We've awakened parts of each other no one else could ever touch."

She pulled him closer, hugging him to her, and spoke against his neck. "Then I never want them to go to sleep again."

Tinkerbell nudged her big, wet head between them.

"I think we need to wash your girl." Finlay smiled as she crawled off his lap.

She pulled at his hand, trying to get him to rise to his feet, but Tinkerbell leapt into his lap and licked his entire face, earning another hearty laugh from her man.

"All right, you spoiled girl." He kissed her snout and pushed to his feet, quickly stealing another kiss from Finlay.

They both got drenched and soapy as they bathed Tinkerbell, and they laughed more than Finlay could ever remember laughing. She swore Bullet was like a different man since telling her more about his experiences and PTSD. She didn't want to change him, and hadn't set out to do it, but the lightness surrounding him right now, at this very moment, was like a gift from the heavens above. A peek at the man trapped someplace deep within him.

Tinkerbell shook herself off so many times, the walls of the washroom looked like it had rained. Bullet used a towel to pat her down. Then she took off running around the yard.

"She won't go in the pond?" Finlay asked as he stalked toward her with a heated look in his eyes. She couldn't stop grinning like a fool, which he seemed to make her do often. Maybe she needed him in her life just as much as he needed her.

"Nope. But she'll be busy for a while." He lowered his mouth to her neck, brushing kisses there and driving her wild. "It's my turn to bathe *you* now."

He lifted the hem of her dress and she grabbed his hands. "What if someone comes over?"

"We'll hear them. No one comes over who doesn't drive a motorcycle." His tongue grazed the shell of her ear, and he guided her hand between his legs.

His hardness electrified her.

"You hold the reins, lollipop. You want to go for a ride?"

"I've never done this before...*outside*." Her voice trembled, but the idea of making love to Bullet right there, with the hot sun baking their damp skin, totally turned her on.

She was too aroused to find her voice, so she squeezed his

erection, and he crashed his mouth over hers. She met his efforts with reckless abandon as they tore at each other's clothes, and he dug out a condom from his soaking-wet wallet and sheathed himself. He lifted her into his arms, his naked body pressing deliciously against hers, as she sank down on his shaft, sighing at the incredible pleasure of becoming one with him. When he was buried to the hilt, he held her there, neither of them moving, both barely breathing, and her heart came tumbling out.

"I love being in your arms. Don't ever let me go."

"Never, lollipop," he said vehemently. "Tell me you're mine."

This time she wasn't taking a chance of him not hearing her promise. She touched her forehead to his and said, "I'm yours, Bullet. Wholly and completely yours."

"Aw, baby."

The emotions in his voice burrowed into her heart as she lowered her mouth to his, sealing her vow. His cock twitched inside her, sending ripples of lust vibrating through her, and she began moving. Riding him faster, harder, taking him as deep as she could with every thrust of his hips. She clung to his shoulders, gasping between messy, frantic kisses. Their moans and sinful noises sailed into the air, and she felt so free, she allowed them to flow, low and needy, each one earning another groan, another greedy noise from Bullet. Every sound he made *for* her, *because of* her, sent her climbing higher, moving faster, chasing the rush of emotions flooding her, until she was out of breath, her control hanging on by a thread.

"Let go, beautiful. Come with me *now*," Bullet demanded.

The sheer need in his voice, the power of his passion, set off a series of explosions inside her.

"*Bullet*—" She dug her nails into his shoulders as her body arched and clenched.

His fingers fisted in her hair as he found his own intense release, and her name fell from his lips like a chant, "Finlay, Fins…*My girl.*"

BULLET MOVED THROUGH the afternoon feeling high and trying to dissect the strange and slightly out-of-control feeling as Finlay padded around his house wearing one of his T-shirts, belted at the waist. The shirt hung nearly to her knees, and the belt was so big he had to put a new hole in it so it would fit her. She looked so damn sexy, with her damp hair and without any makeup, it had been all he could do not to stare at her while they'd eaten lunch. Tinkerbell followed her around the living room as she checked out his things. She looked soft as a feather among his old, masculine furnishings. Her fingertips trailed along the back of his brown leather couch, her gaze gliding over the recliner that was once his father's, a set of black speakers nearly as tall as her, and his grandfather's old wooden desk tucked into a nook beside the windows. She walked around the coffee table, her eyes skirting over the handful of magazines strewn across the top, across the discolored and marred hardwood floors, to the brick walls and unfinished ceilings. He'd seen the exposed wood as rustic and appealing when he'd bought the place. But now, against the calming hum of the dryer he'd never before noticed, Finlay's presence was like a beacon of light in his stark world, and he wondered how *she* saw his home.

He had removed all the interior walls when he'd moved in, leaving only exposed wood and metal support beams on the first floor, which was built behind the garage. The ceilings were eleven feet tall, giving it the spacious feel he so desperately needed. The walls were brick, with a black iron shelf that ran along the far wall, home to family pictures and spare auto parts that had found their way up from the garage. He'd left the barn-wood cabinetry in the kitchen and replaced the countertop with stainless steel, which he could toss his tools on without worrying he would damage them. Several shop lights hung from the ceiling, along with a few black track lights. Dixie had been after him to replace them with something nicer, but he liked their industrial feel.

Finlay walked to the bank of floor-to-ceiling windows over-looking the yard, each flanked by off-white curtains his mother had insisted on. *One day you might want privacy.* He had privacy. That was the reason he'd purchased ten secluded acres and an old barn.

Finlay glanced at him, her finger hovering over the stereo's power button. He nodded, and seconds later an instrumental by Rag'n'Bone Man filled the room. Her hips began to sway, and a playful smile lifted her lips.

Looking like the angel she was, she said, "This is nice. I expected to hear Ozzy Osbourne or something harder."

"It's the instrumental of 'Put That Soul on Me,' by Rag'n'Bone Man. The lyrics are pretty hot, but the instrumental takes me down a notch. I've got Ozzy and all the classics, too. If you hang with me, you hang with them."

"I like this, and I like you, so I'm okay with classic rock." She motioned toward the black iron steps leading up to his bedroom above the garage. "Can I go up?"

He nodded and followed her up. His bed sat atop a black rug on an old concrete floor, with a whiskey barrel as a nightstand on one side. Bookshelves crammed with books and magazines were built into the wall to their left on either side of the window overlooking the front yard. In the corner was a rust-colored oversized armchair, one of Tinkerbell's favorite places to crash. The far walls each sported extra-wide circle-head windows, and the entire room was wood paneled, with the exception of the cathedral ceiling, which was mostly glass.

"It's not much, but it works for me," he said. "I needed space for gardening, and I like having a roof over my head, though it isn't a necessity."

"This is pretty much how I pictured your room would be," she said appreciatively. "Except, what're these for?" She pointed to the wrought-iron rails running the length of the walls in front of the windows.

"I'll show you. Do you know the Bradens?" he asked as he crossed the room. "They own the microbrewery in town."

"Yes. I'm catering a baby shower for one of Leesa Braden's friends next Sunday. I was going to ask if you thought it would be a problem if I used the kitchen at the bar to prepare. There's more room there than at my place, and the renovations should be done by then."

"Next weekend? Sure." It probably made him a dick for hating the idea that on his one day off she'd be tied up, so he kept that to himself. "Dixie's usually there going over the books on Sundays, but she won't mind. I'll go with you."

"Oh, good. That's a big relief. Thank you. What were you saying about the Bradens?"

"I brought in their cousin Beau, a contractor buddy of mine from Pleasant Hill, to adapt this space into something I could live with."

He unhooked the latches across the bottom of the back and

side walls, then pushed a button on the remote control by the bed. The bottom of the walls lifted up and out, until they were parallel to the ground below, like wooden awnings.

Finlay gasped, smiling as she went to the railing and looked out over the gardens and pond. "Holy cow. I've never seen anything like this."

"Neither had I." He wrapped his arms around her from behind. "I thought he'd put on glass doors, or a deck or something. But this is so much better." He kissed her neck. She smelled like his body wash, and hell if that didn't strike every possessive bone in his body.

He turned her in his arms and gazed into her smiling eyes. "I like having you here with me, and I'm sorry my place isn't fancier for you."

"I'm not. Your home is perfect for you, and..." Her gaze moved to the center of his chest.

He sensed her desire to say more, and though he thought he knew what she might say, he posed it as a question. "And you're starting to think that maybe this broken badass biker might be perfect for you?"

She smiled, and her eyes flicked happily up to him. "No."

His gut pitched. He pulled back, but she held tight, keeping him close.

"I don't think you're *broken*," she said vehemently.

"I'm broken, lollipop. I've been as honest with you as I could about all of it. Don't pretend otherwise."

"Well," she said sweetly, "do you think *I'm* broken?"

"You? You've got your shit together better than anyone I know. You express everything you feel, and you find your way to the truth without hesitation."

"Those are things I show outwardly. But remember when I

told you that I had never felt anything for a man since I lost Aaron?" Her gaze went soft.

"Yeah. I remember." He held her tighter.

"I thought I was broken, but I think *broken* is the wrong word for people like us. I think we were *affected* and *hurt*, but not *broken*. Broken implies that we need to be fixed, that we're not good enough to be loved the way we are, or we're lacking in some way. But the more I've gotten to know and care about you, the clearer it's become that fixing isn't part of our equation. You might always have flashbacks or nightmares, and you might never want to be in a house where walls can't disappear."

She shrugged, a small smile lifting her lips as she said, "And I may never get past the hurt of having lost one man I cared about. I don't live my life afraid to love, but until you, I hadn't even come close. You've taught me that I can feel again. And I hope that in time you'll realize that I want to be with *you*, and you don't have to apologize for the parts of you that stem from your past. Those things that make you *you* don't deter my feelings. If anything, they make me want to be there for you if you get a nightmare, or experience a flashback. And don't grind your teeth together like that," she said sharply. "You're still the biggest badass I know. Only now I've seen your badass naked, so I know how *big* you really are."

"Christ, lollipop." He hauled her into his arms and kissed her. "Where have you been all my life?"

# Chapter Fifteen

MONDAY EVENING WHISKEY Bro's wasn't nearly as busy as it was some nights, but the twelve dozen buffalo wings Finlay had brought with her were gone in minutes. The appliances had been delivered, and Crow had nearly finished the renovations. He'd be back tomorrow to complete the job. It was a little after eight o'clock, and Finlay was going over applications for cooks and dishwashers with Dixie while fending off requests for more wings and cookies from customers. She was glad to know her new recipe for Whiskey Wings had gone over well, but after waking up in Bullet's arms, and their visit with Sarah earlier in the day, she was having trouble concentrating on much else.

"Why are you so distracted today?" Dixie asked.

"I'm not," Finlay lied, stealing a glance at Bullet, who was busy talking to Jed behind the bar. "I'm totally focused on dishwashers and cooks." *And your delicious brother.*

Bullet had been tied up with customers since she'd arrived, and even though she was pretty sure Dixie would be happy for the two of them, she was nervous about telling her they were now a couple. When Finlay had admitted that she'd agreed to go out with Bullet the last time they were together, Dixie had seemed shocked, and Finlay hadn't been able to read if it was a good or bad shock. Although Dixie would have had to be blind to have missed Finlay's not-so-furtive glances tonight or Bullet's overt leers.

"Uh-huh. That's why you just put salt in your iced tea." Dixie pointed to the saltshaker in Finlay's hand.

"Oh, geez." She pushed the glass away, thinking about how she'd been startled awake at five in the morning by the feel of Tinkerbell's scratchy tongue on her cheek. She didn't even remember falling asleep. The last thing she remembered was lying on a blanket in Bullet's arms, stargazing. They'd talked well into the night, between hungry kisses and passionate gropes, and Finlay had been surprised to learn that Bullet didn't have many dreams, other than to one day have a *little princess like Kennedy and a little dude like Lincoln* of his own. He loved working with his family at the bar and didn't want much else other than time to ride his motorcycle. As they'd talked, she'd realized her dreams weren't of any great magnitude either. She'd moved back to the harbor, hoping to put down roots, get her catering company off the ground again, and be happy. She'd found her happiness, and he happened to be looking at her right that second.

"Does this have something to do with what's going on between you and Bullet?"

"Um…partially," she admitted. She felt like she and Bullet had spent a month away together on a mini vacation, getting to know—and falling head over heels with—each other. They were so in sync, over breakfast they'd both suggested they visit Sarah, which they'd done together after Finlay had gone home to shower and change. Later, she and Bullet had brainstormed ways to help raise money for Sarah's family's medical bills, but short of a bake sale, they'd come up empty. Finlay hadn't been able to stop thinking about it ever since.

"Are you okay with me and Bullet seeing each other?" she finally asked.

Dixie laughed and tossed her long red hair over her shoulder. "Okay with it? Are you kidding? I wasn't so sure when you told me you'd agreed to go out with him the other day because, you know, you guys seem so different. Really, though, I was only worried that he might be too rough for you. But I was with Crystal and Bear last night, and they said Bullet was like a completely different guy yesterday morning when you stopped by. And today?" She glanced up at the bar, where Bullet was now talking with Jed and Crow. "The man looks like he's been struck by Cupid's arrow. I think he needed you in his life."

Finlay let out a loud sigh. "Thank goodness. I was hoping you would be okay with it, but I was worried. You know, you guys are all so close, and I know I'm different from the type of person most people would expect to be with Bullet." She looked down at her flowery dress, remembering the heat in Bullet's eye when he'd seen her in it this morning. She pushed that image away so she wouldn't blush and said, "Dixie, he's an amazing guy. I mean, truly, just the most loving, kindhearted, bravest man I know. I could go on and on about him. I still can't believe all that he's been through. And yes, he's *possessive*," she said with a smile, "but that's part of his charm. He—"

Dixie grabbed Finlay's hands, silencing her. "Fin, I'm happy for you guys, but if you keep talking about him, you'll end up saying something sisters don't need to hear."

Finlay covered her mouth with her hand and shook her head. "No, I promise. I won't go there." When she lowered her hand, Bullet was stalking across the bar toward her with that almost smile that made her heart race.

"I'm so happy you see him the way we all do," Dixie said. "Do you know that one of my biggest fears was that Bullet would never let a woman into his life? I literally have had nightmares about him harassing every guy I date *forever*." She lowered her voice as he neared and said, "Don't take this wrong, but this is awesome. If he's busy with you, he won't be bothering me."

"Dix." Bullet nodded to his sister. "You gonna be long? It's just you and Jed tonight."

"Not long," Dixie assured him. "We've already chosen several applicants to interview. We're just wrapping things up. I've got it, B. Don't worry."

He turned all his attention to Finlay with that laser focus he did so well, placing one hand on the table, the other on her chair, boxing her in with his body.

She didn't think it was possible for her pulse to go any faster, but she was proven wrong when he lowered his face beside hers. His warm breath seeped into her skin as he said, "I'm heading out back to the clubhouse to meet with the guys. You okay in here?"

"Yeah, I'm good."

"You going to be around tonight?" he asked, gazing into her eyes.

*Yes! Come see me!* She nodded.

"Mind if I come by?"

"I was hoping you would."

He made a possessive show of lifting her to her feet and kissing her goodbye, and she was pretty sure he'd obliterated any chance she had of thinking clearly.

"Geez, Bullet," Dixie said. "I think everyone in here knows

she's yours now."

He came away with a greedy smile. "See you soon, lollipop."

He gave her a softer, sweeter kiss, and then another, and a quick pat on her ass, before heading out of the bar.

"*Lollipop?*" Dixie arched a brow as she lowered herself to the chair. "Boy, you two are as gone as Crystal and Bear."

Finlay took a gulp of her iced tea and nearly gagged on the salt. She spewed it back into the glass. *That cleared the lust from my head.* "*Blech!* Sorry. My mind has been on a hundred things lately."

Dixie handed her a napkin. "More than the big, bearded distraction that just walked out? Is something else going on?"

"Yes. Although he's the biggest distraction of all. You saw how I turned to mush when he *kissed* me. I feel like I'm eighteen, not a woman approaching thirty."

"You've just discovered the *Whiskey magic*," Dixie said with a wave of her hand. "It's a blessing and a curse, really. We can drop people to their knees with a single kiss. Trouble is, I can't find anyone I *want* to drop to his knees."

"I'm sure we can find you a very willing partner. Crow was all eyes on you today, and that guy you were dancing with at Whispers? The doctor? Oh my gosh, Dixie, that guy has serious moves."

"Yeah. Jon Butterscotch touts himself as *fifty shades of sweetness*. My brothers would cut his pecker off if we ever even tried to hook up."

"Yikes. I could talk to Bullet, I mean, if you like Jon."

Dixie shook her head. "No thanks. I think I'll be dating outside of Peaceful Harbor. It's safer for everyone that way. But tell me what else is going on with you. You said you've had a million things on your mind. Is it your catering business?"

"No. I've tabled most of that while I get you guys settled. I'm catering a baby shower next weekend, but that's it until after your kitchen staff is hired and your menus are in place. I'm just worried about Sarah Beckley. Do you know about her family? The accident?"

"Yes. It's so sad. And thank God Bullet was there to help."

"I know. But don't call him a hero or he'll bite your head off."

"Yeah, he's a little touchy about that word. He thinks everyone in the world is as brave as he is." Dixie shook her head. "The truth is, all my brothers are brave, but Bullet? He takes bravery to a new level. My mom said when we were teenagers he'd troll the streets looking for people causing trouble so he could stop them. Like it was his job or something. And before he enlisted, there was some trouble with a gang about fifty miles from here, and he took off and was gone for *four* days. He came back bloody and worn out. My father was so angry. Bullet looked him in the eye and said, 'Your friends won't be seein' any more trouble from them, Pop.' He walked upstairs and slept for two days straight. He never said another word about it."

"Wow, Dixie, I can *see* him doing that." And it no longer scared her to think about him doing that in the way it once had. Now she only worried for his safety.

"The reason I've got a lot on my mind is that I've been bringing Sarah meals, and Bullet and I went to visit her this morning. Bradley is being released tomorrow, but her baby and her brother are still in intensive care. They're going to have huge medical bills, and she's got no family in the area. Her sister came to visit her the first night she was at the hospital, but she wasn't able to stay, and Sarah wouldn't say why, but she doesn't want her ex knowing where she is. I worry about how she's going to handle everything."

"We're worried about it, too. That's one of the things the guys are talking about tonight in the clubhouse."

"I was thinking that I could do a bake sale. Maybe I can get Crystal to make some outfits to raffle off at the boutique. I'm going to talk to Penny about setting up a donation jar on her counter."

"Hey, Dix," Jed called from behind the bar. He nodded toward a group of guys who had been playing pool and were now making their way to a table.

"I'd better get busy. Let me think about Sarah and see what I can come up with." Dixie pushed to her feet. "Are you okay with setting up those interviews?"

"Sure. Of course. Once I finish interviewing, I'll give you my recommendations and then you can bring in the best applicants to screen them yourself. We're still looking at two cooks and two dishwashers, right?"

A guy who had been playing darts called out, "How about more of those cookies from the other night?"

"She's not your personal chef," Dixie hollered across the room. "Maybe if you learn the word 'please,' she'll think about it." She turned back to Finlay with a spark of rebellion in her eyes. "It was my idea to expand the bar and bring in a chef and waitstaff, but I've got to tell you, the idea of bringing strangers in to work here scares the shit out of me. I hope I didn't push for the wrong thing."

"We'll be really careful about who we hire."

Dixie straightened her spine and wiggled her hips. "Time to go work some tips out of these loudmouths. You know, maybe you should talk to Bullet about a fundraising rally. We've done them before for people in the community."

"A rally?"

"Yeah, you know. Host a ride that ends here at the bar or in town, and have a family-friendly community fair sort of thing, sell tickets, raffles, and the proceeds go to the family. I brought up the idea to them when we were talking about expanding the bar."

"Holy moly, Dixie. You're a genius!"

"I'm all kinds of Whiskey magic all rolled up into one hot mama." Dixie laughed.

"Come on, Dix," the guy called over again.

"Keep your pants on, or I'll water down your drinks." She winked at Finlay and strutted across the room.

"A rally," Finlay said to herself as she gathered the résumés and put them in her bag. She took out a notebook and jotted down ideas for a rally fundraiser. Half an hour later she had two pages full of notes. She was too excited to wait to tell Bullet. She stuffed her things into her bag and tossed it over her shoulder.

"Hey, Jed," she said as she passed by the bar. "Where's the Dark Knights' clubhouse?"

Jed hiked a thumb over his shoulder toward the kitchen as he poured a drink. "Out the back door, straight across the lot about a hundred feet. You can't miss it."

"Thanks!" She headed for the kitchen, excited to discuss Dixie's idea with Bullet.

BULLET SAT AT a table in the Dark Knights clubhouse with Bones and Bear, listening as their father, the president of the club, discussed club finances. Bear was busy texting, and he was smiling, which meant he was texting Crystal. Bones sat with his long legs stretched out before him, one arm slung over the back of his chair, the other lifting a beer bottle to his lips. His hair was finger combed, his jeans frayed where they rested on his boots, and his black tank top was untucked. There was no hint of Dr. Wayne Whiskey tonight, just good old Bones. Biker, brother, *friend*.

Bear nudged Bullet, pulling him from his thoughts. He flashed a know-it-all grin and said, "You missed a kick-ass ride, and tonight you look like you're just coming off one, which means Finlay's really gotten under your skin."

Bullet grunted. Yeah, she'd gotten under his skin all right, making him think all sorts of crazy shit—like cutting back his hours at the bar. "You could say that."

"How're you going to get her on a bike?" Bear asked.

Bullet glared at him. He didn't have the faintest idea how, or *if* he ever would, and as shocking as that thought was to him, he knew it wouldn't change his feelings for her one bit. She'd done more than get under his skin. She'd crawled into his heart and staked her claim. They'd fallen asleep outside last night, and for the first time since he was a kid, he'd slept all night, and he'd slept *hard*. Not only was that a miracle, but waking up with his girl in his arms and his pup nuzzled by his side was the best feeling in the world. He wanted more lazy Sundays, more nights with her in his arms. He wanted more *Finlay*.

Bones leaned forward, giving them both the stern Pop's-talking-pay-some-respect look they seemed to take turns passing around like biscuits at a dinner table.

The three of them returned their attention to their father. Biggs was the toughest, most intimidating man Bullet had ever known. Even now, with his thick gray beard and inked leatherish skin, he looked like he belonged on a bike, owning the road. His speech was slower since the stroke, the left side of his mouth interminably weighed down. But he still sported the same worn jeans he'd probably had for a decade, Dark Knights shirts, and leathers. He wore the patches with pride and would be buried with them, like his father and his father's father before him. But a cane had become his constant companion, and riding was no longer in the cards for Biggs. Those deficits did nothing to lessen the man he was. They all knew damn well their father would toss that cane aside and jump into the middle of a fight if it was the right thing to do. Bullet wondered what the man he'd patterned himself after practically since birth would think if he knew Bullet was contemplating cutting back his hours to spend more time with Finlay.

The thought came with a noose of guilt. If he wasn't at the bar every night, who would look after Dixie and Red when they waitressed? Jed was a big dude, but he wasn't Bullet.

Biggs cleared his throat, pushed some papers to the side, and said, "We've got a couple of prospects we need to talk abou—"

The doors to the clubhouse flew open, and Finlay burst in, her bright blue eyes smiling as they coasted over the shocked faces of the members. *Aw, fuck.* Bullet pushed to his feet. Her radiant smile lit up the damn clubhouse like a rainbow. All eyes were locked on her as she ran across the room, her blond hair flying out behind her and her sexy little dress flapping against her thighs.

"Bullet—" She grabbed his hand, apparently oblivious to the fact that the room had gone silent, save for a few curious grumbles. "Oh my gosh! Your sister is brilliant! I know how we can help Sarah's family. A *rally*!" She bounced on her toes like Kennedy did when she was excited. Only Finlay looked hot as fuck doing it, and she had no business in the clubhouse, which meant he was about to send that pretty fucking smile packing.

And it was going to suck.

Bear covered his face with his hand, trying to stifle a laugh. Bones grinned up at Bullet, who ground his back teeth as Biggs's fingers curled around his cane and he pushed to his feet. *Goddamn it.*

"Babe, you can't be here." Only men were allowed to attend *church*, which is what they called the Dark Knights meetings. Bullet put a hand on her back to guide her toward the door, but she was too excited, and the light in her eyes kept him from pushing too hard.

"I know you're talking with the guys, but this is super important."

"Not here, lollipop," he said softer, knowing he'd get hell for that later from his brothers, but he couldn't be harsh to Finlay. "Not now. You can't be in here." Had he forgotten to tell her about church? *Shit.*

"I'm so sorry to interrupt." She turned and lifted her hand in a tentative wave around the room. "I know Bullet's been worried, as I have, about the family that suffered that accident the other night. And Dixie mentioned doing a bike rally and fundraiser, so it would actually be good for you guys to all hear this."

She dug around in her bag as the din of the members rose. The looks being tossed their way were more curious—and appreciative of her beauty—than annoyed, which he was thankful for, because he was not thinking rationally, and if anyone pissed him off, God only knew what he'd do. He loved seeing Finlay in the clubhouse, in his *world*, the place where he'd spent more good times than bad for as long as he could remember. His club brothers might not be blood related, but they were just as much family as Bones and Bear were. And now he thought of Finlay that way, too. Knowing it was inappropriate for Finlay to be there during the meeting pissed him off more than her being there did. And that also brought a bucket of guilt.

"I've got notes," she said happily.

Biggs limped over, serious eyes on Bullet.

Seeing his sweet girl flanked by him and his father, the rest of the brotherhood watching, wondering what was going to go down, made Bullet's gut tense up.

"I've got this, Pop," Bullet assured him.

His father's gaze dropped to Finlay, and his bushy mustache twitched as he said, "Finlay, nice to see you again, darlin'."

"Thank you, Mr. Whiskey...*Biggs*. I still have trouble calling you that." She withdrew a notebook from her bag and turned to Biggs with a happy sigh. "I have some great ideas."

Chuckles from Bear and Bones earned harsh glares from Bullet as he took Finlay by the arm and led her toward the door. "Let's go, babe. You can't be in church."

"Church? I thought you were talking with the guys." She spun around, her gaze surfing over the pool table, dartboards, and about thirty sets of eyes watching her. "There are no women here." Her eyes widened. "Why aren't there women here? This isn't *church*." She stepped out of his reach and headed back toward the center of the room.

"Church is what we call our club meetings," Biggs explained. "And I'm sorry, darlin', but it's just us men." Biggs had been raised by a hard-core biker who lived by the old-school mentality of men bearing total responsibility for everything in life—family, the club, business. And part of that lifestyle meant protecting women at all costs, including keeping them buffered from the darker side of things with regard to the club.

"Really? That's so sexist, and archaic." She shot a look at Bear. "Crystal is okay with this?"

Bear nodded, trying—and failing—to school his amused expression.

"Well, that seems weird in this day and age, but okay," she said. "Can I just tell these guys about my ideas?" She flipped open the notebook.

Some of the guys were shifting restlessly in their seats. Bullet took the notebook from her hands and ushered her toward the door. "Sorry, babe. Not here. Not now."

"But—"

He knew he'd catch hell for it, but he lowered his lips to hers, kissing her deeply as he lifted her struggling body into his arms and carried her out the door. When they were a safe distance away from the clubhouse, he broke their connection and set her on her feet.

"Bullet!" She huffed as she smoothed her dress. "I can't believe you did that!"

"You're a baby chick in the middle of a cockfight in there. Sorry, Finlay, but no sweethearts allowed in the club."

"I *heard* that, but why?" She crossed her arms as arrogantly as she'd faced him the first day she'd come into the bar to meet with Dixie, and it *still* did something funky to his gut.

"Because we discuss guy stuff. Club business."

"Guy stuff." She rolled her eyes. "You said your club held *family-friendly* events, and Dixie's in it, right? She's a woman."

*Goddamn it.* "We do have family-friendly events, and the idea of a rally fundraiser is a good one. In fact, we have a charity ride coming up in a few weeks. We can piggyback off that," he said, hoping to distract her from her other questions. He didn't want to get into a pissing match over women's rights or that kind of shit.

"Perfect, and maybe we can end the ride here at the bar and do some sort of a grand opening for the kitchen." She smiled and said, "Now, back to the *boys club*. What do you guys do in there?" Her eyes narrowing accusatorily. "Are there *no* women, or just no 'sweethearts' or girlfriends allowed?"

She was *jealous*? Women didn't get jealous over him. Well, hell, he felt good and bad about that, and it softened him enough to give her the answers she wanted. "No women at all, okay? Not during meetings."

"Whatever. I'm not used to that." She shook her head.

"I'm sure you're not. But when we're not meeting, when there are events, it's cool; you can be there with me. And Dixie isn't a member like the guys are. As the daughter of the president, she's a princess, well respected."

"And Red? Where does she fit in? And Crystal?"

"Red's my father's old lady. She's the queen, babe, wife of the president. And Crystal's Bear's old lady. Everyone respects them."

"Well, you guys have strange ways of doing things. I hope you don't think I'll take a backseat in our relationship, or let you bully me."

He pulled her closer and gazed into her confident, determined eyes. "The only thing you'll take a backseat on is my bike. Hopefully. Eventually. You're *my* queen, Finlay Wilson, and I'll protect you to the ends of the earth. But I need you to respect the brotherhood in the club. Women add a layer of trouble when you have a group of guys. People start hooking up; lines are drawn, loyalties divided. There are reasons for the archaic nature of the brotherhood, and none of those reasons have to do with a lack of respect for women. It's just the opposite."

Her gaze softened, and a small, reluctant smile lifted her lips. "Well, I'd rather be your *queen* than your *old lady*, but I prefer to be called your *girlfriend*."

"I don't care what I call you, lollipop, as long as I know you're mine."

# Chapter Sixteen

BULLET HELD THE pink ribbon he'd tied to the gift he had for Finlay and dragged the cool metal lightly along her bare hip as she slept Thursday morning. Tinkerbell lay with her chin resting on his calf, her dark eyes following his movements along Finlay's waist and up her arm. Finlay nuzzled against Bullet's chest, making a sweet, sleepy noise. Between interviewing candidates for the kitchen staff at the bar, working on menus, and coordinating the fundraiser, which Bullet had gotten unanimous approval for Monday night, she'd been on a dead run. He was thankful she'd been brave enough to overcome her fear of dogs and get to know Tinkerbell, which allowed them to spend the nights together at his place, as they'd done ever since.

He brushed his beard along her shoulder and kissed his way down her breastbone. She rolled onto her back with a heady sigh, eyes still closed as she reached for him. He loved how she always wanted him as much as he wanted her, but this time he gently moved her hands to the side and lowered his mouth over her nipple, teasing her with his tongue. She bowed off the mattress, mewling, her hands fisting in the sheets.

Tinkerbell sat up, and Bullet whispered, "Down, girl."

The pup slinked off the bed, used to the command she'd heard a lot over the past several days. Bullet set the gift on the pillow, so he could give Finlay the attention she deserved. He moved over her, settling his hips between hers, and laced their hands together. He loved that extra connection. A smile lifted her lips and she blinked sleepily. He loved her sleepy smile as much as he adored all her others—the excited one that reached all the way up to her beautiful eyes, the playful ones that were usually accompanied by a shy fluttering of her long lashes, her seductive smile, the one that turned her eyes midnight blue, and one of his favorites, her sated, happy smile, which she probably didn't realize she made. He saw that one when she was curled up in his arms, her body flushed and warm, still damp from their lovemaking. That was the sweetest smile of all. The one that told him that she was falling for him just as deeply as he was falling for her. The smile that said, *I'm yours. Please don't let me go.*

He knew he never would.

"Mm," she said sleepily. "I do like my Bullet in the morning."

He brushed the head of his cock against her center, and she spread her legs wider. "I seem to remember you liking me in the middle of the night, too."

He dipped his head and glided his tongue over her taut nipple again. When she arched up, he moved to the other one, teasing her with light flicks of his tongue, then circling the tip until she was panting. Her hips rose off the bed, and he pressed the base of his cock against her slick heat. He took one nipple between his teeth and tugged.

"*Oh*—" She whimpered, and he did it again.

With each tug she grew wetter, and her hips rocked faster.

Each time they made love was a new adventure born from his dire need to be closer to her, to have *more* of her. And *more* came in nips, invasions of his tongue and fingers, tugs on her hair, and dirty talk. He wasn't into restraints or other kinky shit, like some guys he knew were, and before Finlay, he'd never given two thoughts to what he liked sexually. Sex was always good, hard, *complete*. A much-needed release. But with Finlay, he wanted to touch *all* of her, to *hear* how much she wanted him and in what ways. Not because he got off on control, but because the trust and emotions they shared in those moments did him in. He craved those things more than the act of sex itself.

He sealed his lips over her nipple and sucked *hard*.

Her entire body craned up. "*Bullet—*"

"Sorry, babe. Too hard?"

She shook her head vehemently, and that seductive smile he loved so much sent rivers of heat washing through him.

"Too *good*," she whispered.

"God, lollipop, you destroy me." He traced the swell of her lower lip with his tongue. "Tell me what you want, babe."

"You," she said breathlessly.

He pumped his hips, pushing his cock along her slick heat, covering his balls with her wetness, thrusting again and again, until he was drenched in her arousal from base to tip and she was trembling.

"Want my cock?" he said against her neck. "Or…" He reached between her legs and teased her with his fingers. She was so wet, he couldn't resist pushing his fingers into her tight heat. He sealed his mouth over hers in a rough kiss as she rode his hand, their other hands tightly laced. She reached between them and fisted his slick cock. He pumped his hips, fucking her hand as he fucked her with his fingers. God, she knew just how tight to hold him, just how fast to stroke, and she did this thing with her thumb over the head that drove him out of his fucking mind.

She moaned into his mouth, her legs flexing beneath him, her sex constricting around his fingers, and he intensified their kiss. He found that spot that made her moan and moved his thumb over her clit, applying just enough pressure to earn a full-body shudder. He quickened his efforts, loving her faster, kissing her deeper, until long, low moans flew from her lungs into his, and she bucked and rocked, squeezing his cock like a vise.

He tore his mouth away and ground out, "You're going to make me come *on* you instead of *in* you if you don't stop."

She blinked up at him. He knew dirty talk was hard for her, and when she stroked him faster, the love in her eyes was the only response he needed. Their mouths came together like a gust of wind, insistent and gentle at once. His emotions reeled as he loved her with his whole body. Their tongues tangled, hands joined as he took her up, up, *up* and she stroked him toward the edge. Blood pounded in his ears, their hearts slamming to their own frantic rhythm, as they both cried out, succumbing to soul-drenching waves of passion.

He collapsed over her, the proof of their love sticky and warm between them as he showered her with kisses. "I need more of you, Fins."

"More?" she panted out. "You have all of me."

"Then I want you to have more of me." He reached for the pink ribbon and dangled her gift between his finger and thumb.

"A key?" Her eyes widened. "Is that to your house?"

He pressed a kiss to her lips. "I don't want to have to call you when I'm finally off work and worry about you driving over." He worked from noon to midnight four days a week, four to twelve on Thursdays, and Mondays from noon until eight, which allowed him to attend *church*.

"I don't mind."

"I know you don't, but I do, babe. You're doing twice as much work with the fundraiser and the expansion of the bar. You need your rest, and part of resting is chilling out, not waiting around for a phone call and then driving across town in the middle of the night." They'd talked about him picking up Tinkerbell after work and coming over, since he couldn't leave Tinkerbell overnight, but that would delay his arrival for at least half an hour, and neither of them had wanted to lose that time together.

She reached up and took the key chain from his hand. "You're so thoughtful, but how will I know you want me here if you don't text or call? I don't want to feel like I'm imposing on your alone time."

"There won't be a time I don't want you here."

She glanced at the key again, looking more closely at the two charms hanging from the key ring. "The Dark Knights emblem? But girls can't be members, and I don't even ride a motorcycle."

"You haven't ridden *yet*," he said, and kissed her again. "You can't be a member, but now everyone will know you belong to one."

"Ah, it's an *ownership* thing," she said with a more serious expression.

"No." *It's a love thing.*

One step at a time.

"It's a protection thing. No one will mess with you, knowing you're involved with a Dark Knight."

"No one messes with me anyway," she said sassily, and then her gaze heated up a notch and she said, "But I'll carry this proudly, as a symbol that I'm yours."

"Good, because I got myself something, too." He reached over to the bedside table and snagged his keys. He lifted the charm he'd bought when he'd had her key made, and laughter fell from her lips.

"A lollipop!"

"You're my sugar rush, baby." As he said the words, he realized they didn't even come close to how important she'd become to him. "You'll always be my sugar rush, but you're so much more. You calm my ghosts enough for me to fall asleep and *stay* asleep, which I can't remember ever doing. You're not only my lover"—he kissed her cheek—"my friend"—he kissed the top of her nose—"and my secret keeper, but you've become an extension of me, always wanting to know more about me, to understand the whys and hows of my thoughts and actions." He touched his forehead to hers and said, "I never knew I was capable of opening up the way I do with you, and I never imagined wanting as much companionship and intimacy as we have, but now I can't imagine going to sleep or waking up without you, Fin. You're my angel, the salve to my wounds. You're my other half I never knew I was missing."

With tears in her eyes, she wound her arms around his neck, the light in those tears matching the light in his heart. As their mouths came together, Tinkerbell leapt onto the bed and barked, and they both smiled into the kiss. Tinkerbell stretched her paws out and lowered her belly to the mattress, inching up beside them until her big body was parallel to theirs. She licked Finlay's cheek, and with a loud, contented sigh, as if they'd righted everything in her world, she rested her chin on her paws and closed her eyes.

He couldn't have expressed it better himself.

CROW HAD FINISHED the renovations at Whiskey's, and the kitchen flowed as wonderfully as Finlay had envisioned it would. She was thrilled to give it a trial run that night. She made a plethora of finger foods, tweaking her best recipes to come up with unique menu ideas for the bar. When she'd arrived earlier in the afternoon, she'd let the customers know there was going to be a tasting session later that evening. She assumed a few people might stick around for it, and she was hoping to discuss the fundraiser with Red and the girls anyway, so staying at the bar would kill two birds with one stone. But word had spread about Finlay's delicious treats, and the place was packed. Even Bones, Bear, and Biggs had shown up for the impromptu event, and it looked as though chatting about the fundraiser would have to wait.

Chicki Redmond sidled up to Finlay by the buffet table. She was Bud's wife. Bud had been a member of the Dark Knights forever, and he was also co-owner of the Snake Pit. "Do you need some help, hon?" She gathered discarded napkins with a *tsk*.

"No. It's okay. I've got it."

Chicki was around Red's age, with beautiful olive skin and chocolate-brown eyes. She wore her dark hair pulled back in a severe bun, and her makeup was done to perfection. According to Red, Chicki was a beautician and had taught half of the women in Peaceful Harbor how to do their makeup. Her black leather pants looked painted on, and her heels were higher than any Finlay had ever worn. On anyone else, the whole look might appear harsh, but Chicki looked elegant, like a model, and she swore like a sailor, a combination that was as foreign to Finlay as it was entertaining. She found everything about Chicki Redmond quite appealing.

"These fuckers think their mothers work here," Chicki said as she looked over the discarded napkins on the table. "What the hell is this? You're not their maid."

Before Finlay could respond, Chicki turned toward the packed bar and clapped her hands. The din of the bar quieted, and she held up the pile of dirty napkins. "Okay, animals, on your feet. This nice young lady is feeding you for free. She is not your maid and she is not your mother. Let's go."

With groans and mumbled apologies, every man in the place began picking up empty dishes and discarded plates and napkins.

Chicki made a show of tossing the napkins in the trash and said, "That, my dear, is how it's done around here."

Dixie sauntered over, balancing a tray of glasses in her right hand as she swiped an empty glass from a table with her left. "Nice, Chicki. Can we hire you?"

"Not on your life," Chicki said. "I did my time at the Snake Pit. A decade, to be exact. Now, give me some grandbabies to watch like Babs, and I'm there." Babs was Bud's brother Viper's wife. She'd recently started babysitting for Kennedy and Lincoln, and the kids called her *Nana Babs*.

Dixie scoffed. "With my brothers around, I can't get close enough to a man for a kiss, much less baby making."

Dixie headed into the kitchen, and Finlay took advantage of the opening to ask about their business. "I've heard good things about the Snake Pit. It's more upscale than here, I know, but what type of foods do you serve there?"

Chicki's eyes narrowed. "Checking out the competition, little miss?"

"No. I, um…"

Chicki crossed her arms, and a slow smile lifted her lips. She put an arm around Finlay and said, "It's okay. Bullet told me he was going to bring you down to compare menus."

She felt her cheeks flush, wishing she had the kind of constitution that would allow her to hide her embarrassment, like Penny or Isabel. They were unflappable. "I'm sorry, yes, that's true, but in a friendly way."

"Honey, there's no competition. We're all family, and now that you're with Bullet, you're family, too. You can come down and get a tour of the kitchen, meet the staff, whatever you'd like. Dark Knights families stick together."

Chicki headed over to the pool table, where several of the club members' wives were gathered. Just a few weeks ago, Finlay had wondered why anyone would want to be involved in a motorcycle club, and Monday night, when she'd learned the women weren't allowed at the meetings, she'd questioned it again. But as she looked around the bar, she took in Tru and Gemma dancing beside Bear and Crystal. Biggs sat at a table with a group of men, each of whom wore Dark Knights patches, including the high school principal. Penny stood at the bar beside Tru's brother, Quincy. Quincy hadn't taken his eyes off her since he arrived. Beside him, two other women who she'd seen arrive with two members she recognized from the clubhouse were leaning in to hear something Jed was saying from the other side of the bar. Bones approached, wearing a leather jacket with the Dark Knights emblem on the back. He put an arm around Quincy and Penny, weaseling right between them. Her gaze shifted to Bullet, who was pushing two drinks across the other end of the bar to a couple of bearded, tattooed guys who were also wearing Dark Knights shirts—men she once might have overlooked, or dismissed as *trouble*. One of them did a fist bump with Bullet, and she saw deep friendships and lasting connections. Now she understood what it really meant to be a member of the Dark Knights.

She barely had time to process her thoughts before remembering she'd been on a mission to refill the food trays. She stacked the empties and carried them into the kitchen and set to work preparing the next round of food for the tasting session. A short while later she was concocting what were quickly becoming known as her specialty—sliders topped with her special Whiskey sauce and coleslaw and sides of bourbon fries—when Red breezed through the kitchen doors.

"How're you holding up, sweetie?" Red set an empty tray down on the counter beside Finlay.

Finlay had learned a great deal about the spunky, take-no-guff redhead since Monday night. Red was no *queen*, that was for sure. She was not afraid to get her hands dirty. It was clear that she was the cog in the wheel that held the Whiskey family, and the club, together. She nagged and pushed when people needed it, and Finlay had quickly realized that Red was the one who coordinated most of the Dark Knights family-friendly events.

She looked up from the sliders she was preparing and smiled. "I'm good. Thanks for asking, but this is fun for me. I can't believe how many people showed up. Thank goodness Jed is here to help with the bar. I'm starting to wonder if having two cooks on staff is going to be enough. We've been interviewing with the thought of hiring two for different shifts. But based on tonight's turnout, I don't think it's going to be enough."

Red helped Finlay finish filling one tray with sliders and fries and another with sandwiches. "Well, that says something about your cooking, doesn't it?"

"I think it says more about Whiskey's reputation and what this place and your family mean to all those people out there. But I am really worried about staffing. You and Dixie can't waitress twelve hours a day, and Dixie has found something wrong with every candidate I've brought in to cook." She hadn't realized how much this was worrying her until just then. "I thought you guys could do this on a smaller scale, but I'm not so sure."

Red set a hand on her hip with an unsurprised look in her eyes. "I hear you on that, sweetheart. I have to believe that the right thing for Whiskey's will show itself at some point. Between the fundraiser and the expansion, there's a lot on our plates. Dixie is either not thinking clearly, or thinking more clearly than ever. Time will tell." She shrugged. "We have a family meeting here Sunday to discuss the hiring. Can you be there?"

"I have a catering job Sunday midmorning, but I'll be here in the morning. Bullet said it would be okay for me to use the kitchen to prepare for the event. Do you mind?"

"Not at all. Our kitchen is your kitchen."

"Thank you. But about the staffing, I'm worried that this might turn out to be more than you guys bargained for. Bullet already works more than sixty hours a week, and Jed isn't full-time. You might need to beef up the bar staff, too."

Red waved a hand dismissively, as if none of that was a big deal. "Bullet could have handled tonight on his own," Red said with pride. "He's run this place for so many years now, he could do it in his sleep."

Finlay didn't understand why Red wasn't more concerned and made a mental note to bring her worries up again on Sunday.

They fell silent as they loaded up the trays. Red lifted her gaze, meeting Finlay's, and said, "Speaking of sleep, my boy seems far less restless than he ever has, and my heart tells me that's because of you."

Finlay warmed, knowing Red had noticed the difference in Bullet, too. She turned toward the other counter to prepare the garnishes. "We talk a lot. I think it's helped to get things off his chest."

"Brandon talking," Red said with disbelief. "My word, girl, what have you done?"

Finlay turned at the somber sound of her voice and was shocked to be met with teary eyes. "Um…Is there something I don't know about? Should he *not* talk about things? He seemed to want to."

Red's hand covered her chest as she blinked several times. She looked up at the ceiling and used a napkin to carefully dab at her eyes, somehow managing not to smear her dark eyeliner. "It's good, honey. So very good." She paused, and her brow furrowed, and then she sighed and said, "My boy is so sensitive. He's struggled his whole life, trying to keep everyone safe, and in doing so, he's turned himself into some sort of…"

"Secret keeper?" Finlay offered. "I've been thinking about that. He hasn't yet shared with me the stories behind his tattoos, but I know they have important meanings. It's like he takes everyone else's pain and doesn't just try to eradicate it, but holds on to a piece of it."

"*Secret keeper*," Red said softly. "I couldn't have defined him better myself. My boys are all so different. Bobby—*Bear*—wears his emotions on his sleeve, while Wayne—*Bones*—has always been able to distance himself from people just enough to see them clearly and evaluate his feelings without getting too involved. But Brandon—*your* Bullet—he struggles with it all. As a boy, if one of the kids got in trouble, he would take the blame, and he wasn't sneaky about it. Imagine trying to keep a straight face when he told me he scratched 'Wayne Rules' into the kitchen table, or when I followed a blue paint trail of Bobby's four-year-old footprints from the patio, up the carpeted stairs, into his bedroom, and back down the rear steps to the utility room, where I found Bobby, his feet stained from the paint they'd washed off and Brandon painting his own feet blue."

Finlay laughed and covered her mouth. "I'm sorry, but I can *so* see him doing that."

"Oh, it gets better, hon. You couldn't argue with Brandon. When he took the blame, it was as if he believed it to his very soul. We tried to punish him for lying, but come on. He lied to protect his brothers. In the end, we'd punish him for what he didn't do, with the hopes the others would learn that there were ramifications."

"And did they?" she asked, unable to stop smiling as she pictured Bullet—her Bullet—painting his feet to save Bear.

"I don't know if it helped, but Brandon then took it upon himself to teach the younger ones right from wrong. I heard him talking to Bobby later that afternoon, and I'll never forget how much he reminded me of my Biggs as he told him about respecting property and how lying was wrong. Bobby asked him why *he'd* lied, and his answers told me everything I ever needed to know about my eldest son. He said, 'Because Papa taught me to always do the right thing. And protecting you is the right thing.' My heart broke *and* grew that afternoon, which I never knew was possible until I had children."

Finlay had experienced her heart breaking and growing at once the first night Bullet had opened up to her, when she'd seen his tattoos, and it had happened several times since. She wanted to share that with Red, but those moments seemed too intimate to reveal.

"We should take these out there before there's a rebellion on our hands." Red picked up a tray and grabbed a handful of napkins. "You already have quite a fan club."

"My mom used to say, if you want to have a happy crowd, all you have to do is feed them and smile." Finlay picked up a tray, smiling as she thought of her mother. She'd told Red about losing her father and her mother moving away, and now, as she picked up a tray, she realized why she wanted to share her thoughts with Red. Red had a way of making people feel special, the same way Finlay's mother did.

Red pushed open the door with her hip and held it for Finlay to pass through.

"I don't think that heart phenomenon is reserved for parenthood," Finlay said as they left the kitchen. "I think it's just reserved for those you care deeply about."

Red leaned in close as they approached the table they'd set up for the buffet-style tasting and said, "Thank you."

"For what?"

Red motioned toward the bar. "Nothing makes a mother happier than seeing her child leading with his heart."

Bullet's gaze was locked on Finlay, and he had what could only be described as a goofy smile on his lips. Finlay's insides melted. She didn't think it was possible for Bullet to do anything that could even be mistaken as goofy, but that I'm-so-*gone*-over-you smile proved her wrong. And *goofy* had never looked so *hot*.

AS THE EVENING progressed, Bullet watched his beautiful girl work the crowd, and a few things became clear to him. That pang of jealousy he felt every time she smiled at another guy needed to be dealt with. No matter how much he'd like to have her all to himself, Finlay Wilson was a people person, and he'd never want to steal that joy from her. Accepting the latter helped him with the former. He knew he'd never slay the green-eyed monster, even though he had never believed it really existed until Finlay came into his life. But he'd dealt with enough painful situations to know this one was a different type of pain. A *good* pain. He looked down at the tattooed letters on his fingers, each one gracing a knuckle—Y-O-U-'R-E on his left hand and A-L-I-V-E on his right—written upside down, because the message wasn't meant for anyone other than himself. He'd thought he'd always need that reminder to push past the pain of knowing he'd left a piece of himself on the battlefield, but now that he'd found Finlay, he didn't need words to move past it. She lit up parts of him he'd thought hadn't existed.

His father's large hands appeared on the bar across from his. The hands that had once carried him across streets, taught him to toss a ball, ride a bicycle, and later, ride motorcycles. The hands that had taught him the importance of embracing and the strength of a handshake. The hands that were now wrinkled and covered with age spots and had never once met his flesh in a slap or a spanking—though Bullet knew there were plenty of times he deserved it. But that wasn't the way Biggs worked. No, lessons were hands- or eyes-on. How many times had his father lifted a chin in the direction of a man saying nasty things to a woman and then pointed a finger at Bullet and said, *Men don't need to demean to make a point. You got a beef with a woman, you sit your ass down and talk eye-to-eye. Hear what she has to say. Got it? A good percentage of the time, she's gonna be right. And when she's not, she deserves your respect for speaking her mind.* Harsher lessons came when Biggs would drag him out of bed to drive a drunk customer home, or tell him to get his ass on his bike and meet the Knights at some address in town, where they were taking a stance against one form of trouble or another.

Bullet met his father's serious eyes, and he wondered how he could have ever been resentful of the man who had not only given him life, but had tried his damnedest to teach him right from wrong.

"Your little filly is quite the salesgirl," Biggs said slowly. He nodded toward Finlay, who was sitting at a table with Dixie, Gemma, Crystal, and Penny, while Red, Chicki, and two other club members' wives leaned over the girls' shoulders. They'd been discussing the fundraiser ever since the crowd had thinned. "She talked with all the members tonight, got the business owners to agree to hold some sort of raffle for the Beckleys. Digger's auctioning off twelve hours of his own time, equipment included. And Bud's offering up a bouquet delivery a month for a full year. You mind gettin' me a beer?"

"Sure, Pop."

As Bullet filled a frosty mug, Biggs continued telling him what Finlay had accomplished.

"Butcher's raffling off a side of beef. Heck, son, she used that sweet smile of hers to convince Rebel and two other firemen to get into a dunk tank, which Crow's going to build. She's got ticket sellers lined up and everything. And your gal's not stopping there. She and the girls have plans to visit local businesses and get them in on it. It's liable to be the biggest event to hit Peaceful Harbor in years."

"She's pretty amazing," Bullet said proudly.

His father lifted his beer in a toast and said, "A miracle worker if you ask me. We haven't been this busy in years."

"People like to eat."

Biggs's mustache twitched as a crooked smile appeared on his face. "They say the way to a man's heart is through his stomach. You and I both know that's not true. We got much needier parts than our stomachs." He took a swig of his beer.

Bullet chuckled. Biggs had never been one to mince words.

"Nope," his father said. "It's not the food that brought everyone here tonight. That helped, of course. Finlay can cook like nobody's business. But word's gotten around that Whiskey's has a new gal on board, and she's got a knack for making every single customer feel special."

"Pop, she's not here for good. You know that, right?"

His father took another pull on his beer, and his expression turned serious again. "I'm aware. But I'm thinkin' you probably ought to fix that."

Bullet shook his head and crossed his arms, steeling himself for an internal battle. "My girl's not going to spend her nights in a bar." He wanted Finlay where he was every minute of the day, but no matter how much he wanted that, he knew it wasn't best for her. She had dreams of expanding her catering business, and she hadn't come to Peaceful Harbor to give those dreams up.

"She's got a catering business to get off the ground. Hell, Pop. We're coming in Sunday so she can use the kitchen to get ready for an event."

"You're coming Sunday? Not going riding with your brothers?" Biggs wrapped his fingers around the head of his cane and pushed to his feet.

"Maybe while she's at the event, but Sunday's my only day off. If she's here, I'm here."

His father's gaze drifted down Bullet's torso to his hands. "Sometimes words take on new meanings and what seemed like a penance turns into a celebration." He motioned for Bullet to reach across the bar, and he gave him an awkward one-armed hug. "I love you, boy, and if I don't tell you enough, I'm damn proud of you. Always have been."

Bullet cleared his throat in an effort to quell the surge of emotions his father's praise unleashed. He watched Biggs limp over to Red and pull her into his arms. He must have said something charming because his mother's gaze softened, and she touched his cheek before pressing her lips to his. Bullet looked away, his eyes immediately finding his girl, and his father's words pushed through his mind. *Sometimes words take on new meanings and what seemed like a penance turns into a celebration.*

He had reason to celebrate life all right, and she was sitting across the room holding up her phone. She and the girls were talking on a video call.

As quickly as his father's words had come back to him, they were drowned out by another thought. *She's not here for good. You know that, right…? I'm aware. But I'm thinkin' you probably ought to fix that.*

Maybe his father wasn't referencing the tattoos on his fingers after all.

Finlay's eyes shifted, as if she felt the weight of his stare, and she waved him over. "Bullet! We want to ask you something!"

He headed over to the table and ran his fingers through her hair. "What's up, lollipop?"

"Lollipop!" came from the phone with a snort.

He recognized the voice as Finlay's mouthy friend, Isabel. They talked often, and he liked her; she was a firecracker.

"How many licks does it take to get to *Fin's* sweet cent—"

"Izzy!" Finlay cut her off, earning giggles from the peanut gallery.

*Christ.* He didn't want to get involved in this hen party. He started walking away, and Finlay grabbed the back of his shirt.

"Wait, please?" She glared at Isabel. "She'll behave. She's just had too much wine to drink."

Isabel held up an empty wineglass. "That might be true, but I'd say it anyway, because it's funny."

"How about we *not* talk about my girl's body parts." He glanced at Finlay, who was smiling so brightly, he couldn't help but smile, too. "What's up, angel?"

"We were just thinking. If we bring on kitchen staff, we might need another bartender and a waitress, and we were thinking about hiring Izzy. She could work for my catering company part-time, and work here part-time."

His mind selfishly went to cutting back his hours. He looked at Dixie, then at his mother, and that guilt noose he sported tightened again. He needed a fucking clone to protect the people he loved, so he could spend more time with the one he loved most.

"Why don't we discuss it Sunday?" Red suggested.

*Sunday. My only day off, and I'm spending most of it without Finlay.*

Sunday was going to fucking suck.

# Chapter Seventeen

SUNDAY BLEW IN with a sudden drop in temperature and fierce wind. Finlay had lived in Boston for so long, she'd forgotten how Maryland could be hot as Hades one day and sweater weather the next. As much as she was looking forward to catering the baby shower, she really wanted to curl up on the couch with Bullet, shut out the rest of the world, and disappear into him for an entire day. Since that wasn't an option, she hung up her raincoat, slipped one of her aprons over her long-sleeved gray-and-white minidress, and began unpacking the groceries as Bullet carried them into the kitchen of Whiskey Bro's. His family hadn't arrived yet, and she hoped to get most of her baking done before their family meeting.

Bullet was supposed to go on a ride with his brothers after-ward. She had a feeling he needed it, because he'd been a little edgier than normal this week, waking earlier and irritated about work. The only time he seemed completely at peace was in the mornings. He didn't leave for work until eleven, which gave them several uninterrupted hours together. When he came home at night, once she was in his arms, their worlds came back together like a long-overdue sigh, draining the tension from his body and settling all the longing that had built up inside her all day.

"Will you still go on your ride in this weather?" she asked as she laid out the groceries and supplies. They'd gone down to the Snake Pit yesterday before Bullet had gone to work. As Chicki had promised, they'd gotten a tour of the kitchen, which was three times the size of Whiskey's, and she'd talked with the chef about their menus. By the time they left, several guys had asked when he was going to ride with them again, and he'd been vague with his answers.

"If it clears up." Bullet shrugged off his leather jacket and tossed it on a chair. His tattoos bled out from under the sleeves of his faded black T-shirt. He pushed a hand through his thick hair and shook off the rainwater. A chain hung from his belt loop to his back pocket, making it almost look as if he'd accessorized with his silver rings.

The thought of her man accessorizing gave Finlay a tickle. Bullet's wardrobe consisted of dark jeans, faded T-shirts, and a host of leather bracelets and wrist cuffs. He always wore two or three skull or hammered metal rings, but she knew it had nothing to do with aesthetics. She was sure they all had meanings behind them, because one thing she'd learned about Bullet was that everything he added to his body was done purposefully.

He moved behind her and wrapped his arms around her waist. He was always doing that, touching, kissing, wanting more of her. And oh, how she always wanted to touch him, too!

"You said this baby shower will go on until two or three? If I ride, I'll make sure I'm back by then."

"Don't cut your ride short. You don't need to rework your life around me. I'll be available when you get back. Just enjoy yourself, and your brothers." She turned in his arms, and the fluttery sensation in her stomach she'd come to expect when they were close climbed into her chest. She reveled in that feeling.

"I've enjoyed myself and my brothers for thirty-plus years." He lowered his lips to hers, taking her in a delicious kiss that brought her up on her toes. He rubbed his beard along her cheek and said, "I love when you do that."

"Get hot and bothered?" she teased.

"Go up on your toes, like you can't get enough of me."

She'd never needed anyone before, but the closer she and Bullet became, the more she realized she'd needed him all along. She'd buried herself so deeply in work for the past several years, she hadn't realized how much emptiness she'd been harboring. Bullet, and even Tinkerbell, completed her in ways no one and nothing ever had. Whether they were taking walks or Bullet was working on one of his bikes in the garage while she sat nearby preparing menus and kitchen schedules, or if they were lying in each other's arms beneath the stars, which she didn't think they'd be able to do too much longer, as fall was moving in, the three of them were together, and they were happy.

*We're putting down roots.*

"I will never get enough of you." She pulled him down for another kiss.

A little more than an hour later, Dixie came in through the back door, her fiery hair whipping around her face from the wind. Finlay looked over her shoulder as she put the wild king salmon, salads, seared spinach, and coriander yogurt sauce in the fridge.

"Wow. I half expected the Wicked Witch of the West to blow in." Dixie peeled off her jacket and hung it on a hook by the door. "It's so windy out there. I think we should have indoor options for the fundraiser, just in case."

"I was hoping it would die down," Finlay said as she began decorating the frosted sugar-cookie pizza with slices of strawberries and kiwis.

Dixie eyed the pink and blue cupcakes in a catering box on the counter and the Oreo-rattle pops and peanut-shaped tarts cooling on racks by the sink where Bullet was peeling hardboiled eggs. She put a hand on Bullet's shoulder and said, "You're so domestic, I almost didn't recognize you."

"Finlay bribed me with sex." He winked at Finlay.

"I did not!" She felt her cheeks burning. After Bullet had set her on the counter and tried to eat *her* for brunch, she'd promised to *blow his whistle* later if he let her get her cooking done. She couldn't very well attend the event reeking of sex. Even though she'd learned her lesson when Bullet went with her *anywhere* and always carried extra panties. Sometimes that was enough, but when he *devoured* her, she got so hot and bothered, she needed a full-on shower afterward—a *cold* one, or the aftershocks alone nearly made her come again.

The doors to the bar opened, and Bones strutted in wearing his black leather jacket, a bike helmet in his hand, and the rest of his family on his heels. "Damn, it's nasty out there. But it sure smells good in here."

Bones set his helmet down and put his arm around Finlay as she prepared the frosting for the baby bundles, the peanutshaped tarts she'd decorate to look like swaddled babies. Half the finished cookies would be blue, and half pink, with chocolate chips for eyes.

"What've you done with my brother? Soon he'll be wearing a dress and an apron."

Bullet scowled.

Finlay whispered, "I bribed him with sex."

Bones pushed Bullet away from the sink. "Give me the damn eggs."

Bullet grabbed him by the back of his collar and hauled him away from the sink with a look so dark Finlay feared she'd caused real trouble.

Bones threw his arms up in the air and laughed. "I'm kidding, bro." He shoved Bullet's shoulder so hard Bullet released him, still glowering.

"Bones has a death wish." Bear sank down to a chair at the table.

Dixie laughed as she headed toward the door to the bar. "I'm going to get the ledgers from the office. Be right back."

Red sidled up to Finlay and said, "There are three things you don't kid about in our world. Women, bikes, and family."

"I didn't mean to cause trouble," Finlay said. "It was a joke."

"You didn't cause trouble, honey," Red assured her. "Bones did. He knows Bullet's been acting like he's got a gorilla on his back lately."

Finlay made a mental note not to step out of her comfort zone and tease like that again. She was surprised Red had noticed Bullet's edginess, and she wondered if she had any clue as to what was behind it. Finlay had tried asking Bullet, but he'd brushed her off each time, changing the subject.

Biggs sat beside Bear and pointed his cane at Bones. "Cut the shit. One day Bullet's going to let loose on you and you're going to be sorry."

Guilt speared through Finlay. She knew Bullet and Bones had a special connection, and she'd hate to mess that up.

Bullet's lips tipped up and he held a fist out to Bones, who tapped it with his own.

Relief swept through her. She moved a tray of cookies to the counter, distracting herself by spreading pink frosting over the lower half of each cookie and creating tiny pink bows at the top, making the baby bundles.

Bullet wiped his hands on a towel. "Sorry, man," he said to Bones.

"No worries." Bones leaned against the counter. "The weather's supposed to clear up by noon. You coming with us?"

Bullet nodded. "For a few hours."

Dixie returned with the ledgers, and Bear said, "Let's get this show on the road. Dix?"

An uneasy look passed over Dixie's face. She crossed her arms, uncrossed them, then crossed them again. Finlay waited for an explanation, as Dixie had nixed every candidate she'd interviewed for the cook positions, having found something *off* about each applicant.

"We haven't filled the positions yet," Dixie explained. "Fin spent all last week interviewing, and the applicants are all qualified. But they just didn't feel right. I'm not sure about hiring a stranger."

"You're the one who wanted this," Bullet reminded her.

The gruffness of Bullet's comment rattled Finlay. She'd almost forgotten he hadn't wanted her to work there in the first place, much less to expand the bar.

She concentrated on adding the chocolate-chip eyes to the cookies.

"I know, and, Dad, I know you want the expansion so we have a legacy to carry on for generations, but did you see how busy we were the other night when Finlay did the tasting session?"

"Sure did," Biggs said. "Finlay's got quite a reputation around here."

"We're not just looking at hiring a cook and a dishwasher anymore." Dixie looked pleadingly at Finlay, and understanding finally dawned on her.

Dixie was as worried about the staffing as she was.

Finlay wiped her hands on a towel and said, "She's right. The turnout the other night concerned me, too. It was wonderful, but worrisome."

Bullet reached for her, and when she went to him, his arm circled her waist. She loved his support and wasn't sure if he'd noticed she was nervous, or if he just wanted to hold her, but she sensed it was both.

"We started out looking for two part-time cooks and dish-washers so we could offer shifts, but based on the turnout the other night, which had zero publicity, I think you're looking at a much bigger endeavor than you initially wanted." She felt like she'd somehow let them down, even though she knew this was business, and she'd done nothing more than evaluate their needs.

"I told you I thought this was a bad idea," Bullet said.

Biggs held up his hand, silencing him. "Let's hear what Finlay has to say."

She looked apologetically at Bullet.

He kissed her temple and said, "You're good, lollipop. Go ahead," and she breathed a little easier.

"My recommendation is to decide what you really want out of this expansion. I believe the goal was to increase profits, which I think you can achieve on a large or small scale, depending on what you want. Jed's only part-time, and Bullet already works more than sixty hours a week. Dixie and Red can't be expected to waitress full-time seven days a week. So if you offer food all day, then you'll probably need at least two more waitresses, another full-time bartender, two full-time cooks so they're not working more than forty hours a week, and then you still need to hire the dishwashers. And if you go that route, it's clear you'll need a manager as well, unless Bullet takes that over. Dixie is fully qualified, of course, but she's managing the auto shop, waitressing here, and doing the books. You'll need someone to handle schedules, and I don't know if you've thought this far ahead, but full-time employees should have health and vacation benefits, too."

Bullet and Bear shook their heads.

"That sounds about right," Red said.

"That's what worries me," Dixie explained. "Then our family business will turn into something that's so much bigger, it's not going to feel the same. I think Bullet was right about that."

"There is another option," Finlay said. "You could offer food only for lunch, for example. Then you'd need a cook, a waitress, and a dishwasher for, say noon to three, or similar hours. Twenty hours a week should do it. You'd still want a backup cook, I think, just in case that employee got sick or hurt, or went on vacation. Or you could offer only dinner, but dinner tends to be busier, in my experience, and would probably require more bartending staff."

"Finlay, what would you prefer, if you were working here? What hours?" Biggs asked.

"Me? Well, I think you might find employees eager to work during the day rather than at night, so probably lunchtime."

Bullet tightened his hold on her. "She didn't move back here to work at the bar."

"He's not asking me to work here," she said. "But I do enjoy being here. I love the people, and I get more time with you and your family. I think it's a great place to work. It's friendly, and sure, the crowd is rougher than what I'm used to, but they're kind and funny, and—"

"Stay," Biggs said.

Finlay startled. "Excuse me?"

Biggs shrugged. "You're already here. You know the customers. You're the one coming up with the menus. You're with our boy, like family. Stay. Work whatever hours you want."

"Work here?" Her mind zoomed through the idea. Working with Bullet was wonderful, and she'd meant all the things she'd said about enjoying the people. If she worked part-time, she could still do catering. She looked up at Bullet, who was frowning, and her stomach knotted up. "I...I don't know if that's a good idea. I haven't had time to find a place to rent for my catering company. That'll probably take me a while, so I really couldn't commit..."

"I don't want Finlay giving up catering, and she's not working nights at *any* bar," Bullet said. He looked at his watch and whispered, "You've got to get finished, baby. You have to leave soon."

How could she have gotten so sidetracked? Her head was spinning with the offer, and with Bullet's comments. He worked nights. Why didn't he want her there?

"I'm sorry, but I really do have to finish up," she said to Biggs, and went back to frosting the other tray of cookies. She mentally walked through the steps of turning the hard-boiled eggs into baby carriages, using deviled-egg mixture for the blankets and sausage slices for the baby's faces, with chocolate sprinkles for the eyes. She could get it done in twenty minutes if she hurried.

"Let me help." Red went to the sink. "What can I do with the eggs?"

"Thank you. If you can cut them into halves and remove the yolk, I can make the deviled-egg mixture and then slice those sausages." She pointed to a tray of sausages.

"I've got the sausages," Dixie said, and grabbed a knife.

"Thank you," Finlay said.

"Finlay, we don't want you giving up catering, either," Biggs said. "You can use this kitchen for your catering business, and as I said, work whatever hours you'd like."

Her eyes nearly bugged out of her head as she turned to face them again. Dixie nodded, smiling like it was the greatest idea ever. Bear and Bones were talking in hushed voices, but their agreement was obvious. Her mind reeled with possibilities.

"I..." She looked at Bullet, but couldn't read his expression. "What do you think?"

He slid an arm around her shoulder, pulled her ear beside his mouth, and whispered, "No nights, lollipop. Please leave them open for us. And I don't want you giving up your catering job. You love it too much."

Her heart swelled. "But you're okay with it otherwise?"

He nodded and pressed a kiss to her cheek. "I'm okay with whatever you want."

"Really?" she asked softly. "This is your place, and I know you didn't want me here at first."

"I want you with me every second, baby."

"What do you say?" Biggs asked.

Her heart was beating so fast. Bullet wanted to be with her, and they were offering her so much all at once. She forced herself to rein in her spinning emotions and think rationally.

"It could be complicated," she finally answered. "I wouldn't want to let you guys down, but if I were the only cook, what if I got sick? What if I got hired to cater an afternoon event that was too good to pass up? It could put us all in an uncomfortable position."

Red's hand stilled over the cutting board. "Uncomfortable position? Sweetheart, you'd be our saving grace. I don't think any one of us wants to hire a crew to take over, or worry about managing people who aren't part of our family."

"Yes, but customers need to know they can rely on what you're offering. If you offer lunch, someone should be here to cook it, and if I get sick, I can't be the one to do it."

Red and Biggs exchanged a knowing smile, one that Finlay wasn't in on.

"Sweetheart, this business isn't successful because we run a tight ship," Red explained. "Whiskey Bro's has lasted this long because of the connections we create and the bond we have with the community. Trust, and those connections, are the very essence of this family business and what we all hoped to preserve when we looked at expanding. Having the right person holding it together is far more important than if you can serve lunch on a Friday."

"This is so much to process. Please don't think I'm ungrateful, but can I take some time to think it over? To talk to Bullet in private?"

"We're in no hurry," Biggs said.

"But she is," Bullet reminded her.

Fifteen minutes later, Bullet had loaded up her van, the rain had stopped, and Finlay hugged everyone—including Bones—and promised to make a decision quickly.

Bullet leaned into the van and kissed her. "You good? Know

where you're going?"

"Yes. Thank you for your help. And, Bullet, if you don't want me to work at the bar, that's okay. It won't hurt my feelings."

"I want you with me. I just don't want my girl working nights. But during the day? That's cool with me, babe. The closer you are, the more often I get to make out with you." He nipped playfully at her neck. "Now, get out of here before I throw you in the back of the van and make you miss the baby shower."

"You can't leave me with that thought in my head." She grabbed him by the collar and pulled him into another kiss. "My van has never been christened, so while you're out riding, maybe you should think about all the things you'd like to do to me in it."

His eyes went coal black, and in her most innocent voice, she said, "Ta-ta, sweet man of mine. I must be leaving."

BULLET WATCHED FINLAY drive away. Then he stalked back into the kitchen, determined to demand a change in his hours.

"Hey, B." Dixie reached into a cabinet and handed him a pink box. "Finlay said to give this to you later, but I'm heading out in a sec."

Red and Dixie were watching him expectantly, and guilt swallowed him again. He couldn't reduce his hours. He had to be there to protect them when they were waitressing. *Motherfucker.*

"Open it," Dixie urged.

He opened the box, took one look at the heart-shaped tart with *B + F* written on it in blue and pink frosting, and said, "*Fuck.* I need to get out of here." He turned to go outside and smacked into Bear's chest. Without thinking, Bullet grabbed him by the shirt and lifted him off his feet.

"What the hell, B?" Bear pushed from his grip, and Bullet released him. "What crawled up your ass and died?"

"I can't fucking do this anymore." He paced by the door, gritting his teeth to keep from saying more.

"Do what?" Red asked. "What's got you so upset, baby?"

Bullet glared at her. "Nothing."

"That's the lyingest *nothing* I've ever heard," she challenged.

"It doesn't matter. There's no resolution." He stormed out the door, and his family followed him out. He turned, ready to give them hell, but Biggs stood in front of the others, leaning on his cane, a barrier to absorb Bullet's wrath. Bullet bit his tongue out of respect for his father.

"Talk to me, son," Biggs said. "You don't have room to keep any more demons trapped inside you."

Bullet clenched his jaw.

"You are one stubborn son of a bitch," Biggs said. "Spit it out before it kills ya."

Bullet reached behind his neck with both hands and tipped his face up toward the sky, slamming his eyes shut. Never before had he wanted something so badly. He tried to fight it, tried to do the right thing and keep his damn mouth shut, for the sake of his family. But his love for Finlay was too strong, and the words flew fast and furious. "I can't do this anymore, working until midnight five days a week, having no time off with Finlay. But I can't cut my hours back. I'm fucked, and there's no way out of it."

"About damn time," Bear said under his breath.

"What?" Dixie asked. "We were just talking about hours. You couldn't have said something then?"

Biggs held his hand up without turning, silencing her.

Bullet glared at Dixie. "I can't cut my hours. Who would protect you and Red?"

"Protect us?" Dixie strode right past Biggs until she was in Bullet's face. "Thought you didn't want to be a hero?"

"Dixie," Red snapped.

"No, I'm not going to shut up." Dixie crossed her arms, holding Bullet's stare.

"I'm not anyone's hero," Bullet seethed.

"Bullshit. You're the very definition of a hero any way you look at it. The question is, whose hero do you *want* to be?"

"I don't know what the hell you're talking about. Someone has to protect you and Red."

"Yeah?" Challenge rose in Dixie's eyes. "Well, here's a news flash. I can protect myself, and no one would dare mess with the wife of the president of the Dark Knights."

Bones and Bear approached, taking a stance on either side of Dixie. Arms crossed, heads held high. Fuck, he'd taught them too well. He just never thought he'd be the one facing them down.

"She's right, B. No one is going to screw with them in our bar," Bones said. "You've seen to that, Bullet. You've built iron bars around that place. You've threatened anyone who even *thought* about causing trouble. You've protected the people in that bar for years to come. That's all you, B. You've given a lifetime to our family and then some. Don't rob Finlay of the life you two deserve."

"You've got a girl now, bro," Bear said. "You're right to feel all churned up inside and to want to turn your life inside out for her. I know what that feels like. It hit me like a truck when I fell for Crystal, and it still does every damn time I see her. Go with that feeling, Bullet. You're not getting any younger, and God knows how you suckered that gorgeous woman into your life, but don't fuck it up out of some misplaced responsibility."

Bullet looked away, choked up with emotions.

"Whose hero do you want to be?" Dixie asked again. "Mine and Mom's? Or Finlay's? I hope to God you choose the right one, because I'm pretty damn sick of you being my hero." She waved her hand toward their other brothers and said, "That goes for all of y'all. I could use some space, and God knows getting Bullet out of the bar for a few hours at night would be a great start." She smiled at Bullet and said, "I love you, but I'm overdosing on being protected lately."

Bullet shook his head. "Something happens to you or Red, I'll never forgive myself."

"The list of things you won't forgive yourself for is already too long, Bullet. Don't let losing Finlay be at the top of it," Bones urged.

"I'd give my life for her," Bullet said honestly.

"How about *living* your life *with* her, son?" Biggs stepped up beside Bones. "That'd be a much-deserved step in the right direction."

Swallowing past the lump in his throat, he said, "Thanks, Pop."

Biggs nodded, and Red came at Bullet with open arms. "My boy's growing up." She hugged him so tight it made him laugh.

"Ma..."

"Shush up, you big oaf," she said. "Just let me be happy that another of my boys has found the other half of his heart."

Bullet's phone rang in his pocket, and his mother released him as he pulled it out. Finlay's name appeared on the screen, and he put the phone to his ear. "What's wrong, babe?"

"I left in such a hurry, I forgot the salmon, salads, and dip. They're in the fridge. Do you have time to run them over to 101 Kastler Street?"

"No problem. Be right there." He ended the call and threw an arm around Dixie's shoulder, following the others into the bar. "You think you can get someone to take over from eight to midnight Tuesday and Wednesday? And from five to midnight Friday and Saturday? Someone big and mean?"

"No, but I can get Jed, and I'm sure Fin would go crazy if we hired Isabel." She smiled and said, "You're doing the right thing, Bullet, even though I know you have a hard time accepting that. You've protected me my whole life. It's Finlay's turn, and more importantly, it's your turn. She loves you, B. I can see it in her eyes."

TWENTY MINUTES LATER, Bullet was walking through a living room filled with women and baby paraphernalia, where he gazed into Finlay's gorgeous blue eyes. The women were gathered around Leesa Braden, who was trying to calm her screaming baby girl. Bullet set the dishes on the table by Finlay.

"Thank you so much," she said, and went up on her toes and kissed his cheek.

"Everything okay?" He eyed the unhappy baby, remembering when Truman had first brought Lincoln and Kennedy home after rescuing them from a crack house where their mother had overdosed. They were scared and fussy, but when

Bullet had held them, they'd calmed right down. He didn't know if it was his size or what, but to this day, those babies were happy when they were in his arms. And Lord knew he loved holding them.

"Leesa's baby, Avery, has been fussy since she got here. She's nursing, so she didn't want to leave her, and the party is for one of her best friends."

He walked over to the crowd of women, and they parted like a deck of cards. He nodded at Leesa, whom he knew well, as she was married to Cole Braden, one of Beau's cousins, who lived there in Peaceful Harbor. "Hi, sweetheart. Can I try to calm your baby girl?"

"Bullet? What are you doing here?" Leesa asked.

"Fin's my girl. She forgot something, and I brought it over for her." He thrust his hands forward. "Give me your princess so you can enjoy the party."

"Um, sure, but she's having a hard time," Leesa said, and handed him the baby.

He settled the baby over his shoulder and spoke softly to her. "It's okay, sweetheart. Calm down for Uncle Bullet." He spread his hand over her back, rubbing in slow circles. As he paced the floor, the baby quieted, save for a few whimpers. She smelled as new and fresh as a warm summer's breeze. "That's it, li'l princess. That's a good girl."

"Oh my gosh," a brunette woman said. "Who *are* you?"

"I've got twin eight-month-olds who could use a manny, if you're free," a petite blonde with wide brown eyes pleaded.

"Wait," another blonde said anxiously. "I've got a colicky four-month-old. I get dibs."

Finlay was watching him with an amused and dreamy expression. If he'd had any lingering doubts about his decision to cut back his hours and where he needed to be at night, that look silenced them.

"Sorry, ladies, but all my free time"—*and my heart*—"is spoken for."

# Chapter Eighteen

FINLAY AWOKE TO the sound of Penny's ringtone. She rolled toward Bullet's side of the bed and realized she was alone. It had been two weeks since Bullet had mentioned cutting back his hours and ten days since Jed had modified his schedule to accommodate the change. Bullet had been far less edgy ever since, and he'd been sleeping soundly again, which was why she was confused about waking to an empty bed.

She reached blindly for her phone and put it to her ear. "Hey, Pen. What's up?"

"Obviously not you."

"What time is it?" She turned to look at the clock and found a sticky note blocking the numbers. She snagged it and read Bullet's blocky handwriting. *Meet me out front.*

"Time for you to get up," Penny said way too cheerily. "I gotta run. I'm meeting Tegan at Jazzy Joe's for coffee. Love you!" The line went dead.

Jazzy Joe's was a café in town run by twins Jasmine and Joe Carbo. Coffee sounded really good right then. She sat at the edge of the bed, wondering what the heck was going on, then padded over to the bathroom and found another sticky note on the mirror.

*Wear jeans and those sexy lace-up boots.*

She couldn't stop smiling as she used the bathroom and brushed her teeth and hair. Her life had changed so much, so fast. The morning of the baby shower, she'd thought her life couldn't get any better. Then one of the women at the event had hired her to cater a surprise party for her mother and Bullet had broken the news about cutting back his hours at work and told her that Dixie had mentioned the possibility of hiring Isabel. Finlay had been so excited, she'd accepted the part-time job with the Whiskeys that very night. In the two weeks since, she'd had the menus designed and printed, and Isabel had worked out an *almost* full-time schedule with Dixie, giving her time to also work with Finlay, and she'd already put in her notice at the restaurant in Boston.

Last Saturday they'd pulled together the final details for the fundraiser, which was taking place in two weeks, after the charity ride. Sarah's brother was out of ICU, and with any luck, he and the baby would be discharged before the event. The fundraiser was being held on the grounds of Whiskey Bro's, and they would use it to announce the opening of the kitchen. Finlay was going to cook, and all proceeds from food sales as well as the rally itself would go to the Beckleys.

She gazed out the bedroom window at the backyard as she pulled on a pair of skinny jeans. She and Bullet had worked in the gardens together last Sunday. His passion for nature, and for *her*, was boundless, and she loved working with him in the gardens as much as she loved working with him at the bar. It was easy to see how working with his hands, concentrating on bringing life into the world, nurturing it, and watching it grow, was cathartic. *Just like loving him.*

As she laced up the boots he loved and threw on a comfy gray sweater, she wondered what he had up his sleeve this morning.

Downstairs, she found a Pillsbury cinnamon bun on a plate in the kitchen with raisins in the shape of the letter *B* on top, along with a cup of instant coffee. He was so thoughtful, but she had to laugh that his possessiveness carried over to the *B* on the top of the cinnamon bun. Could she fall any more in love with him? She quickly ate the bun, getting more excited by the second, and downed the coffee, which was too bitter, but Bullet had gone to the trouble of making it. It could have been thick as sludge and she still would have drank it.

She put her dishes in the sink and ran out front. "Bullet?"

He came out of the garage wearing his leather jacket and jeans and carrying something behind his back. "There's my angel."

Tinkerbell trotted over to Finlay, and she knelt to love her up, remembering the first time she'd seen her and screamed and the morning she'd come over to meet her. She'd been terrified, but Bullet and his family had made her feel safe, and they hadn't stopped since.

Bullet knelt beside her and kissed her cheek. He'd trimmed his beard, but it was still long enough to tickle. "Hey, baby. I got you something."

"Was that something a phone call from Penny?"

He chuckled. "Someone had to wake you." He handed her a box wrapped in sparkling silver paper with a big pink bow around it. "She told me about your dad and his gifts. I hope you don't mind, but I'd like to carry on that tradition of celebrating your milestones."

Tears brimmed in her eyes. "Bullet? What's this for?" she

asked as they both rose to their feet. Tinkerbell leaned against her leg.

"Because you're my girl."

She untied the bow and lifted off the top. "Oh my gosh, is this leather?"

Bullet took the box as she withdrew a gorgeous black leather biker jacket with big silver zippers, just like his, only made for a woman.

"Turn it around."

She did, and her heart leapt. WHISKEY'S was embroidered across the back in script. "You got me a jacket from the bar? I love it."

He set the box down and gathered her in his arms. "That's not a bar jacket, babe." A spark of possession glimmered in his eyes.

"You're *branding* me?" She giggled.

"*Protecting.*"

"More like *claiming.*" She tugged him down for a kiss and said, "I love it. Thank you."

"Try it on." He held it as she slipped her arms into it.

"It's so soft. Does it look okay?"

He made a guttural noise and hauled her in for a greedy kiss, leaving her breathless.

"Wow. I like getting presents from you."

"You look hot as fuck, baby. Seriously, I shouldn't let you go out wearing those painted-on jeans and that jacket."

"*Let* me? Do we need to have a talk about this?"

He chuckled and shook his head.

"Good, because now that I've seen your reaction, I'm going to make a point of wearing jeans around you more often."

His arm swooped around her waist, and he lifted her with

one arm and kissed her again. "You might never leave the house if you do."

"I'm not sure my employers will be happy about that. You know, I have a real job now."

"This employer has no qualms with you spending all your time in his bed." He set her on her feet and put an arm around her neck. "Come on, babe. We're going for a ride."

He led her into the garage to his shiny black motorcycle and patted the leather seat. "Hop on, baby girl."

"I've never been on a motorcycle before."

"Until a few weeks ago you'd never had sex outside, and until two nights ago, you'd never had sex on top of the washer while it was running. I seem to remember you enjoying both so much, we needed repeat performances."

She was unable to deny the thrill of either.

He put his arms around her again and said, "You can always trust me, baby. I'd never put you in harm's way, and I promise to go slow."

He tucked her hair behind her ear and his gaze softened and somehow intensified at once. "I love you, Finlay, and I want you with me when I ride. Please do this for me?"

"You..." Emotions clogged her throat.

"I love you, baby. I love how you stand up for what you believe in. I love how you believe in me and how you love Tinkerbell. I love you in your frilly dresses, and I love you lying naked beneath me. I love all of you, and I want, I *hope*, you'll try this for me because riding is a big part of who I am."

She could barely breathe as she struggled to keep the tears in her eyes from falling. "I love you, too." She threw her arms around his neck and he lifted her into his arms, both of them laughing and kissing. "*So much*, Bullet. I love you so much."

"Me too, baby." *Kiss, kiss.* "God, it feels good to finally tell you."

"For me, too." She kissed him again, and as he set her feet on the ground, she said, "I'll try to go for a ride, but if I get scared, you'll stop?"

"Always, baby."

"Where will we go? Do you have a favorite place you like to ride?"

"No. The open road has always been my place."

He put Tinkerbell in the house and gave Finlay a lesson in motorcycle safety. She tried really hard to concentrate, but she was busy silently repeating everything he'd said about loving her so she'd never forget a word of it. When he helped her onto the bike and gave her a pink helmet with WHISKEY'S written in black cursive on the sides and said, "I had it made to match your jacket," she fell even more in love with him. The emotions were so overwhelming, they mounted inside her, taking up all of her until she couldn't keep them in any longer.

"I love you," she whispered. "I love you more than words can say, Bullet, and I just want to tell you over and over again, so you never forget."

"I'll never forget, baby. But I hope you'll never stop telling me anyway."

He helped her onto the bike, then climbed on in front of her and showed her how to hold him. Wrapping herself around Bullet felt as natural as baking a cake. *This* was where she belonged, with Bullet, no matter where he was.

"Ready, angel?"

"As ready as I'll ever be."

The motorcycle roared to life, vibrating like thunder beneath her. As good as that felt, it didn't feel half as incredible as the way it rumbled up Bullet's body, humming through his back and radiating against her heart.

"I think I'm going to love this!" she yelled.

He lifted her hand to his lips and pressed a kiss there before pulling her arms around him tighter and putting on his helmet.

As he drove down the driveway, she felt like she was flying. She inhaled the grassy, leafy scents of fall, which took on a sharper, more vibrant aroma. He stopped at the end of the long driveway to ask how she was doing and she gave him a thumbs-up. He revved the engine and turned onto the main drag, heading out of Peaceful Harbor and toward their newest adventure.

BULLET STOPPED TO check in with Finlay two or three times during the beginning of their ride, and he was thrilled that she not only wasn't freaking out, but was bubbling over with enthusiasm. Seeing her on his bike, with that leather jacket and helmet, was almost the biggest aphrodisiac he'd ever encountered. But *nothing* was more of a turn-on than Finlay Wilson wearing one of her frilly little dresses and that sunshine smile.

About an hour outside of the harbor, he turned off the highway, heading up a narrow mountain road, to give Finlay the experience of riding the back roads. The sun had kicked up, gracing them with a gorgeous day. If he were riding with the guys, he'd keep on going for hours, but as incredible as it felt to have Finlay pressed up against him, he wanted her in his arms. He physically ached with love for her. Like his heart had never fully functioned, and she made it work harder than it ever had.

That was a new and exquisite pain, one he hoped never ended.

He followed the windy mountain roads until they came to a meadow, when Finlay yanked at his jacket, indicating she wanted to stop. He pulled over and removed his helmet, stepping off the bike to see his bright-eyed girl.

"You okay?"

She tugged at her helmet, and he helped her take it off.

"That was amazing. *Fantastic*. It was so romantic, holding on to you. I can't explain it, but…" She rose onto her toes, still straddling the bike, and pressed her lips to his.

"I wish I knew more about romance for you, baby."

Her smile cut straight to his heart.

"Just saying that is more romantic than anything I could dream up." She grabbed him by the jacket and pulled him closer. "I get it now. *All* of it, Bullet. The closeness of the club, the way these rides become a part of you. The reason you sometimes get edgy when you don't have a chance to ride."

"I don't get that way much when I'm with you, do I?"

"No, but sometimes I see something there, and then when you come home from work and step off your bike, that look is gone."

"That's me coming home to *you*, baby." He lifted her off the bike and kissed her hard. He ran his fingers through her hair and held on tight with both hands, angling her face up so he could gaze into her eyes. "You slay my demons and make everything seem possible. I want everything with you, Fins. I want days of riding and nights of making love until the sun comes up. And right now, pretty girl," he said as he lifted her into his arms and carried her across the meadow, "I need to love you."

She laughed and kissed him as he carried her through the

tall flowers and grass to the far side of the meadow, out of sight from any passersby. He lowered her to her feet, taking her in another sensual kiss.

"You okay here?" he asked against her lips.

She pushed his jacket from his shoulders without hesitation or embarrassment, and that trust nearly did him in. He tugged off his shirt and laid it on the ground. Their mouths came together in slow, loving kisses as they undressed each other and sank down to the grass. Cool air brushed over their skin, but her flesh was warm to the touch, gorgeous in the sun's rays.

"God, I love you, baby," he said between urgent kisses as he loved every inch of her body, worshipping her scars and that heavenly paradise between her legs. He guided her legs over his shoulders, devouring her, teasing over the special spot that made her quiver and shake. She pulled at his hair, holding his mouth tight against her swollen sex as he took his fill.

"*Please*, Bullet."

He lifted her hips, feasting on her, feeling the rush of her approaching orgasm in her quickening breaths, the flexing of her thighs. He gripped her ass, holding it tight in the way he'd learned made her climaxes even more intense. She cried out, her body bucking wildly as she shattered against his mouth. He didn't relent, holding her tighter, plunging his tongue deeper, through the very last pulse of her release. Then he sheathed his cock and drove into her in one hard thrust.

"*Ah!*" she cried out as his mouth came down over hers.

She was right there with him, meeting every thrust of his hips, every stroke of his tongue, with an eager, loving motion of her own. Every breath she took, every noise she made, roused his passion. Long, surrendering moans came from both of them as they yielded to their love. As they soared up toward the clouds, he was filled with an incredible sense of completeness.

They lay together for a long while afterward, until Bullet had no choice but to reluctantly break their connection so he could take care of the condom.

He helped her on with her panties and sweater and put on his briefs, still too hot to be dressed. Then he lay on his back with Finlay tucked against his side. Her thigh moved over his, and she ran her fingers along his chest. He laced their hands together and kissed her knuckles.

"When we're close," she said softly, "I feel like we fall into this world of our own, and nothing else matters or exists. Is that terribly selfish? I mean, the real world is out there. Poor Sarah is struggling to heal her family and make ends meet, and people around the world are suffering, and here we are in this blissful meadow."

"You're the least selfish person I know."

"No, not even close. That would be you." She unlaced their fingers and touched his skull ring. "Is that for the Dark Knights?"

"No. It was my grandfather's. The other one I wear was my uncle Axel's, my father's brother. He died when I was on tour, and Bear held on to it for me."

"But you wear three sometimes."

"The third was my old man's. He gave it to me when I went into the military."

"Do you think you'll ever tell your family about the time you were in the hospital? The truth of how you almost died?"

He shifted his eyes up to the clear blue sky. Talking with Finlay about his past was easier now, since they'd talked about it quite a few times. She was too curious to let many questions go unanswered, and he knew this one bothered her because not only did she hate lies as much as he did, but she loved his family. She was too bighearted to let it go.

She straddled him, and his blond angel smiled down on him. "How long were you in the hospital?"

"Several weeks in the hospital and a couple months of rehab. I came home about eight months after I was discharged."

"You're not going to answer me about telling them, are you?"

She didn't say it accusingly. She said it with acceptance and without judgment, and that made him hurt in a whole new way. "Babe, I can think of a hundred reasons not to tell them, but not one reason to do it."

Her expression turned serious. "Do you think they'd be hurt knowing you didn't tell them in the first place?"

"Definitely. They'd want to know all the details, and who knows what kind of shit that'll bring up. Some things are just better left unsaid."

"Are you protecting them, or yourself?" Again, there was no judgment, just the need to understand shining in her eyes.

"Both, to be honest."

She nodded and ran her finger over the names tattooed on the right side of his chest. "Would it bother you to tell me whose names these are?"

"Fallen brothers. Guys I couldn't save."

She squinted, lowering her face so she could look more closely. "There are so many I can barely read most of them."

"They're not for anyone else to read. They're for me."

Her gaze met his. "Should I not try?"

"No, babe. My body is your body. Go ahead."

She shifted so she was lying on his other side and began whispering the names as she read them and pressing kisses over each one. "Dreamer." *Kiss*. "S. Nelson." *Kiss*. "Brinks. Michael Z." *Kiss. Kiss*.

He closed his eyes against the pang of painful memories accompanying each one. When he'd started honoring his fallen brothers, he hadn't known if he'd remember them, but with each name she spoke, he knew he'd never forget. Many he hadn't known well. Some he'd met on missions, known them for only minutes or hours before they were killed. Others he'd known for years. He listened to her sweet voice, concentrating on that instead of the heartache.

"Daniel." *Kiss*. "Gunner." *Kiss*. "Chip. Buzz." *Kiss. Kiss*. "M. Martinez." *Kiss*.

Her hand stilled on his skin, and a chill rushed down his spine. The air around them, the very atmosphere, turned colder. His eyes flew open, and he grabbed her hand, unsure of what she'd sparked and afraid he'd tumble into a flashback. But when his eyes met hers, the fear in them revealed the chill he'd felt. Her hands trembled within his, and he bolted upright. "What is it? What's wrong?"

"*I. A. Rush...?*" Tears streamed down her cheeks.

Wails burst from her lungs, and she turned away, sobbing into her hands. He knew. He just fucking *knew* that was her guy. The man she'd lost in the war. He scooped her into his lap, holding her as she cried. "Baby, I'm so sorry. *Aw, Christ*, Finlay. That's the man I was carrying when I got hit. I tried to save him."

His mind reeled back to the battlefield, and he fought against the mounting fear, the uncontainable anger that consumed him when he thought of that last battle. And then like he'd stepped in front of a moving vehicle, the realization crashed into him. Jesus, he'd fucking killed Finlay's guy.

"Ian Aaron Rush, that was his name," she said through her tears. "He went by Aaron."

She buried her face in his neck, her tears soaking his skin, her heartache drowning him. He felt sick, needed air. His head fell back, and he gulped long, painful inhalations. He was vaguely aware of her stilling against him, of her hands on his cheeks.

"Bullet. Bullet? It's okay. You were with him. I always thought he died alone. But you were there."

Her words flew at him like darts. How could he tell her the truth?

She climbed off his lap with panic in her teary eyes. He sat up on his knees, dragging air into his lungs.

"Bullet, breathe, honey. Breathe. You're okay. You're here with me, not back there."

She put her shaky arms around him, but he broke free and pushed to his feet, the spiky grass poking into his skin. He didn't care. He deserved the pain. *Fuuuck.* "It's not a flashback. It's the fucking truth of it all."

Confusion rose in her eyes. "I don't understand."

"I *killed* him, Finlay. If I hadn't been carrying him, he wouldn't have been hit in the chest, and you'd be with your guy right now, not here with the one who killed him."

Her jaw hung open, her entire body shaking. "No. No, no, no. No, Bullet."

She pushed to her feet, lifting them in quick succession as she stepped on the prickly grass, and hopped back onto his shirt. Fresh tears tumbled down her cheeks. "Don't do this. You didn't kill him. Aaron died of the wound in his leg. It severed his femoral artery. They told his family he had other wounds, but it was the one in his leg that killed him."

He tried to process what she said, but his head was spinning. "I was there. I looked into his eyes."

"Yes, which is why I'm so *relieved. That's* why I'm crying. His family—*I*—always thought he died alone on the battlefield. But he *didn't*, Bullet. You were with him. You held his hand. You comforted him in the end." She went to him, but he took a step back in disbelief. "Bullet...why are you doing this?"

He turned away, grabbed his head, and pitched back on his heels, eyes clenched tight against the blazing sun. "Aw, *fuck*, Finlay." Could she be right? All these years he'd been sure he'd killed the man. He shook his throbbing head as her hands came around him from behind.

"You didn't kill him, Bullet. Don't do this to yourself. Don't do this to *us*."

He folded his arms over hers, the weight of her words crashing over him like shattered glass, and he sank to his knees.

"You didn't kill him," she said into his ear. "Don't let his death kill you."

Tears burned in his eyes as she rested her head on the back of his shoulder, whispering, "I love you. You didn't do it, Bullet. I promise it's true. It's not your fault."

Struggling against the emotions clawing for release, he inhaled deeply, unwilling to fall completely apart in front of Finlay. "I'm so sorry. I wish I could have saved him."

She came around and climbed into his lap, her arms around his neck, her head on his shoulder, and she held him tight. "Nobody could have saved him out there. But you consoled him. And now you've healed the piece of me that was still broken, the one holding on to the image of him alone as he took his last breath. Don't you see, Bullet? No one could save Aaron, but now that we know this, maybe Aaron can save you."

"I don't need *saving*."

"Not *saving*. That's the wrong word," she said quickly. "You can give his family the closure they've never had, and it might help you move forward and finally leave the guilt of that awful time behind. Ed and Helen Rush live right outside Pleasant Hill, on Mercer Street."

He closed his eyes, doubting anything would ever ease the guilt that had strangled him since that fateful day. "I don't know if I can do that."

"Of course you can. You're the strongest man I know."

Anger erupted inside him like a volcano, abrupt and unstoppable. "Stop it, Finlay. You *know* what's at risk for me. I don't know if seeing his family and relaying what happened out there will slam me back into another flashback, or worse, into full-on PTSD. And if it does, I don't know who I'll be if, or when, I come out on the other side." He tried to lift her off his lap, but she refused to let go.

"I'll go with you. I'll help you," she offered. "You've been okay talking to me. Talking seems to help."

"Goddamn it, Finlay. I just found you! I'm not risking everything for a family I don't even know."

Tears brimmed in her eyes, and she swallowed hard. "Bullshit," she said softly.

The curse hit him like a shotgun round.

"You risk yourself for strangers all the time, and I believe with my whole heart that this will help you as much as it will help his family. As much as it's helping me. They're not strangers to me, Bullet, and I wouldn't ask this of you if I thought I'd lose you because of it. But you've obviously been harboring tremendous guilt over what happened out there, and it's not yours to hang on to anymore. Not now that you know the truth."

"Finlay…" He'd do anything for her, but this?

"Please think about it for me? For us? I honestly believe it'll help you let go of that part of your past."

She climbed off his lap, and they dressed in painful silence. For the first time since he'd been with Finlay, he needed space away from her. He needed to clear his head. He felt like he was standing on the edge of a ravine with Finlay rooted on the opposite cliff and a world of fucked-up nightmares between them.

The drive back to his place was long and cold, and when Finlay climbed off his bike, he took her in his arms and said, "I gotta go ride, baby. Gotta clear my head."

"I know," she whispered, and he gathered her in his arms.

"I'm sorry. I want to be the man you need, but I just don't know who I am right now."

Several tortured hours later, long after darkness chased away the light of day, Bullet sat in front of the dark house, struggling to make sense of all that he'd learned, needing an anchor to settle him in the dizzying sea of worries.

He pulled out his phone and called Bones, who answered on the first ring.

"What's up, B?"

"I don't know, bro. Some shit went down. That guy I was carrying when I got shot was Fin's boyfriend, man." His chest constricted.

Bones cursed. Several long moments later, he said, "Where are you?"

"If I fuck this up, if I lose her…" Tears burned in his eyes, and he gripped the phone tighter.

"Bullet, where's Finlay?"

He glanced up at the house again, pain slicing through him anew. "Keep your phone on."

# Chapter Nineteen

"ARE YOU SURE I can't come over?" Penny asked for the millionth time since she'd called an hour ago.

"I really need to be alone," Finlay answered. She lay on the couch bundled up in Bullet's flannel shirt, needing to feel closer to him, with Tinkerbell curled up beside her. Tinkerbell seemed to sense that something was wrong and had been by her side since she'd arrived several hours ago. She'd made the mistake of answering Penny's call earlier, and now Penny and Isabel, who Penny had patched through on a three-way call, didn't want to let her get off the phone. They'd called to hear about Finlay's first motorcycle ride, and she'd been too distraught to pretend like nothing had happened, so she'd told them *everything*. From the amazing ride, to the devastation of realizing that for all these years Bullet had believed he'd killed Aaron. As thankful for their company as she was, she didn't want to talk to anyone but Bullet.

"Should I go to my place?" Tears stung her eyes again at the thought of not being there when Bullet got home. "Do you think he'll want to be alone when he finally comes back?"

"Definitely not," Isabel said. "He's working through things

the best way he knows how, but he'll want you there, Fin. Otherwise he would have dropped you off at your place."

She petted Tinkerbell, hoping Isabel was right. "I shouldn't have pushed him to talk to Aaron's family," she said for the hundredth time, which was only about half as many times as she'd thought it.

She'd tried to distract herself for hours before the girls called, but she'd even been too upset to cook, which had never happened to her before, and she felt utterly and completely lost without that outlet. But every time she looked at the kitchen, she felt sick to her stomach about pushing Bullet into a corner. She'd alternated between pacing and curling up on the couch. She'd even tried taking a walk with Tinkerbell, but the yard seemed too big and empty without Bullet. That struck her as funny, considering her man needed space and, without him, she needed to be confined. To be wrapped up in his shirt, surrounded by his belongings, his scent, his *energy*.

"Aw, Fin," Penny said. "You love him so much. I don't think you'd ask him to do something you thought he couldn't handle."

"But he *left*, Penny. He's so protective of me, for him to leave for this long can only mean—"

"That he's working his way through what you've asked of him," Isabel said adamantly. "That's all it means, okay? Bullet is crazy about you, and he let down his guard, but he's still *Bullet*. He's got more walls inside him than any of us can imagine, and right now he's figuring out if he can scale them or not."

She stared at the ceiling, wishing she could talk to him, to take back their conversation. She'd texted Bullet earlier, but she knew if he was riding he'd never feel the vibration. "I made everything worse for him. After the most incredible day ever, I screwed things up. What if he shuts down completely? What if I sent him over the edge and he can't see his way clear to forgiving me?"

She sat up, feeling worn out and too sad to stay on the phone. "I'm hanging up—"

"No!" Penny and Isabel yelled.

"Sorry, you guys, but my heart hurts too much. I just need time to"—*curl into a ball and cry*—"think things through. I love you. I'll call you tomorrow."

After ending the call, she went up to the bedroom with Tinkerbell and sat on the edge of the bed, looking at the sticky notes from that morning. Bullet was so thoughtful. Had she slowed down enough to think things through, instead of seeing a path for him to clear his conscience, she might have offered to tell Aaron's parents herself. If Bullet couldn't handle doing it, then at least she could help them get closure.

*But he needs it just as much.*

Did he? Or was she just hoping it might help? Ugh. She'd asked herself the question too many times and couldn't even ponder an answer any longer.

She lay back on the bed, and Tinkerbell lay beside her. She grabbed Bullet's pillow and curled up around it, allowing the tears that had been coming and going all evening to flow. She closed her eyes, and when sleep came, she welcomed the escape.

THE ROAR OF a motorcycle engine sent Finlay's heart into her throat. She pushed from the bed and ran down the stairs with Tinkerbell on her heels. She flew through the house and out the front door as Bullet climbed from his bike. She rushed toward him, nearly falling over Bones, who was sitting on the front step. She'd forgotten he was there. He'd shown up hours ago, before she'd talked to Penny and Isabel. She'd heard his motorcycle and run outside thinking it was Bullet. She'd been devastated, but she'd tried not to let that show. She must have failed because when she'd invited him inside, he'd insisted on waiting out front. What was it with Whiskeys feeling the need to stand guard?

Tinkerbell beat her to Bullet, trying to climb his leg. Bullet's shoulders were rounded forward, and his eyes lacked the spark of vigor they usually held. When he shifted his gaze from Finlay to Bones, he looked...*defeated.*

Good Lord, what had she done to him?

She stopped moving, and when he opened his arms, she fell into them.

"You don't have to talk to his family," she said quickly. "I'm sorry I asked you to. I was wrong. You've been through enough. You don't need to be anyone's hero. I'm so sorry."

He kissed the top of her head, his big hands caressing her back. He didn't say a word, just held her tighter, and that sent fear trampling through her. She looked up at him and opened her mouth to speak, but it was too hard. She didn't know what else to say, so she buried her face in his chest again.

"Can you see my eyes in the dark, angel?" he finally asked.

She gazed up at him, her heart hammering against her ribs. She searched his solemn expression, and when she met his eyes, they were unlike anything she'd seen before, and she didn't know how to read them. But she nodded, because she could see them.

"I'm sorry I took off. I had to figure things out."

"I know. It's okay. I'm sorry. I won't ever ask you to do

anything like that again."

"You won't have to," he said evenly. His gaze shifted to Bones.

"I came over thinking you were here," Bones said. "And when I saw your bike was gone, I couldn't leave Finlay alone. I'll take off now, unless you need me."

"You've been here the whole time?" she asked.

Bones shrugged. "Of course."

*Of course?* More tears streamed down her cheeks.

"Thanks, bro. You should hear this." Bullet looked down at Finlay. "I went to see Aaron's family."

Her mouth fell open. "You saw them?"

He nodded. "I couldn't risk letting you down, baby. Not when you've done nothing but lift me up."

"You went...?" she said, unable to believe it. "And you're okay? You don't hate me?"

"I could never hate you. I did it because I love you, Finlay. You needed this, and I need you. I just had to wrap my head around the idea. But you were right. It helped." He walked over to Bones and embraced him. "Thanks, man."

"I didn't do anything," Bones said.

"You answered your phone and you stayed with my girl. That's everything." He reached for Finlay again, and the three of them sat on the porch steps. Finlay and Bones sat on either side of Bullet, and Tinkerbell climbed onto his lap, licking his face.

"Any flashbacks?" Bones asked.

Bullet stared out into the darkness without answering for so long, Finlay wondered if he was going to answer at all. She placed her hand on his thigh, and he covered it with his, lacing their fingers together.

"They had pictures all over of their boy they'd lost, and pictures of you with him," he said to Finlay. "I didn't know him well, had only met him on that mission, and didn't even know he went by the name Aaron. He was just *Rush* to me. But for you to have been with him, I'm sure he was a great guy. I didn't have a flashback. Not even when I described his last moments, which shocked the hell out of me. I was bracing for the worst, but it never came. Then his parents lost it. They were so relieved, because like you said, they thought he'd died alone. I cried right along with them like a fucking pussy, but I didn't feel like one. It felt good to give them peace."

"You've been with them all this time?" Bones asked.

Bullet shook his head. "I went to see Mom and Pop. I figured if I was facing my demons, I should give it all I had."

"Oh, Bullet." Finlay leaned against him.

Bones leaned his elbows on his knees, worrying with his hands. "And…?"

"Pop knew."

Bones held his hands up. "I swear I didn't tell him."

"I know. Goddamn motorcycle community. Some doc who worked on me at Walter Reed, the military hospital in Bethesda, recognized my back tat. Biggs has known the whole damn time."

"And he never said anything to either of you?" Finlay was unable to disguise the awe in her voice.

"He said…" Bullet paused, his eyes glistening in the moonlight. He cleared his throat, sat up a little straighter, put one arm around Tinkerbell, the other around Finlay. "He said he'd thought he'd lost me once. He didn't want to piss me off and lose me again."

"And Red?" Bones asked.

"Red..." Bullet repeated. "She didn't give it up. I have no idea if Biggs told her or not. She just hugged me and cried. You know how she is. She's either setting us straight or loving us up. I was on the loving side of things tonight. Tomorrow she'll probably want to kick my ass."

"Won't we all?" Bones pushed to his feet and embraced Bullet. "I'm proud of you, man. I love you. You had me worried tonight, but I shouldn't have been. You're invincible."

Bullet scoffed. "Hardly. Love you, little bro." He patted Bones on the back and then patted his leg to call Tinkerbell and reached for Finlay. Tinkerbell came to his side as Bones started up his bike and drove away.

Bullet gathered Finlay in his arms and said, "I'm sorry for taking off and making you worry. Thank you for not giving up on me."

"Thank you for not giving up on us." She was so full of love for him, he'd become even more of a hero, but she'd never dare let those words slip out again.

"I wasn't sure if you'd be here or not, so I drove by your place first, and, baby..." A world of emotions rose in his eyes. "That's not your place anymore, lollipop," he said with all the strength and passion she'd grown to love. "I need you here with me all the time. I know I've got baggage, and that probably makes you unsure, especially after tonight—"

She reached up and pulled his mouth to hers, kissing him into silence.

"You don't need me, Bullet. You *want* me. I'm so thankful I'm the one you chose, because I do need you...and Tink. And more than that, I want you both in my life. I moved here to put down roots, and I thought those roots would include only sisterly love. But you've shown me I'm still capable of loving and being loved. I've got baggage, too, but our love is so *big*, it's help-each-other-unpack-our-baggage love, the kind of love that lasts forever."

"Thank you, angel," he said softly. "But I do *need* you, and I'm not ashamed to admit it." He brushed his lips over hers, his beard tickling her skin as he said, "Earlier today, you asked me if I had a favorite place, and I said I'd never had one, that I needed the open road. But I was wrong, baby. I found my place. It's right here beside you."

He lifted her into his arms and carried her inside. "How about we go upstairs and make up for the time we lost?"

"One orgasm for each hour we were apart?"

"That'll never be enough."

# Epilogue

"IZ, CAN YOU grab the pigs in blankets? Dix, do we need more plates? I think we need more plates—" Finlay started when Isabel grabbed her by the shoulders.

"Fin, *stop*. We've got this. Don't worry." Isabel's hazel eyes danced with confidence. She'd moved to Peaceful Harbor last weekend and had taken over Finlay's lease, after Finlay had moved in with Bullet.

"Don't make me go get your mother," Dixie teased.

Finlay's mother and stepfather had come down for the event, and last night, her mother, Penny, Isabel, Dixie, Gemma, Crystal, Red, and even Chicki and Babs, had helped prepare food for today's fundraiser just so Finlay could go on the charity ride with Bullet this morning. While Finlay had been a nervous wreck, fussing over every little thing they cooked, her mother had been the eye of the hurricane, calm, cool, and collected.

"Why are you so nervous anyway?" Isabel asked. "You've been acting like you had drugs for breakfast ever since you got back from the charity ride."

"I don't know. I just want things to go well for Sarah, and I'm so full of adrenaline from the ride, I can't seem to calm down," Finlay said. The ride had lasted for three hours and had ended at Whiskey Bro's, where the fundraiser was in full force. It had been two weeks since that fateful day at the meadow, and she and Bullet had been going for rides almost every morning since. Riding was just as addictive as Bullet was.

"Okay, girls, let's go. We have to get this food out there." Finlay picked up two trays of burgers and headed for the door.

Isabel and Dixie followed her outside, where hundreds of people milled about the tents and activities. They weaved between the dunk tank run by a host of handsome firefighters and a line of people waiting for a chance to get their pictures taken with the wooden photo props Truman had painted. For two dollars, they could put their face through the hole and become a woman in a bathing suit, a biker sitting on a motorcycle, or a child sitting in a sidecar.

They passed the obstacle course of orange cones beside the food pavilion, where a dozen or more children raced Big Wheels toward the finish line, their parents cheering them on. Bones came around the pavilion carrying Bradley on his hip and holding baby Lila, who was patting his cheek with her pudgy hand. Bradley's eyes were damp with tears, and his knee was scraped up. Sarah walked beside them, rubbing Bradley's back and carrying Lila's blanket, her favorite stuffed hedgehog, and a bottle.

"Oh no. What happened?" Finlay asked.

"I falled on a rock," Bradley said. "But I'm not going to the hospital. Bones said he'd fix me right up here."

"Bones is good at that," Finlay said. "Sarah, how are you holding up?"

Sarah patted her burgeoning baby bump and looked adoringly at her children. "I'm good, thanks. Just glad to have my babies and Scott home." Lila had recovered completely, and the plastic surgeon said the scars on her face and arms should become almost undetectable over time. Scott was still in a wheelchair with pins in one leg, the other casted, but his lungs were healing well.

"We'll catch up with you guys later," Bones said. "I've got to get B-boy cleaned up. Bullet was looking for you a few minutes ago, Fin."

"Isn't he always?" Dixie teased.

Finlay smiled, thinking of yesterday evening, when they'd skipped dinner and made love for hours. They were together as often as they could be, and when they weren't physically together, they were together in their hearts.

"For the record, Penny and I are jealous. The man worships you," Isabel said as they passed the moon bounce.

"You can bring those trays over here," Bear hollered from beside it, where Kennedy was peering through the mesh at him.

"No, they can't," Crystal said as she came out of the tent where the raffles were being held and took one of the trays from Finlay. "I'll bring you and Kennedy plates," she said to Bear, then to Finlay and the girls, "I'm so glad my stomach is better. I think Bear was hoping I was pregnant. Now he's got babies in his eyes every time he looks at me."

"Babies are amazing," Isabel said. "You should have one!"

"Please keep her away from my husband," Crystal teased. "There must be five hundred people here. Some of the raffles are up to thousands of dollars. Did you see the local newspaper guy? He's taking pictures, and said he would do a whole write-up on the expansion of Whiskey Bro's."

"It's amazing what this community does for their own," Finlay said as they entered the food tent, which smelled heavenly and was bustling with people. She was pleased as punch with the turnout, even though the food was gobbled up as quickly as she could cook it. Thankfully, Nate Braden, who owned Tap It, a local restaurant, and Jasmine and Joe Carbo from Jazzy Joe's Café, were also taking part in the event, so no one was going hungry.

Finlay looked across the tent at Penny, who was surrounded by families waiting for ice cream. Tegan and Isla, Chicki and Bud's daughter, had come out to help her run the ice cream station. Several of the Dark Knights members' wives and daughters were helping out with the food stations. Finlay felt lucky to have found her small hometown to be just as close-knit and welcoming as it had been when she was young. As she set the tray on a table, she spotted Red talking with her mother in front of the drinks station. It warmed her heart to see her two worlds coming together.

"Would you mind watching over things so I can go find Bullet? I'll be quick," she asked Isabel, who was glaring at Jed as he snagged three cookies from the tray.

"What? I'm sharing with my friends." Jed motioned toward Quincy, who was waiting in line for ice cream.

"Mm-hm." Isabel shook her head. "The only thing Quincy has on his mind is getting a *luscious lick* of Penny."

Jed leaned across the table and said, "I could go for some licks." He waggled his brows.

Isabel rolled her eyes. "Why did I agree to work with you again?" She laughed and looked at Finlay. "Oh, right, because my bestie is here. Did Bullet like your surprise?"

"He loved it," she said, smiling to herself. When she'd shown him the tattoo she'd tried to get yesterday, he'd gotten a sad look in his eyes. At first she'd thought it was because she'd meant to have his name tattooed over her heart, but it had hurt so much, she'd gotten only one line, the left side of the letter *B*. But later, as they were lying in front of the fireplace, the flames casting shadows over their naked bodies, he'd run his finger over the line and said, *I love that you wanted my name on you, but I wish I could have been there with you. I want to be there for all the important things in your life.* Finlay had lined up a few catering jobs after the baby shower, and even though Isabel would be there to help her, Bullet had offered to go with her, too, when he could. The man claimed not to know anything about romance...

"Go ahead, Fin," Isabel said, and smirked at Jed. "I'll keep the vultures away."

Finlay stepped outside the tent, scanning the grounds for Bullet as she made her way through the crowd. Even with so many leather-clad men milling about, her man was easy to spot, holding Lincoln near the temporary tattoo booth. She melted at the sight of her big, burly man with that sweet little one in his arms. As he pressed his lips to the baby's head and closed his eyes for the briefest of seconds, she remembered what he'd said about wanting children. A heavy hand touched her shoulder, pulling her from her thoughts.

"You done good, darlin'," Biggs said as he stepped beside her.

"This was a collaborative effort, and I'm so happy it's going well."

"The event is going well, too, but I meant with my boy."

She looked across the lawn at Bullet just as Kennedy barreled into his legs, and he scooped her up into his other arm. He was the most loyal, loving man Finlay knew, and even though he'd struggled with what that meant when he was younger, she knew the man he was had everything to do with the parents who had raised him. Thinking of the life lessons Biggs had taught Bullet and the way he'd waited years, silently holding on to what must have been extreme curiosity until Bullet was ready to share his secret with him, she said, "You done good, too."

With that thought, her mind turned to her parents and how much she missed her own father. She thought about her mother moving away after they'd lost him. Then her thoughts turned back to the man across the field, the one who had become an even bigger part of her life as he'd come out from under his guilt a little more each day. Bullet saw things in Finlay that no one else—including her—ever had. Finlay hadn't realized she'd needed closure with Aaron's family, too, but Bullet had, and he had secretly set up a meeting with them. Little had she known when they'd set out for a ride last Saturday morning, they'd end up in Pleasant Hill having breakfast with Aaron's parents. Or that later, as they'd driven home, she'd realized that if anything ever happened to Bullet, moving away from the harbor wouldn't be enough to help her move forward. Their love was too deep and too big to ever leave behind.

AS IF THEY were connected by energy bigger than the eye could see, Bullet couldn't look away from Finlay as she crossed the grass in a long plum-colored dress that hugged her luscious curves. Her blond hair cascaded over her shoulders, softening the edginess of the black leather jacket she wore. Bullet was struck with the images he'd begun seeing in his mind lately. Images of their future. He'd never thought past the day he was living until he'd found Finlay, and now he couldn't stop visions of her, her belly round with their baby, or cooking with a child on her hip and Tinkerbell by her side, from finding their way into his mind on a near-daily basis. He envisioned himself lying beneath the stars with Finlay and a gaggle of their children, Tinkerbell standing sentinel over them all. Sometimes, like now, as he stepped toward her with Kennedy and Lincoln in his arms, he imagined he and Finlay old and gray, riding over the bridge that led out of Peaceful Harbor and off into the sunset on his bike—knowing they'd be coming back over that bridge together.

"Look how pwetty Aunt Finlay looks in her dwess, Uncle Bullet." Kennedy waved at Finlay.

"She sure does."

Finlay waved and blew a kiss to Bullet. Kennedy pretended to catch the kiss and pressed her hand to her cheek.

"Hey, that was my kiss," Bullet said.

Kennedy giggled and pressed her hand to Bullet's lips. "Now you have it, too." She reached over and pressed her hand to Lincoln's cheek. "And Linc has one, too."

"Thanks, princess."

Finlay smiled and kissed the babies. "Your uncle Bullet sure does have a way with you guys, doesn't he? He always keeps you smiling."

Kennedy nodded, and Lincoln shyly pressed his face into Bullet's neck.

"Wait until we have our own," Bullet said.

"You're going to have a baby?" Kennedy asked with wide eyes.

"No, honey," Finlay said, giving Bullet a why-would-you-say-that look. "Uncle Bullet is just being silly."

"Uncle Bullet doesn't know how to be silly," Kennedy said

with a serious look on her pretty little face. "Mommy said he is too good at protecting everyone to be silly."

"I know how to be silly," Bullet said, and blew raspberries against Lincoln's cheek, making him giggle up a storm.

"Do me!" Kennedy pleaded.

Bullet did, earning lots of sweet little-girl giggles. He spotted Bear, and motioned for him to join them. "Can you take these little darlin's for a bit?"

"Absolutely." Bear took Lincoln from him as Kennedy wriggled from Bullet's arms.

Kennedy took Bear's hand and dragged him toward Bones, who was headed toward the food tent with Bradley. "I want to see Uncle Boney!"

Finlay laughed. "I don't think I'll ever get used to hearing her call him that."

"What do you think our kids will call him?" He draped an arm over her shoulder and headed for the bar.

"I don't know. You mean our little leather-wearing, ring-bearing, bike-riding kids?" she asked as they headed into the bar.

"Don't you mean our cake-baking, bike-riding kids?" He groped her ass as he closed the door behind them and guided her over toward the bar.

"Bullet," she whispered, as if the whole world might hear her chastising him for groping her. "I told Izzy I'd be quick."

"God, I love you, baby. You know that?"

She blushed, and his heart swelled.

"We'll be as long as we'll be," he said as he took her in his arms and gazed into the eyes of the woman who had changed his life. "Do you remember our first kiss?"

"Yes. I still get the chills when I think of it."

"So do I, lollipop. And when I think of the way you stood up to me, right over there"—he glanced across the bar—"in that pretty dress, your gorgeous eyes boring into me with such strength and conviction, I knew right then I'd met my match."

As he dropped to one knee and took her hand in his, he knew he should be more nervous than ever before, but he was dead calm, because this—him and Finlay—was the rightest thing he'd ever done.

Her eyes widened, and "Bullet" slipped from her lips like a prayer.

"Finlay, my angel, I have no idea how or why you agreed to go out with me—"

"It was the kiss," she said through her tears.

He chuckled. "It *was* a hell of a kiss, and I thank God every day that you were wearing rose-colored glasses that night, because I adore you, and I never want to imagine a single day without you by my side. I told you that I'm not Prince Charming, and our lives will never be a fairy tale. But if you marry me, I will spend every moment of our lives worshipping, protecting, and loving you with everything I have."

As he rose to his feet, he slipped the rose-gold, princess-cut solitaire ring from his pocket, running his thumb over the black diamonds in the shape of an infinity symbol on either side of the band. He gazed into Finlay's eyes and said, "Marry me, lollipop. Be mine, and let me be your man."

Nodding, with tears sliding down her beautiful cheeks, she said, "I've been yours since that very first kiss, and I'll be yours until my very last."

For years Bullet had wondered if his life might have been better if he hadn't enlisted in the military, if he hadn't nearly lost his life or watched other men lose theirs. But now, as he took Finlay in his arms and sealed their promises with a kiss, he realized all that pain had led him to her—and knew he would live through it all over again just to be right there with the woman he loved. His sugar rush. His angel. His *everything*.

**Ready for More Whiskeys?**

**Fall in love with Bones and Sarah in *Wicked Whiskey Love***

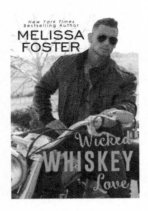

This caring (and naughty) doctor is the most mysterious of all the Whiskeys. Find out more about this big-hearted, passionate Whiskey, in *Wicked Whiskey Love*.

### Want MORE Whiskeys?

The following books are **waiting for you** at all book retailers
*River of Love* (First introduction to the Whiskey family)
*Tru Blue* (Truman and Gemma)
*Truly, Madly, Whiskey* (Bear and Crystal)

### Love Melissa's Writing?

Discover more of the magic behind *New York Times* bestselling
and award winning author Melissa Foster with the series that
started the phenomenon:

### LOVE IN BLOOM Big-Family Romance Collection

Fiercely loyal heroes, sassy, sexy heroines, and stories that go
above and beyond your expectations! Free downloadable series
checklists, reading orders, and more can be found on Melissa's
website, as well as FIVE free eBooks to get you started! Book
links are available on the next page.

# Book List

## LOVE IN BLOOM SERIES

### SNOW SISTERS
*Sisters in Love*
*Sisters in Bloom*
*Sisters in White*

### THE BRADENS at Weston
*Lovers at Heart*
*Destined for Love*
*Friendship on Fire*
*Sea of Love*
*Bursting with Love*
*Hearts at Play*

### THE BRADENS at Trusty
*Taken by Love*
*Fated for Love*
*Romancing My Love*
*Flirting with Love*
*Dreaming of Love*
*Crashing into Love*

### THE BRADENS at Peaceful Harbor
*Healed by Love*
*Surrender My Love*
*River of Love*
*Crushing on Love*
*Whisper of Love*
*Thrill of Love*

### THE BRADENS at Pleasant Hill
*Anything For Love*

## THE BRADEN NOVELLAS

*Promise My Love*
*Our New Love*
*Daring Her Love*
*Story of Love*
*Love at Last*

## THE REMINGTONS

*Game of Love*
*Stroke of Love*
*Flames of Love*
*Slope of Love*
*Read, Write, Love*
*Touched by Love*

## SEASIDE SUMMERS

*Seaside Dreams*
*Seaside Hearts*
*Seaside Sunsets*
*Seaside Secrets*
*Seaside Nights*
*Seaside Embrace*
*Seaside Lovers*
*Seaside Whispers*

## BAYSIDE SUMMERS

*Bayside Desires*
*Bayside Passions*
*Bayside Heat*

## <u>THE RYDERS</u>

*Seized by Love*
*Claimed by Love*
*Chased by Love*
*Rescued by Love*

## SEXY STANDALONE ROMANCE

*Tru Blue*

*Truly, Madly, Whiskey*
*Driving Whiskey Wild*
*Wicked Whiskey Love*

## THE MONTGOMERYS
*Embracing Her Heart*
*Our Wicked Hearts*
*Wild, Crazy, Heart*
*Sweet, Sexy, Heart*

## BILLIONAIRES AFTER DARK SERIES

### WILD BOYS AFTER DARK
*Logan*
*Heath*
*Jackson*
*Cooper*

### BAD BOYS AFTER DARK
*Mick*
*Dylan*
*Carson*
*Brett*

## HARBORSIDE NIGHTS SERIES
Includes characters from the Love in Bloom series
*Catching Cassidy*
*Discovering Delilah*
*Tempting Tristan*

### More Books by Melissa
*Chasing Amanda* (mystery/suspense)
*Come Back to Me* (mystery/suspense)
*Have No Shame* (historical fiction/romance)
*Love, Lies & Mystery* (3-book bundle)
*Megan's Way* (literary fiction)
*Traces of Kara* (psychological thriller)
*Where Petals Fall* (suspense)

# Acknowledgments

Thank you for reading Bullet and Finlay's story. I hope you adored them and all their witty and wonderful family members and friends, each of whom will be getting their own happily ever after.

If this is your first introduction to my work, please note that every Melissa Foster book can be read as a stand-alone novel, and characters appear in other family series, so you never miss out on an engagement, wedding, or birth. You can find information about the Love in Bloom series and my books here:
www.melissafoster.com/melissas-books

I offer several free first-in-series ebooks. You can find them here:
www.MelissaFoster.com/LIBFree

I chat with fans often in my fan club on Facebook. If you haven't joined my fan club yet, please do!
www.facebook.com/groups/MelissaFosterFans

Follow my author page on Facebook for fun giveaways and updates of what's going on in our fictional boyfriends' worlds.
www.Facebook.com/MelissaFosterAuthor

If you prefer sweet romance, with no explicit scenes or graphic language, please try the Sweet with Heat series written under my pen name, Addison Cole. You'll find the same great love stories with toned down heat levels.

Thank you to my awesome editorial team: Kristen Weber and Penina Lopez, and my meticulous proofreaders: Elaini Caruso, Juliette Hill, Marlene Engel, Lynn Mullan, and Justinn Harrison. And last but never least, a huge thank-you to my family for their patience, support, and inspiration.

Melissa Foster is a *New York Times* and *USA Today* bestselling and award-winning author. Her books have been recommended by *USA Today's* book blog, *Hagerstown* magazine, *The Patriot*, and several other print venues. Melissa has painted and donated several murals to the Hospital for Sick Children in Washington, DC.

Visit Melissa on her website or chat with her on social media. Melissa enjoys discussing her books with book clubs and reader groups and welcomes an invitation to your event. Melissa's books are available through most online retailers in paperback and digital formats.

Melissa also writes sweet romance under the pen name Addison Cole.

www.MelissaFoster.com
Free Reader Goodies:
www.MelissaFoster.com/Reader-Goodies